Google
Husband Back

By

Julie Butterfield

Also by Julie Butterfield

Did I Mention I Won The Lottery?

Did I Mention I Was Getting Married?

Lucy Mathers Goes Back To Work

Eve's Christmas

Agony Auntics

Chapter 1

When Kate's husband announced that he was leaving her, she was only mildly surprised. He broke the news as he stood in the doorway of the kitchen and Kate was preoccupied with the large smudge of porridge she'd just noticed on her shoulder and the butter that was dribbling down her fingers. She'd just remembered that she was starting her new diet today, one that would shift the baby pouch still sitting on her midriff – and butter on her toast had not been part of the plan. In fact, there should be no toast at all, buttered or otherwise; she was meant to start the day with half a grapefruit and some hot water with a slice of lemon. She looked at the toast, already half eaten and decided it was a shame to waste the rest. The diet could wait until tomorrow. As for the porridge, well the jumper could join the rest of Kate's crusty tops in the washing machine. Porridge smeared shoulders seemed to be par for the course with a baby in the house.

'Did you hear me Kate?' asked Alex impatiently.

'Yes, I heard. I thought it was next week.'

She wiped the runny butter from her fingers before deftly catching Millie's cup as it flew towards the floor.

'Next week?'

'Yes, next week.'

She was confident that it was next week Alex was going away. She remembered because a few weeks before he'd been very grumpy, claiming she didn't pay enough attention when he was talking about work and they'd had a brief but intense argument about just how much interest she should pay when he came home at the end of the day. Kate was of the opinion that having spent her day with a grouchy nine-month old baby, washing, cleaning, singing, playing with squeaky toys, washing some more and cleaning again - she deserved more than a re-run of Alex's day. But she had accepted the rebuke, smiled apologetically at her husband and resolved to pay more attention in future. She had even taken to writing down snippets of information so she could have a quick read before he came home and remember to ask him how his meeting had gone or what his boss thought of his latest report.

So Kate was very confident that it was next week that Alex was going to spend four days in the North of England, looking at demographics showing why the population all seemed much happier living in the South of England.

Alex was staring at her and with a sigh Kate finished the toast, put the feeder cup back on Millie's highchair and grabbed her cup of tea.

'You said that you were going to Northumberland next week ...Tuesday morning, meetings until Thursday evening, round up Friday morning, lunch, arrival home Friday evening,' she repeated parrot fashion.

Alex carried on staring.

'You said,' repeated Kate a little impatiently, 'that you would definitely be back on the Friday evening but you would be away on the Saturday morning for...' she paused. Actually she had stopped listening at that point and wasn't sure what Saturday had in store for her overworked husband. 'Er, for something else. Anyway, it was Tuesday coming home Friday. I listened,' she finished triumphantly.

There was a moment of silence. Millie was tipping her cup so that contents sprayed onto her hand and Kate was sipping her tea, watching Alex who stood in the doorway staring at Kate.

'Kate I – I - that's not what I'm talking about. I'm leaving. I mean I'm actually leaving. You. I'm leaving you. Today, now. I'm… well I'm leaving.'

Kate stared at him.

'What?'

He ran a hand through his hair, the floppy fringe that neither Kate nor gel had ever managed to control and she suddenly noticed how tired he looked. How absolutely drained of colour he was. She noticed how the groove between his eyebrows seemed to have deepened overnight. And she noticed the two large suitcases that stood by his feet. They were the suitcases they used when going on holiday, not the small one Alex always used when he had to spend a few days away with work.

'What do you mean? Leaving to go where? Northumberland is next week. You said Northumberland was next week, I was listening!'

There was a bang as Millie threw the cup back onto the floor but Kate didn't turn round.

'What are you talking about Alex? Where are you going?'

'I'm sorry Kate, I'm so sorry. I have tried to tell you, to explain. I'm sorry...' he shrugged, trailing into silence.

Kate frowned, fairly certain she would have remembered a conversation that involved her husband telling her he was leaving. She waited but it seemed Alex had run out of words. With a loud sigh he shrugged his shoulders again, a helpless look crossing his face. Refusing to meet her eyes he turned, grabbed the handles of the cases and with a few steps he was across the hallway and out of the front door.

Kate stood perfectly still, staring at the empty space he had filled seconds before. Millie grunted indignantly as no one retrieved her cup, gave Kate a moment then yelled a little louder to get her mother's attention.

'Sorry Millie darling.'

Blindly Kate reached out and stroked her daughter's silken head.

'Daddy's being silly sweetie. He said he's leaving!'

She looked down into Millie's big blue eyes staring back, listening to her mother's words, waiting for her cup.

'He wouldn't leave us Millie,' Kate laughed. 'He would never leave you. That's just silly isn't it?'

She picked up the cup, kissed Millie's head and stood staring at the sink. She wasn't sure how it managed to get so full each morning. She washed, dried and put everything away each night so she could start with a clean kitchen the next day. But by the time Alex left for work it invariably looked as though they'd had a party with the detritus spread across every surface.

Why on earth would Alex say such a thing? It wasn't at all funny.

Kate was ever so slightly smug in the knowledge that they had a perfect marriage. They had fallen head over heels in love eight years before and nothing had changed since. They had been taken somewhat by surprise the previous year to find that a new member of the family was expected but Alex adored his daughter, even if he did complain that for a tiny being she took a huge amount of time, space and attention. But he wouldn't leave her. He wouldn't leave Kate because they still loved each other.

So why Alex would come out with such a strange statement on a normal Monday morning was beyond Kate and shaking her head she rolled up her sleeves and set to work on the mountain of things in the sink. He must have been teasing decided Kate, although she found it very unamusing and it was an elaborate tease to actually bring two suitcases downstairs.

And why did he say he'd tried to explain things? What things? Alex wasn't unhappy. Neither of them were. They were both tired, most definitely tired. Life was always hard with the arrival of a new baby but they were still very much in love and eventually things would get easier, they both knew that. When Kate had left work to have Millie they'd both decided that she would not return until their daughter was at school. They wanted Millie to have a stay at home parent and Kate wanted to be that person. It had resulted in a strain on their budget that took some juggling, leaving Alex working harder than ever. There were days when in a fog of exhaustion and mind numbing baby orientated activity, Kate wondered if perhaps they would all be better off if Millie spent a couple of days a week at nursery and Kate found a part time job somewhere. Anywhere really – as long as she was with adults who didn't have an overwhelming need to turn everything into a song. But they had decided it was best if Kate stayed at home so they stuck with the plan.

Alex had occasionally complained about spending every evening in the house, listening to the sound of Millie's soft breaths through the baby monitor. Why couldn't they have the occasional evening out he had mumbled? But Kate had thought about the effort of washing her hair, finding clothes that weren't covered in dried porridge or sticky fingerprints, the effort of finding a baby sitter and decided that a night cuddling in front of the TV was just as acceptable.

But they were still happy. Very happy.

Millie was grizzling. She had abandoned the cup and was rubbing her eyes with tiny fists as she whimpered. Scooping her out of the highchair, Kate headed upstairs where she ran a bath full of sweet smelling baby bubbles, washed Millie until she gleamed, fluffed up the blonde baby curls and dressed her in a clean, fresh vest, pink woolly tights and soft pink dress

She breathed in the delicious aroma of clean baby.

'Why would he say such a hurtful thing Millie? Why on earth would he say he was leaving?'

Millie shook her head fractiously and Kate held her close, feeling the warm little body relax and go loose. She laid her down in her cot, watching for a moment as Millie struggled to keep her eyes open briefly before giving in to the demands of sleep, her eyelashes resting like smudges on her cheeks.

Wandering back into her bedroom, Kate stood in the doorway staring at the wardrobes against the far wall. She really couldn't understand why Alex would say such a thing. Perhaps he was actually going somewhere with work this week and he was angry because she hadn't remembered. She did try to listen but when he came home tired, a little grumpy and wanting to tell her the minutiae of his day, she did sometimes find it hard to be enthusiastic. What Kate really wanted was for Alex to come bursting into the kitchen with a huge smile at the sight of his wife and child and a kiss on the lips for Kate. Then he would take over the making of the evening meal and leave Kate to get Millie bathed and in bed using both hands and her full attention. Or perhaps he would scoop Millie into his arms and insist on carrying out her nightly ritual so Kate could pour a glass of wine and relish the idea of cooking a meal without having a tired baby stuck to her hip. What actually happened was that Alex would throw his briefcase into the corner of the room and follow Kate round the kitchen telling her about his day and chatting as she prepared their meal and Millie grizzled in her arms. Then he would sit and catch up with the news while Kate bathed Millie and by the time their daughter was in bed and Kate and Alex sat at the table to eat, she was often too exhausted to bother with any further conversation. Alex had suggested that Kate should put Millie to bed a little earlier but Kate had been outraged at the idea he was happy not to see his daughter each evening. Most fathers, she told him firmly, would welcome the chance to spend an hour at the end of the day with their new child. So Kate continued to keep Millie up until Alex came home, acknowledging that exhaustion was an inevitable side effect of a baby in the home and she tried to smile and listen to Alex's tales of office life and murmur the right things in the right places to show that she supported him.

Kate thought hard about the last few days. Could Alex have said that the meeting had been moved and she hadn't paid attention? Or maybe he was just trying to catch her out. Alex did that sometimes if he didn't think Kate was listening, properly listening. He would throw some outrageous comment into the conversation and see if she picked up on it, sending an accusing 'I knew you weren't listening' in her direction. Like the day he told her that Athens had frozen over and everyone had been evacuated and Kate had replied 'I see'.

Maybe she'd not been listening and he was teaching her a lesson. Of course he hadn't actually left, that was a ridiculous thought.

But she carried on staring at the wardrobes. One door was slightly ajar, Alex's door. Kate nibbled at her nails and walked over to stand a little closer. She couldn't really see much, just a dark space and taking another step forward she stretched out a hand, pausing slightly before letting her fingers curl around the handle and then slowly, carefully, pulling open the door.

It was empty. Kate felt her breath catch. She felt the air leave her body in a sudden whooshing movement that left her dizzy and breathless. She stared in the empty wardrobe and felt her heart hammering inside her chest so loudly that it hurt her ribs.

She stepped back, still staring at the wide open doors and the empty space. She tried to breathe but oxygen didn't seem to be reaching her lungs and she gulped for air. Shaking her head, she looked around. The book Alex was reading was no longer on his bedside cabinet. The bits and pieces that he always left on the dressing table were gone. She walked into the bathroom. His toothbrush was missing, his shaving foam and the old fashioned shaving brush she had bought him for his birthday – gone. She threw open the bathroom cabinet. The second shelf down was empty. His indigestion tablets, his migraine tablets, his aftershave, the nose hair trimmer she had slipped in his stocking the previous year and he had laughed at but secretly used – gone.

She walked into the spare room on unsteady legs and checked the wardrobe where he kept his older clothes, some of his suits, his jackets. Gone.

There was nowhere else to look. All traces of Alex had disappeared and Kate was left with only one conclusion.

That when her husband had announced that morning he was leaving her, maybe he was telling the truth.

Chapter 2

When Millie woke up an hour later, Kate was still shaking. It took several attempts to get the little wriggling figure inside her quilted coat, the mittens over her baby fingers and a snug hat covering her blonde curls. Kate strapped her into the buggy, wrapping a blanket around her legs and went out of the front door turning in the direction of the shops. Her mind whirling with possibilities she walked along the pavement, listening to Millie's gurgles and trying to control her breathing. It was a misunderstanding she told herself, it was a joke, it was something to do with work, it was something she had forgotten because it was simply not possible that Alex had actually left.

Consulting the list that was in her pocket she went into the corner shop for beans, rusks and half a dozen eggs; to the bakery for a loaf of bread and the thick bread cakes that Alex liked and then into the butchers where she joined a queue that was so long the door couldn't close and the smell of freshly baked pies was drifting out onto the street.

Lost in a world of uneven, disjointed thoughts, Kate only realised that it was her turn to be served when the elderly lady behind gave her a little nudge of her elbow.

'Oh sorry,' she said, moving closer to the counter. She stared blindly at its contents. She had thought about making lasagna for tea. Alex loved lasagna and Kate would spend time making the béchamel sauce, flavoured to perfection and exactly the right thickness because she loved the look of happiness on Alex's face when she placed his plate in front of him. There again he loved pork chops served with good old fashioned mash, peas and carrots with homemade onion gravy.

'What can I get you darlin'?' asked the butcher, a touch impatiently.

Kate looked up from the selection spread out before her.

'I don't really know,' she half whispered.

There was a slight movement in the queue behind her, a general shrug of impatience that made its way in a wave down the waiting people to rest on Kate's shoulders.

'You don't know? Well if you don't know I'm sure I don't.' The butcher tried to laugh, his shoulders tensing slightly under his white jacket.

'How about some sausages? Steak? Pork chops?'

Kate stood quite still, staring at him as he made his suggestions.

'What do you fancy?' he asked desperately, 'what does your old man like for his tea?'

'Pork chops,' said Kate shakily, 'he likes pork chops.'

'Now we're getting somewhere!' announced the butcher triumphantly to the queue as the woman behind Kate sighed loudly.

'Pork chops it is then! How many darlin'?'

Kate shook her head. She could feel the tears begin to gather behind her eyes. Her hands had started to shake again and she bit her lip to stem the sobs that she could feel rising from deep within her chest.

'I don't know,' she said shakily. 'I really don't know. I'm not sure if he's coming home tonight. You see, he said this morning that he was leaving me. But I didn't believe him because why would he?'

She turned to the queue now rigidly still and looking anywhere but at Kate as an enormous sob forced its way out.

'Why would he leave me, why would he leave Millie?'

At the sound of her name Millie stopped chewing the ear of the cuddly donkey she held and sent an angelic smile in her mother's direction.

'He said he's tried to tell me he was going but I don't think he did. I would remember a conversation like that, wouldn't I? And anyway, we're happy, we love each other so why would he want to leave? Maybe he is coming home,' Kate was doing her best to control the sobs but they had started coming thick and fast, making her shoulders judder as she gripped the buggy, shaking her head in confusion.

'Maybe he's joking … or punishing me … or …I don't know. Maybe he'll be back tonight and what if he comes home and I haven't got anything for tea? Maybe he'll just go again,' and finally she lost the battle bending her head over the buggy and weeping uncontrollably, huge tears splashing down onto Millie's hat.

There wasn't a sound in the shop, not a movement in the queue as Kate wept at the fearful thought that maybe her husband wasn't coming home that night.

She felt a hand on her shoulder and looked up through her tears at a grey haired woman who had moved to stand at Kate's side. 'I think you need to go home my dear,' she said softly, tucking a strand of tear sodden hair behind Kate's ear. 'Take your beautiful little baby home and phone a friend. You shouldn't be alone right now.'

Kate nodded. She turned the buggy in the direction of the door as everyone pressed themselves backwards so Kate could leave the shop without her distress touching them.

'Just a minute!' Another hand on her shoulder as the butcher stepped from behind the counter, his eyes suspiciously bright as he pushed a plastic bag in her hand. 'Two chops darlin', on the house. You know... just in case he comes back....'

And then Kate was out of the shop, the relief of the other shoppers palpable as she turned the buggy left and strode down the pavement, the wind stinging her face and almost freezing the tears that were raining down her cheeks.

Five minutes later she turned into a small pathway leading to a Victorian semi. The plants and shrubs either side were overgrown and the pebbles that were meant to neatly edge the borders were scattered across the path catching at the wheels of the buggy. Kate pushed on, reaching the shiny red door and banging at the knocker with a desperation that transmitted itself into the house beyond.

'Hold on!' the door flew open, a slight woman with tousled red hair peering anxiously out.

'Kate! Good God I thought it must be …
Kate, what on earth is the matter?'

A shocked hand flew to Fiona's mouth as she
took in the tear soaked cheeks and heaving
shoulders of her friend.

'Kate honey, whatever's happened?'

Kate struggled to speak, every time her mouth
opened sobs erupted but swallowing hard she
wiped the tears from her cheeks.

'He's left me Fee, Alex has left me!' and
breaking down completely she sank down onto
the cold, hard path, awash with tears.

There were several minutes of carefully
controlled panic as without saying another word
directly to Kate, Fiona grabbed the buggy and
hauled it inside the narrow tiled hallway before
clutching at Kate's arm and pulling her inside as
well. With the door shut behind them the warmth
of the house took only a few minutes to defrost
Kate's icy face and she watched numbly as with
soft cooing noises Fiona unstrapped Millie and
stripped her of mittens, hat and warm coat and
tickled her tummy until she squealed with
laughter. Making a quick diversion to the under
stairs cupboard she pulled out the play mat and
toys reserved for Millie's visits and the little girl
was soon happily laid out on Fiona's breakfast
room floor chewing on her donkey's ear.

Kate still stood by the front door, her eyes
glazed. Fiona took hold of one of her hands and
led her into the room, peeling off her coat and
pushing her gently down onto the settee. Still not
saying anything she stepped into the large messy
kitchen and flicked on the kettle, watching Kate

anxiously as she made the tea, setting the mugs out of Millie's reach before sitting down next to her friend.

'What's happened Kate?' she asked softly taking hold of her hand. 'What's happened?'

Kate's lip was wobbling, the tears still rolling down her cheeks but the sobs were quieter, almost a hiccup as she relayed her morning to Fiona.

'He's left?' repeated Fiona, her hazel eyes like saucers.

Kate nodded miserably.

Fiona looked stunned. 'I can't believe it Kate, I mean I genuinely can't believe it. You two always seemed so happy!'

Kate sniffed, 'We were, we are! I know Millie wasn't planned, well not right now and money is tight and Alex works so hard. But despite all that, we're still happy. At least I thought we were. I know things are a struggle at the moment. It's not been easy but we both said it would soon get better and the main thing was we still loved each other.'

A solitary tear trickled down her cheek. 'How can I think that we're happy while Alex is so unhappy that he walks out? How can I have got it so wrong Fee?' she wailed, the tears turning back into a flood.

Her friend threw a protective arm around her shoulders, holding Kate tight, trying to send some comfort into the trembling figure by her side.

'Oh Kate honey, I'm so sorry. I can't believe Alex would just walk out!'

'He said he's tried to talk to me, to explain,' sobbed Kate.

'Explain. Explain what?'

'I don't really know,' whispered Kate rubbing her eyes much like Millie did. 'He never told me he was unhappy, he never said anything - apart from the usual stuff.'

Fiona's eyebrows raised slightly. 'What is the usual stuff?' she asked carefully.

'Oh you know, money, paying the bills. He was a bit fed up that we'd stopped going out. He said children shouldn't mean that life ended and he was a bit grumpy because I didn't go to the work's Christmas do … the usual.'

Fiona nodded. 'Right.'

'Oh Fee, I really didn't think it would be such a big deal skipping the work's bloody Christmas do! Millie was teething, I was exhausted, I had nothing to wear and couldn't really afford to buy anything! I thought Alex would enjoy going by himself and letting his hair down for once.'

Kate wondered if it was her imagination or did she just see a flash of something in Fiona's eyes?

'And that's your only argument, not going out since Millie arrived?'

Kate chewed her lip. 'Well that makes him sound selfish,' she defended her missing husband. 'It's not like we were arguing all the time. We are happy Fee! Really happy. He just doesn't realise how hard it is to do things on impulse when you've got a baby in the house. You know what it's like,' she appealed to her friend, 'just going out shopping takes a morning of planning!'

Fiona nodded sympathetically. 'I know honey, believe me I know!'

Her eyes rolled slightly in the direction of the school photograph on the dresser showing three mischievous looking boys, all with Fiona's rich red hair and a smattering of freckles across smiling faces.

'But' started Fiona carefully, 'having a baby in the house doesn't mean that everything stops.'

Kate's eyes opened wide and Fiona carried on quickly.

'What I mean is that it's still important that you and Alex go out occasionally, have an afternoon shopping, go for lunch, go to the pictures, out for a meal … anything really,' she trailed off.

'But Millie...' began Kate defensively.

'Millie can always go to a babysitter,' said Fiona firmly. 'You know I would have her any time you asked. She could go to your mum's for the night,' they both winced slightly and Fiona hurried on, 'or you can take her with you. I'm just saying that life doesn't - shouldn't stop when you have a baby.'

Kate's lip started to tremble again. 'You're saying I've neglected Alex and now he's left me because I wouldn't go to the Christmas ball?'

'No! No Kate! Of course not honey, I'm just saying that maybe you've taken the whole stay at home with baby a little more seriously than you had to, that's all. But that doesn't excuse Alex walking out like that. Oh Kate!' and putting her cup of tea down, Fiona wrapped her arms around Kate's shuddering shoulders as a new wave of sobs overcame her.

When the tears had stopped and Kate was calmer, Fiona tried again.

19

'You really had no idea he was thinking about leaving? He didn't say anything before he left?'

Kate shook her head soggily, 'Nothing. And I've been wondering, how on earth did he pack so quickly and how did he get everything into two suitcases?'

Fiona's eyebrows shot under her spiky fringe.

'He's taken everything Fee, his suits, his casual clothes, even his summer clothes from the storage chest. How did he wake up at 7.15 and have everything packed in less than an hour? I couldn't begin to manage that. And to get it all in two cases?'

'You think he may have already moved some things out?'

Kate shrugged unhappily. The thought that Alex wanted to leave her was bad enough. But she had been clinging to the hope that he'd woken up depressed and on impulse had thrown some things in a case and walked out. To consider that he'd been planning his departure, that he'd sat on the settee each evening chatting to her about his day, cuddling Millie while all the time thinking that soon he'd be free, that soon he would be able to leave, was almost more than she could bear.

Her eyes welled with tears again. 'Why do you think he left Fee?' she whispered in anguish. 'Why would he leave us? Do you really think it's because I wouldn't get a baby sitter and go to the Christmas party? Would he leave us over something so trivial?'

Her voice caught and Fiona clasped her hand reassuringly. 'Oh no Kate, surely not! I think he's just going through a bad patch that's all!' She ran a hand through the already wild red hair, 'I'm as surprised as you are Kate, I always thought the two of you were as happy as it was possible to be!'

They sat in silence for a while watching Millie. She had played with everything on the mat happily chattering to herself and was now laid with her head on her donkey her eyelashes drifting towards her cheeks.

'Kate,' began Fiona delicately, 'were things alright elsewhere?'

Kate looked at her questioningly.

'I mean, with you and Alex. Where things, you know okay?'

At Kate's blank look Fiona rolled her eyes with impatience, 'For God's sake Kate, in the bedroom. You and Alex, was everything okay or was that one of the things you argued about?'

'Oh!' Kate's face cleared. 'I see. Everything was fine Fee, like I said, we were – we are happy.'

Fiona nodded thoughtfully and a shiver went down Kate's spine.

'Why do you ask Fee,' she demanded urgently. 'Do you know something. Oh my God, is Alex seeing someone else?'

The tears were back as she clutched at her friend's arm.

'Don't be silly Kate,' said Fiona firmly. 'If I knew that Alex was having an affair I would have told you. No matter how unpleasant it might have been - for both of us. I was just going through the possibilities. I mean, why do husbands suddenly pack all their belongings and leave?'

Kate had an unpleasant prickling along the back of her neck. 'But you think he might be having an affair?'

'Of course not! Like I said, I'm just checking the possibilities.'

'But he could be having an affair and neither of us know anything about it?'

'Stop it Kate, don't be silly!'

Both women sat in silence for a moment.

'What happened at the Christmas do Fee?'

Fiona looked startled. 'What do you mean?'

'Something happened didn't it? I mentioned the Christmas party earlier and you looked – funny. Something happened at the Christmas party – something with Alex. What was it? Tell me!'

Her voice had risen, strident and forceful and for a moment Millie's eyes flew open at the unfamiliar sound of her mother shouting.

Kate lowered her voice but gripped Fiona's arm. 'You need to tell me everything you know Fee. Absolutely everything. My husband has gone, I don't know why or where but if you know anything, if you suspect anything you must tell me!'

The tears had vanished, a determined look taking their place.

'Kate ...' began Fiona.

'Tell me!'

Fiona shook her head, 'It was nothing Kate, really nothing. It's just with Alex leaving, I thought, I wondered ...'

'TELL ME!'

Fiona looked down defeated. 'Alex wasn't his usual self at the party.'

Kate stared at her friend. 'How?'

Fiona wriggled uncomfortably on the settee. 'He was very much in the party spirit. I hadn't seen him like that before.'

'How?'

'Oh nothing serious Kate. Nothing to worry about, just a bit - flirty I suppose.'

Kate nodded. She didn't waste time looking shocked or upset.

'Go on.'

'Just flirting that's all.'

Fiona looked at the set of Kate's chin and sighed.

'It just surprised me. He was like a child given a free run in the sweet shop and I wondered at the time how unlike him it was. But I just put it down to too much drink and ...' her voice trailed off and she looked at her knees.

'Who with?'

'What?'

'You heard me Fee, who was he flirting with? Oh God, was he flirting with you? Did he try anything with you?'

Fiona looked shocked. 'No! of course not. And if he had, don't you think I would have mentioned it before now?'

'Sorry I didn't mean ...'

Fiona waved away her apology.

'So who was he flirting with?'

Fiona shook her head dismissively. 'He was just being really flirty Kate, sort of quite desperately flirty. The way some husbands are when they're not getting … when things aren't good at home. Which is why I asked if you and Alex …'

'Who with?'

'No one in particular. It was just the way he was behaving …'

Kate gripped her friend's hand so hard they both flinched.

'Who with Fee?'

Defeated Fiona gently freed her fingers, wiggling them back to life.

'Sandra Maddison in the accounts department.'

Kate looked blank.

'You've met her, she's been there for a couple of years.'

Kate trawled through her memory banks for a Sandra but came up blank. Although Fiona was one of her closest friends and her rock, Kate had only known her for a few years. Both their husbands worked at the same company and Kate and Fiona had met at one of the regular company social events, instantly gravitating towards each other. Alex and Stuart, Fiona's husband, worked in separate departments and had very little to do with each other but Fiona and Kate were delighted to discover that they lived only minutes apart and although Fiona was a few years older than Kate they had quickly moved onto a strong friendship that didn't rely on company outings. Stuart had worked at the company for years and there was no-one that Fiona didn't know. At some of the more tedious events she would entertain Kate by feeding her delightful little titbits of gossip about the rest of the staff.

'What's she like' demanded Kate curtly.

Fiona shrugged. 'Blonde, trying to be thin, not overly attractive but always got the full make up thing going on, highlights, lowlights - a bit desperate I always think.'

Kate nodded, liking the description.

'And you think Alex has left me for her?'

'Whoa! I never said that Kate. You're jumping to massive conclusions! I just said that Alex was flirting with her. The kind of flirting that lonely husband's often take up, which is why I asked if you and Alex were ... okay.'

Kate chewed her lip, thinking frantically back to six weeks before and the Christmas party.

Alex had been really disappointed when she said she wasn't going to join him. Even Fiona had tried to persuade her to go but Kate was exhausted. Millie had been teething and had a snuffly nose. Kate hadn't managed more than three hours of straight sleep for days and the effort just seemed too much at the time.

Alex had announced he was going regardless and she hadn't been at all upset; she'd actually enjoyed having the evening to herself. Millie had gone to bed and against all the odds slept soundly and Kate had enjoyed a long soak in a bath full of bubbles, a glass of wine by her side. She'd watched one of her favourite programmes and then slipped into bed to have an amazing night's sleep. In the morning she'd woken to the sight of Alex's clothes all over the floor as he lay beside her like a starfish, his hair still smelling of smoke and beer from the night before. She had slipped out of bed and collected Millie before making him a full English breakfast which she took upstairs. Was it her imagination or had he seemed a little subdued? She had wondered if he felt guilty about going out without her but now Kate thought more about it, he had been very pleasant and helpful that rest of the weekend. Was he feeling guilty for other reasons? Her mind racing through every possibility, she didn't hear Fiona talking to her.

'Kate!'

Blinking Kate looked at her anxious friend.

'Please don't make too much of it Kate. I just mentioned that he was flirting. I did actually mention to him that he seemed to be very - happy. He said it was just good to have a night out.'

Fiona was smiling reassuringly, but now the idea was in Kate's head it had taken hold and was spreading its tentacles thick and fast.

Kate tried to smile, 'It's okay Fee, it's okay.'

She patted her friend's hand absently. 'I think I better get back home.'

'No! Stay here Kate, stay for the day. I don't think you should be ...'

Kate stood up stopping Fiona in mid-sentence. 'Really Fee, I'm okay. I need to go home. I need to think. Don't worry, I am okay,' she repeated nodding fiercely to emphasise just how okay she was. 'Really.'

Under Fiona's worried gaze she gathered Millie into her arms, wrapping her up against the bitter February weather and strapping her back in the buggy. She kissed Fiona on the cheek, giving her a tight hug before she pushed the buggy out of the door.

'Kate I really think …'

'No! It's okay, I just need to go home. I've probably misunderstood it all Fee,' Kate tried for a laugh but it sounded almost like a yelp.

'I'll see you later,' she called over her shoulder and waving goodbye to a rather dazed Fiona, she set off in the direction of home.

Kate walked briskly, pushing the buggy ahead of her as though she were in training. The jolting didn't seem to bother Millie who was waving her hands in the air, laughing and watching as everything rushed by. Kate just needed to get home. She needed to think. She needed to sit down and think really long and hard because Alex had left her and she needed to find out why.

And she especially needed to find out if it was anything to do with Sandra Maddison.

Chapter 3

By the time Kate arrived home the tears had become something of a permanent addition. She would become aware that her face was wet and would brush aside the constant stream of despair.

It was lunch time and despite Millie's smiling face Kate knew that a five minute delay would bring on tears to equal anything that Kate could produce, so taking deep breaths and trying to control her shaking hands, she stripped Millie of her outdoor clothes and sat her in the highchair. Millie watched eagerly as Kate prepared some lunch, her daughter was easy to feed, Kate had yet to find something that didn't meet with Millie's approval.

'Shepherd's Pie Millie, what do you think?'

Millie clapped her hands together in glee although Kate seriously doubted she understood what was being offered and for the next half hour her attention was given to her small daughter who ate the mashed up shepherd's pie, wolfed down the baby yoghurt and emptied her feeder cup. With a satisfied burp Millie sat back to look at her mother through a smeary face and hair containing more than its fair share of yoghurt.

Kate smiled sadly. 'Oh Millie darling, what is going on?' she whispered, her cheeks once more wet with tears.

It was clear that Millie wasn't too upset by the morning's activities and she smiled happily at her mother before throwing her cup on the floor and pointing to it with a delighted smile.

Retrieving the cup Kate looked at the sink, full once more with cup and plates and the surface sprinkled with crumbs.

The kitchen was usually immaculate by now. When Millie had her morning nap Kat would whirl through the house restoring order and throwing things in the washing machine so when Millie finally woke Kate could devote her time to her small, demanding daughter.

Kate shrugged her shoulders. The kitchen would have to wait and wiping Millie down with a flannel she lifted her out of the highchair and took her into the living room. Even in here the absence of Kate's routine was visible. Normally she would have dashed in at some point to plump the cushions, placing them back on the settee in the correct order (who has a correct order for cushions Alex often asked), shaking out the throw and replacing it with the fringe straight and hanging neatly downwards, folding the newspaper that Alex usually left on the floor and putting away any magazines or books that Kate had read the night before. But this morning Kate didn't give the disorganised cushions a second glance as she dropped Millie into her bouncing chair with donkey for comfort and pulled open one of the sideboard drawers so violently that it flew from its runners and landed heavily on Kate's foot. Wincing with pain but not stopping to examine for any damage, Kate upended the drawer on the settee and began looking feverishly through its contents.

Hundreds of photographs were stuffed into envelopes, all supposedly waiting to be transferred into the scrapbook that Kate had decided to create. The scrapbook lay in the second drawer, still wrapped and waiting for the day Kate found a spare few hours.

She pulled out envelope after envelope throwing them to one side with a tsk of annoyance until her fingers pulled out one that made her stop. She held it close, taking a deep breath. Carelessly she brushed her hand across the settee, pushing everything onto the floor before holding the envelope upside down and scattering its contents across the seats. She spread the photographs out, face upwards, her fingers desperately seeking the one she knew was there until with a sharp intake of breath she stopped. She could see it, half hidden by others but she knew it was the one and slowly she shook it free and raised it to eye level, her eyes flitting over every figure in the captured scene.

Fiona had given her the pictures. There was always a Christmas photographer at the work's party and anyone who wanted could have a copy of the evening unfolding and caught through the lens of the camera. 'You didn't come but at last you can see what happened!' Fiona had said as she presented the envelope to Kate.

They had spent a lovely afternoon looking through the photographs with Fee giving a running commentary as to who said what, who disgraced themselves at the bar, who embarrassed themselves on the dance floor and who threw caution to the winds and indulged in a little Christmas fling! No mention had been made of Alex's flirting and Kate had looked on indulgently at the evidence of her husband enjoying a night out with his colleagues.

But one photograph had been burning its image into Kate's mind as she walked home. One photograph of the group that had included Fiona and Alex, a line of people all leaning in to wave their glasses in the air as they shouted Happy Christmas. She worked her way along the picture, putting names to faces until she came to Alex, then stopped. Standing beside Stuart, Alex was holding his glass aloft like the rest of the party as he smiled into the camera. On his other side, the last person in the shot, stood a woman. Kate vaguely remembered asking Fiona at the time who she was and being satisfied with the answer. She couldn't remember what Fiona had said but now, staring at the figure, she knew without a shadow of doubt that she was looking at Sandra Maddison.

She was tall and slim as Fee had described. Her hair was upswept and still immaculate compared to others in the group whose hair was becoming untidy and losing its pre-party shape. She was pretty, very pretty. And there was no air of desperation that Kate could detect no matter how long she looked at the picture.

She was standing very close to Alex. Kate tried to excuse this as a necessary party pose and her eyes travelled along the rest of the gathered figures. They were all standing close together she reasoned, and yet ….

Was it her imagination or was Sandra Maddison leaning in towards Alex, almost relaxing against the length of his body. Was there a suggestion of intimacy as she raised her glass in the air? Were the back of their hands touching as their glasses moved upwards? Were Sandra's eyes moving in the direction of Alex's own rather than towards the camera and more importantly, was Alex's other arm actually around Sandra's waist, resting on the curve of her hip just out of shot?

Kate was breathing rapidly. She brushed her hand impatiently against her tear soaked cheeks and stared at the picture trying to see beyond the image and into the night itself. Sandra Maddison wouldn't have been sat on the same table as Alex. She was not part of the group that would traditionally be seated together. So to be on the picture she must have gone to the table to talk to someone … Alex? Had she slipped into an empty seat wondered Kate? Had she sat beside Alex and asked him what he thought of the meal, the evening? Had he turned to her with a smile and said that the turkey was a little dry, the vegetables were too hard and there weren't enough potatoes? No of course not. That was the sort of conversation he would have had with Kate. This was a beautiful woman, with no sign of a baby pouch still sitting on her stomach. She was wearing an expensive new dress and Kate had doubt there was a recent visit to the hairdresser and quite possibly the beauty salon showing on her credit card. No thought Kate, the conversation would have been far more relaxed, much more intimate. Perhaps Sandra had rested her hand on Alex's arm and asked him how he was enjoying the evening. He would have put his head close to hers so she could hear him over the music pounding through the room and explained that his wife had refused to come because she was too tired. Perhaps Sandra had given a little pout and offered a 'poor you' to which Alex had no doubt nodded his head vigorously and agreed, yes indeed poor him.

Fiona had mentioned flirting. Is this how it had started? A little sympathy at the dinner table. And then afterwards? Had they walked onto the dance floor hand in hand to twirl and whirl, exchanging lingering looks when their eyes met, holding hands briefly as though to steady themselves, feeling the chemistry shoot up their arms and straight into their hearts. Had they declared they were going to grab some fresh air and separately made their way to the dark terraces outside, gliding towards each other, neither saying a word as their lips met? Had Alex run his hands over her body, pulling her closer to him as they shivered from both passion and the freezing temperatures of a dark December night?

Kate realised that she couldn't see the photograph any more for the shimmer of tears that had fallen onto its surface and weeping in anguish she clutched the photo to her heart and cried as though she would never stop while Millie chewed donkey's ear and watched her mother slide from the settee to sit on the floor racked by sobs.

Ignoring the state of the kitchen Kate put Millie down for her afternoon nap and still clutching the picture of Alex and Sandra in one hand, she pulled out the other envelopes, all crammed full of photographs. Recently any photos taken went straight onto the computer but these envelopes contained Kate and Alex's early relationship, a series of snapshots that featured two smiling faces now spread across the settee and the floor.

They had met when Alex, a serious young man with his first job in marketing still in its infancy, came into the café where Kate, a carefree spirit with no career to speak off was working until she decided what to do next. Alex had been in every day for a week and Kate had taken to the tall rangy figure with the blonde hair that flopped onto his forehead no matter how many times he pushed it back. Alex in his turn had fallen head over heels for the slender young woman with the strawberry blonde hair that hung down her back in a thick curly plait, trying hard to escape the pins keeping it in place. Her dark gray eyes were wide, framed by dark lashes that caught and held Alex's gaze. But it was Kate herself that fascinated him, the bubbly, infectious joy of Kate's manner that left him quite enchanted.

Little did Kate know that Alex was potentially damaging his career by spending every lunch hour in the small tea room instead of joining the other thrusting young executives at the funky new sushi bar around the corner. And little did Alex know that Kate had left her letter of resignation in her pocket all that week as she waited each lunchtime for the tall young man to walk through the door and give her a shy smile as he ordered a ham salad sandwich. By the end of a week that had progressed to names but little else, Kate had decided to take the step that Alex didn't seem quite able to reach and gently suggested that maybe they should meet one evening, away from the café.

Kate looked at the photographs she had spread around the floor; there were so many of them. Their third date when they joined a couple of Kate's friends and drove to a pub by the canal, Alex gazing adoringly at a windswept Kate who sat in the crook of his arm and watched the boats glide past.

Another taken the first time they went to Kate's mum's for Sunday lunch, dressed up for the rather exacting standards she imposed and looking a little strained as they sat ramrod straight at the table. Their first holiday together, laying on the beach in Malaga and looking sun kissed and totally in love; their first flat; their engagement party where Kate, beside herself with happiness drifted around the room showing everyone her diamond ring and a smile that wouldn't disappear while Alex stood at the bar looking inordinately pleased with himself.

It was all there, the story of their lives together. Kate stared at them for hours, lining them up in an order that charted the progress from the very first few days of their relationship to the small but elaborate wedding Kate's mum had insisted on hosting and paying for; their eventual move to the house where Kate had imagined they would spend their next decade together and culminating in a shot of Kate and Alex staring anxiously down at a tiny red faced figure in Kate's arms.

Kate picked up each photograph, searching Alex's face for clues. Did he look less loving in this photo than the one before? When did that adoring look leave his eye? At what stage should Kate have seen that he had moved away from her and would now spend his Christmas parties flirting with slim blonde women called Sandra as they trailed their hand along his arm and whispered seductively in his ear?

Kate was struggling. In every photo the smile Alex sent in her direction was as loving as the previous one. Sometimes he was laughing, his arm thrown around Kate's shoulders, sometimes his face was serious as he looked adoringly into her eyes.

But no matter how hard Kate looked, no matter how many times she looked, there was no sign, no clue at all that Alex Patterson had decided that Kate was no longer the love of his life and he was about to pack his case and walk out of the door.

Chapter 4

Later that evening there was a knock at the door and Kate shot up from her semi sleeping state, skidding through the newspapers and photos that littered the floor as she flew to answer it, her heart hammering.

'Oh,' she said, disappointment clouding her face, 'come in.'

Fiona followed her into the hall.

'I just wanted to check that you were alright,' she said giving Kate a quick hug. 'Have you heard from Alex? I thought you might need someone to talk to.'

Kate shook her head. She hadn't been able to suppress the tiny fragment of hope that it had been Alex who was knocking at the door, Alex who had come home having decided she had learnt her lesson.

'He would have used his key honey, he wouldn't be knocking on his own front door.'

Kate's eyes flew to her friend. 'Mind reader,' she accused trying to smile.

'Not really,' sighed Fiona, 'it's written all over your face.'

Kate shrugged. 'Tea?' she offered and turned to walk away, shoulders sunk with depression.

Fiona only just managed to stop the exclamation as she followed Kate into the kitchen. Fiona was notoriously untidy and constantly teased Kate for refusing to relax her high standards even with a small baby creating chaos around the house. But the kitchen looked like a student flat. Every surface was covered with something, pots were piled high in the sink, the kettle was sitting on the dresser and the milk sat on top of the hob which mercifully was turned off. As Kate looked round for the kettle, her bleary eyes wandering unfocused around the room, Fiona slipped off her coat and took Kate by the arm.

'Go sit down honey. I'll make the tea, you put your feet up.'

Kate nodded and wandered aimlessly back into the living room as Fiona looked round her in dismay, rolled her sleeves up and attacked the chaos.

Twenty minutes later she carried a tray of tea and biscuits through to the living room. The sink was empty, the dishwasher loaded and turned on, the misplaced items returned to their homes, surfaces tidied and cleaned.

Having restored order in the kitchen she almost dropped the tray as she entered the living room. Kate was curled up in an armchair by the fire. The TV was a blank screen in one corner of the room and the lights were off but in the glow of the street lighting Fiona could see the mayhem that covered every inch of the room. Balancing the tray, she flicked on a light so she could walk through the piles of photographs spread across the floor and make it safely to the small table by Kate's chair, one of the few surfaces not covered with memories.

Biting her lip, she touched Kate's shoulder to rouse her from her reverie as she stared through the window to the dark garden beyond. Looking around, Fiona failed to find anywhere to sit so she slid to the floor at Kate's feet and reached out to touch the line of photos that snaked around the room, overlapping, crowding on top of each other, sweeping across the floor, onto the sofa and back onto the floor, all clearly set out with some path in mind.

'Having a clear out?' she asked lightly.

Kate shook her head listlessly and for the first time Fiona noticed that she was clutching something in her hand.

Reaching out she gently uncurled Kate's fingers from the fist they had formed and smoothed out the crumpled photo.

Suddenly Kate came back to life and jumping out of the chair she squatted down by Fiona's knees.

'That's her isn't it?' she demanded eagerly. 'That's Sandra Maddison!'

Fiona stared at the picture. It was hard to see who anyone was anymore. Clutched in Kate's hand for hours the surface had broken and caused white lines to form across the faces of the people gathered. But Fiona obediently looked at the line of people toasting Christmas and at the blonde woman who Kate was stabbing at with her finger.

'No,' said Fiona in surprise. 'that's not Sandra. That's the head of sales, Gwen. You met her at the last social we had. Remember? She'd just spent two years working in California and we both said how we'd love to visit there one day.'

Kate stared at Fiona in bemusement. 'So that's not Sandra?'

'No of course it's not.'

Kate grabbed the photo from Fiona's hand.

'But I was so sure. Look at them … look at them Fee!'

Fiona obligingly looked at the figures standing side by side.

'You can tell can't you, you can tell just by looking - can't you?'

Fiona bit her lip. 'Tell what honey?'

'That they're together, that they want to be together!'

Fiona looked hard at the photo, at Alex smiling into the camera and Gwen standing by his side, leaning forward so she was in the shot, her hand raised in a toast, smiling.

'Kate, they're not together …'

'They are!' Kate's voice was almost a scream and she snatched back the photo. 'Look how close they're standing, look how she's leaning on him, look at his arm … LOOK!'

She waved the photo in Fiona's face, almost scratching her friend's nose as she thrust it closer. But Fee shook her head, worry etching a line between her eyes.

'Kate they're not together. Look at everyone else, they're all standing close to each other. We had to so we could all get in the photo. And what do you mean look at Alex's arm, I can't see his arm …'

'Exactly!' shouted Kate clutching her stomach and doubling over with grief. 'Because he's touching her with it, it's out of shot because he's touching her, I know he is!'

Fiona sat up pulling Kate into her arms, smoothing her hair frantically as she stared at her friend's anguished face.

'Oh my God Kate, you need to stop this. I'm telling you that there is absolutely nothing between Alex and Gwen. This is a picture of two people at a Christmas party, drinking together, having their photograph taken. It is not a sign that they're together in any way.'

Fiona stroked Kate's face, trying to get her to focus on what she was saying. 'Listen to me Kate, please listen to me.'

She felt Kate relax a little, a fraction of the tension leaving her shoulders.

'It's not Sandra Maddison?' whispered Kate.

'No, absolutely not,' answered Fiona.

Kate nodded, looking down at the crumpled picture in her hand

'Right,' nodded Kate and Fiona slumped in relief pressing a shaking hand to her mouth.

'Kate darling you must …'

But Kate had gone, breaking free from the protective circle of Fiona's arms and dropping the photo to the floor without a second glance.

'Well if that's Gwen,' began Kate following the photographic trail towards the last few weeks of its timeline and the bright blur of the Christmas party, 'where is Sandra Maddison?' she asked, her eyes frantically searching for the blonde woman she suspected had stolen her husband's heart.

Fiona watched in horror as Kate grabbed at each photograph, searching the background for some glimpse of Sandra, throwing them to one side if they didn't fulfill the requirements.

Suddenly she snatched at one almost throwing it at Fiona. 'This one ... is that her?'

'Kate please calm down ...'

'IS THAT HER?'

Fiona shook her head, 'Of course not that's Olivia from ...'

Kate had already turned away scrabbling through the pile.

'What about this one?'

'Kate you're going to make yourself ill if you keep this up. I should never have mentioned Sandra's name. I just said Alex had been flirting that's all. I never meant you to think that they were having an affair or ...'

'What about this one?'

'Oh God Kate please!'

'Is this her? Is this Sandra Maddison?'

Fiona shook her head in despair, tears pricking at her eyes. She wondered if she should phone a doctor, phone Kate's mum, phone Alex.

Kate grabbed at her arm, her eyes boring into Fiona's own. Her voice was soft, pleading.

'Please help me Fee,' she whispered. She held up her hand to stop Fiona from replying, 'I know you don't think there's anything going on but I just want to see her picture. I'm just trying to understand what went wrong and I feel, somehow, that if I see what happened that night it will help.'

For a moment neither of them moved and then with a heavy sigh, Fee joined her friend on the floor her hand smoothing over the rumpled pictures in her search. She stopped, picking at the corner of a photograph somewhat distastefully and examining it for a second before handing it to Kate.

'There,' she instructed, pointing to a figure just in range of the shot. 'There, that's Sandra. And as you can see Alex is nowhere near her.'

Kate stared silently at the figure caught at the very edge of the photograph. She was standing slightly apart from the group the camera was following, half turning in their direction so her face was caught almost full on but with her body still mainly in profile.

Kate smiled. How could she have ever thought that Gwen was Sandra Maddison. They were nothing alike.

Gwen had been stylish, smooth, expensive. Kate had imagined her gazing seductively at Alex and he would have been unable to do anything about it. She would have bared her perfect teeth outlined by her glossy, expensive lipstick and he would have succumbed immediately. Kate had felt defeated when she saw Gwen's picture because she knew she wasn't able to compete.

The woman in this shot was just as Fiona had described her. She wasn't as tall as Gwen. She wasn't as slim. Oh she wasn't fat and she didn't have Kate's baby pouch but neither did she have the natural long, lean slenderness of Gwen. Her dress was not the expensive designer model worn by Gwen, although it had been chosen carefully to make the most of her figure, emphasising an undeniably impressive cleavage. The fabric travelled across her stomach in gentle folds but

43

stopped too high up her thigh. Her hair was blonde but not the natural soft sheen of Gwen's hair, it was an altogether more brittle colour, swept up at the back in a similar style but it hadn't been set by a hairdresser and was already tumbling down in a birds' nest at the back of her head. Her face was ever so slight out of focus and no matter how much Kate stared she couldn't make out the individual features. A normal face, over plucked eyebrows, red lips, that was about as much as she could determine. But the overwhelming impression, much to Kate's delight was almost exactly as Fiona had described, okay and maybe just a little desperate.

'Kate?' asked Fiona nervously, 'are you alright.'

Kate carried on staring at the photo. She had scoured every inch, every shadowy shape but had been unable to find even a glimpse of Alex. He was nowhere to be seen.

'Kate?'

Kate looked up her yes blinking.

'Are you okay honey?'

Kate nodded, turning her eyes back to the picture.

'You see what I mean,' asked Fiona, happy that the crisis had been averted. 'She's nothing Kate, nothing at all to worry about. There's no way that Alex would leave you for her.' Fiona sat in the chair recently vacated by Kate and sipped at her cup of tea. It had gone a little cold and she wrinkled her nose.

'I asked Stuart, when he came home. I told him what had happened – I didn't think you'd mind?' She shot a quick glance at Kate who shook her head, a new photograph now clutched in her fist. 'He was as shocked as me. He said he hadn't heard anything about Alex, nothing at all. No gossip at work, not even a tiny little rumour that Alex might be having an affair so I really don't think it's anything to worry about darling. Really. Alex is having some sort of - crisis and doesn't know what he's doing right now. That's all it is.'

She leaned over to touch Kate on the shoulder, 'You will be alright by yourself tonight Kate? I can stay you know. I've put Stuart on notice that I might not go home and I ...'

'No - thank you,' smiled Kate. 'Thank you so much Fee but I wouldn't do that to you. A morning having to get your three to school on his own and Stuart would be walking out as well!'

Fiona chuckled. 'It might do him good, make him appreciate me more!'

Kate shook her head and yawned. 'Truly Fee, I'm okay. I just need to get some sleep.'

Fiona looked doubtful but gave in and hugged her friend as she headed for the door.

'I'll come round tomorrow, after the school run,' she promised as Kate opened the door. 'I know it's easy to say but try and get some sleep Kate. It will sort itself out I'm sure and in the meantime you need to look after yourself.'

Kate smiled wryly. They both knew that sleep was unlikely for Kate that night but she allowed her friend to reassure her, allowed her to wrap her arms around her and smooth her hair

'I'll be okay Fiona, really I will,'

'And forget all this business about Alex having an affair! I'm certain that he's not. I would have heard something – well Stuart would have heard something, no-one at that office can keep anything to themselves!'

Kate nodded obediently.

'Sandra Maddison was just someone he flirted with at the Christmas party, nothing more. I don't know why Alex has gone but he'll be home as soon as he realises what a stupid thing he's done.'

Kate nodded again then said 'Goodnight' and watched her friend walk down the path, her breath freezing in the bitterly cold night air, before closing the door. She knew she would not be able to sleep. She knew that visions of Alex standing in the doorway saying he was leaving would hound her through the darkness.

But obediently she locked the door, turned off the lights and climbed into bed to lay staring at the ceiling with tears rolling down her face as she sobbed and wondered why the man she loved had left and whether it had anything at all to do with Sandra Maddison.

Chapter 5

It was after midnight when Kate phoned Fiona. After her friend had left, Kate had gone to bed but was unable to sleep, tossing and turning for hours. In her mind she could still see the snaking line of photos that recorded her life with Alex; happy, smiling images of a young couple in love and she'd suddenly realised how silly she was being. She loved Alex with all her heart and she knew he loved her just as much. Why would he suddenly decide to leave her? And as for the idea that he had left her for a woman he'd met only weeks before at a Christmas party – Kate had thrown back her head and laughed. He was obviously cross with her, maybe he was teaching her a lesson but he hadn't left. And certainly not because he was with Sandra Maddison. He was coming home, Kate just knew he was coming home. So she had ignored the time on the clock and decided to recruit Stuart to help her find out for sure where Alex was.

'I think he's gone away with work,' she announced triumphantly as Fiona was still trying to work out which way up to hold the phone.

'He's cross with me so he took all his clothes to make it look like he was leaving,' Kate laughed as she carried on breathlessly. 'He's coming home at the end of the week like he always does but he's letting me think he's not because he's angry.'

Fiona didn't answer and Kate continued. 'Of course he hasn't left! People don't leave when they're happy and Alex was happy, we were happy, so he hasn't left. And Sandra Maddison,' another high pitched laugh, 'Oh God what was I thinking? You tried to tell me it was nothing Fiona and I wouldn't listen. But you're right. Alex wouldn't leave me for someone else. If he was having an affair I would know! And why would he want to have an affair anyway? He was happy, here, with me.' Kate's voice started to break slightly and she took a deep breath. 'Anyway, I've realised that I'm just being hysterical and of course Alex hasn't left me. He's away with work and he'll be back in a day or so. If I phone the office tomorrow and ask to speak to him someone will tell me he's in Warrington or Rotherham or somewhere else doing something for the company.'

'Kate …' Fiona tried to interrupt.

'But I was thinking Fee, I wondered if Stuart could ask? He could go to Alex's department and just ask where he is, as though he needed to talk to him about something.'

'Kate honey…'

'I just need to know. It will just help me stop wondering Fee. I mean I know he's coming home and he hasn't really left me. But it would be good to know for certain.'

There was a pause as Kate finally stopped talking.

'Kate, why don't I come round? I can stay with you tonight and …'

'No, don't be silly. Really I'm fine Fee. I just wanted to ask if Stuart could check for me. Because he works there and he can ask without it sounding strange. If I phone, people will think I don't know where Alex is.'

Neither of them said the obvious and Fiona sighed. 'Kate …'

'Please Fiona! Please ask Stuart if he will find out for me!'

There was the slightest hesitation. 'Okay Kate. I'll speak to Stuart and I'll come round to see you tomorrow.'

'Thank you,' breathed Kate.

'Now please try and get some sleep.'

And saying goodnight Kate actually fell into a deep if somewhat troubled sleep, her dreams full of images of a happy and smiling Alex but with a feeling of dread and panic swirling through her mind that she couldn't quite place.

The sun was shining through the curtains where Kate hadn't pulled them together tightly enough, the light resting on her face.

Alex was smiling at her, the smile that always made her feel so special because it was clear that it was a smile just for Kate and no-one else.

'More potatoes Alex?' asked Kate's mother and Alex stopped smiling at Kate and turned instead to smile at Marcia Brady as she proffered a serving dish still holding plenty of perfectly cooked roast potatoes.

'Yes please Marcia,' answered Alex politely and heaped several more on his plate. 'These are delicious.'

Kate grinned, Alex loved his potatoes. She must ask her mum how to make them so deliciously fluffy. Kate wasn't exactly a star in the kitchen, mainly from lack of interest but now she had Alex to cook for, well she needed to be able to provide him with a pile of roast potatoes cooked just like her mum's.

When they had finally finished, Marcia refused Alex's offer to help clear the table and waved him into the living room. Kate knew better than to follow and she began to carry the tableware into the kitchen.

'He seems very nice my dear,' said her mum as she slipped on a dark blue apron over her dress and began washing.

'Responsible, grown up and obviously keen to make a name for himself with his new job,' she continued.

Kate couldn't help but smirk a little, deciding to overlook the clearly surprised tone of her mother's voice. It was the first boyfriend who had ever received even the slightest hint of approval from Marcia Brady even though Kate had long made a habit of only bringing home young men who she thought may stand a chance and leaving many potential candidates at home by themselves when she was summoned for Sunday lunch.

Kate's parents had divorced when she was nine and even at that tender age Kate could tell it was the best thing for all of them. Kate's mum, far from being traumatised at being left on her own with a nine-year-old, just seemed slightly relieved to have one person less in the household. Over the next few years Kate had the definite impression that her mother was playing a waiting game until Kate also departed leaving Marcia without the interruption of other people in her life. Once Kate had finally moved out and there was no-one else to disturb the status quo, the house spent its days in a showroom condition regardless of the time of day. Tea was always made in a rose covered teapot which was placed on a tea tray along with a matching milk jug before being poured into china cups. The everyday china was used Monday to Saturday but the best china was always used on Sunday even if Marcia was the only one to sit at the mahogany dining table, and sit at the table she always did, nothing so common as a plate on her knee for Marcia Brady.

Kate's hand hovered by one of the wine glasses she had collected from the very same mahogany table.

'You're not going not put that in the dishwasher are you dear?'

Kate's hand moved as though burned, 'Of course not Mum!'

'Good, crystal doesn't go in the dishwasher.'

Kate set it next to the sink, beside the gold rimmed plates which also didn't go in the dishwasher. In fact, thought Kate as she looked around, very little of the Sunday dinner service seemed to belong in the dishwasher. Reluctantly she picked up a tea towel and started drying.

'How long have you known each other?' asked Marcia, her eagle eyes watching Kate as she dried a plate. 'Do be careful Kate, they are part of a set you know.'

Kate hated being in the kitchen with Marcia. The intense scrutiny made her so nervous she dropped more in her mother's kitchen than she dropped anywhere else combined.

'Oh a couple of months,' she said carefully drying the plate and setting it to one side.

'Mm. Do you spend much time with him?'

Kate stared. 'Of course we do, we're going out.'

'Do you spend much time in the house?'

Kate blushed. Her mother was obviously trying to find out if Kate was sleeping with him.

'Quite a lot,' she mumbled, drying another plate and adding it to the pile. 'We are both old enough you know!'

Marcia's eyebrows raised. 'I'm sure you are dear. I'm not actually asking if you've had sex.'

Kate's blush threatened to cover her entire body. This was a conversation she simply couldn't have with her mother.

'I was just wondering if he actually spent any time with you at home. If he knew how appallingly untidy you are, how disorganised. Has he ever had the misfortune of eating any of your cooking for example?'

Kate pouted. 'He loves me mum, he loves me because I'm messy and disorganised and can't cook!'

Actually Kate suspected the last part was not true, that Alex loved her despite her quite appalling untidiness and total lack of cooking skills. But only the other day when she had been unable to find her door keys in the disaster that was her flat, Alex had laughed and hauled her into his arms and instead of being annoyed that they were now fifteen minutes late for the cinema he had told her that he loved the chaos that she brought into his life. They ended up missing the entire film as Alex insisted on showing Kate just how much he loved her disorganised ways. She'd found the keys the next morning in the cutlery drawer when she went to make a cup of tea.

Kate realised she was smiling at the memory and her mother was watching her with a raised eyebrow.

'It's all well and good in the beginning,' said Marcia briskly, rinsing the last plate and taking off her apron. 'But give it a few years and I guarantee that other people's mess and clutter becomes far from romantic.'

Her voice was stern and Kate had a fleeting memory of one of the many arguments that used to greet her every evening when she came in from school.

'Oh Graham, can't you put anything away!'

'For God's sake Marcia, I'm still using the wretched thing, stop being such a pain!'

Kate had been in no doubt that her mother had found her husband's natural inclination towards untidiness less than appealing. It had been an act of rebellion on Kate's part that made her refuse to follow in her mother's footsteps and instead adopted her father's untidy, cluttered approach to life.

Kate shrugged her shoulders. 'Well Alex loves me the way I am,' she said defensively, 'I don't need to change!' and the conversation had stopped as Kate finished the plates in silence and

Marcia poured some water into the rose covered teapot and set out the tray with her china cups and saucers.

Later that day, when they were back in Kate's shambolic flat, she had recounted the story to Alex and he had thrown her onto the settee and announced that he would never get annoyed with her untidy ways. Although he did say, with a solemn face, that her cooking had better improve because he refused point blank to eat one more round of burnt cheese on toast and then they had laughed and kissed and tumbled into bed. But there was a little nagging doubt in Kate's head. Maybe her mother had said the same sort of thing to her father when they were in the first flush of love and romance, maybe she had found his messiness sweet and laughed at the chaos he left in his wake. But eventually it had driven an untidy wedge through their relationship. So just to be on the safe side, Kate resolved that she would try and be a little neater, nothing too over the top, just a little tidier, a little more organised. She would make sure that Alex could never give untidiness as a reason to leave her.

The light was still tickling Kate's eyes, forcing them to open and for a moment she stared at the dust mites dancing in the sunlight peeping through the gap.

'Alex,' she murmured, suddenly unsure where she was. She was staring at a wardrobe that she didn't remember.

'Alex?'

She rolled over and remembered that she wasn't in her old flat. She was in her house. Her grown up house. The house she and Alex had bought together. The house into which they had brought their adorable daughter. And the house which Alex had left the day before.

'Oh.'

Sitting up Kate looked around her. Her old bedroom would have been covered with clothes and shoes, every drawer and wardrobe ajar. It always looked as though it had been ransacked. She remembered Alex's look of alarm the first time he was invited back. He'd asked if she had been burgled and she had been indignant and defensive until she saw the twinkle in his eye. Then he'd thrown her onto the pile of clothes laid on her bed, reflecting her lack of decisiveness over what to wear that morning and pretended to be climbing a mountain as he hauled himself beside her.

That seemed such a long time ago thought Kate. This bedroom was an oasis of calm. Designer wardrobes and drawers filled with well organised clothes, all folded and put neatly away into drawers covered with scented liners or hung on padded hangers next to the small sachets of vanilla freshener in the wardrobe. Kate had taken her tidiness and organization to a level that impressed even the impossible to impress Marcia Brady.

The morning light was getting stronger and with a sudden burst of energy Kate leapt out of bed. Alex was coming home. He hadn't actually left, Kate had misunderstood or Alex was playing a rather cruel joke but he hadn't left. She needed to get dressed. No she needed to shower and get dressed. She needed to wash her hair and put on something nice. She needed to tidy the house. The house! If Alex came home now he would think she had gone back to her old untidy ways, she needed to clean and fast. And Millie. She needed Millie looking her best as well. Kate cocked her head to one side to see how awake Millie sounded on the baby monitor. Early morning sounds, she was waking but Kate had a little more time before her tiny daughter would start to vent her rage at any lack of attention and with a skip in her step, Kate launched herself under the shower, scrubbing and polishing until she came out glowing.

An hour and a half later Fiona was at the front door, her eyebrows raised at Kate's changed demeanor. She was dressed, hair gleaming, face smiling with a happy chuckling Millie dressed in an adorable pink denim dress sitting on her hip.

'Fee!' Kate dragged her friend into the kitchen, putting Millie in her highchair. The kitchen had undergone the same transformation and the work surfaces shone, not a thing out of place.

'Did you ask Stuart for me? Will he do it? Will he check where Alex is? Does he mind?'

Kate was filling the kettle, passing Millie a chopped up banana to gum and taking cups and saucers out of the cupboard all at the same time.

'Kate.' Fiona stopped. She took the cups out of Kate's hand and drew her friend to one of the kitchen chairs. 'Sit down Kate. The tea will wait.'

'No I ...'

'Kate sit down.'

Kate was shaking her head, her shoulders tense. 'I know I'm right Fee,' she said defiantly. 'I know I'm right and I just need Stuart to check it for me, that's all. I just …'

'He already has Kate.'

Silence fell in the kitchen, broken only by happy mumblings from Millie as she smeared banana over her face.

'He's asked already? He's been to Alex's office and …'

'He went there first thing.'

'Right,' nodded Kate. 'And what did they say? Where is Alex? Did they say when he was expected back?'

'Alex was in the office honey. He was sitting at his desk when Stuart walked in.'

'Oh.'

It was a small sound, uncertain, confused.

'Stuart asked him what was happening, as a friend. He said you were upset and seemed to think Alex had left.'

Kate seemed not be listening, she was staring out of the window her eyes darting round the garden but her shoulders were tense, her body was still.

Fiona took her friend's hand. 'Alex said that he …' Fiona bit her lip, trying to look into Kate's wild eyes. 'He said that he had left, that you two had split up.'

Kate shook her head. 'No.' she said decisively, 'No. We haven't split up. He's just angry about something and…'

'Kate darling, please listen. Alex has gone. He has left you. He isn't playing games, he's left.'

Kate let out a cry, a piercing cry that stopped Millie, hand halfway to her mouth as she turned to look at her mother and which made Fiona's eyes fill with tears.

'I'm so sorry Kate darling, I'm so very sorry but Alex has gone.'

Chapter 6

The day passed in a blur of tears and pain. Kate looked after Millie, she made her daughter some tea, bathed her, loved her – all with tears rolling down her face. The pain was unimaginable. Alex had left her. The husband she adored had gone, her perfect marriage, it appeared, had not been so perfect after all.

She had asked Fiona if it was because of Sandra Maddison but Fiona had shaken her head and said 'Of course not Kate. I really wished I'd never mentioned the woman. I can't believe that Alex would have an affair.'

'Didn't Stuart ask? Didn't he ask Alex why he'd gone and where he was staying and …'

'It wasn't really an appropriate time and place to ask anything, standing in the middle of the office. Stuart was trying to be discreet and he's a man at the end of the day, they don't do the whole let's talk about what's happening thing!'

Kate had smiled wanly and asked Fiona to thank her husband for at least going to find out where Alex was.

'There's no gossip though Kate, no-one seems to know that Alex has gone. He may not have told you what's happening but he hasn't told anyone else either.'

Later in the afternoon Kate insisted Fiona left to pick up her children from school and turned down an offer to join her and Stuart for supper. She said she had a lot of thinking to do and although she sat in the armchair, hugging the fire while Millie had her afternoon nap, she actually thought very little, her mind a haze of confusion.

She had refused to phone her mother. She couldn't bear to see the rebuke in Marcia's eyes, the inevitable feeling of failure. 'I did tell you it was hard Kate. I told you that you would have to change your ways to keep your husband.' No, Marcia would have to wait for a little while longer, at least until Kate could explain what had happened and why Alex had walked out on their supposedly happy marriage.

So Kate had gone through the motions for the rest of the day, her heart a physical ache inside her body as she smiled and cooed at Millie and held her little daughter tightly to her chest. At nine o' clock when Fiona walked round to Kate's house to see how her distraught friend was coping, she found the lights off, the curtains closed and the house in darkness; although if she'd listened very hard she may have been able to hear Kate sobbing as she curled up in her big empty bed wondering where she had gone so terribly wrong.

It was a lovely warm day and Kate could feel the weight of Alex's arm around her waist as they stood at the patio door admiring the flower strewn garden. 'Your mum has a lovely house Kate.'

Kate snorted. Marcia Brady had always kept a tidy house. She was fanatical about order, everything had its place and there was a place for everything. Kate's dad had been very different. He would wander in from his shed and put a spanner on the work surface, right next to the potatoes Marcia was peeling. He would take off his muddy boots at the door as directed but leave them upended on the floor and not side by side on the mat. He would look for things in the sideboard and leave the contents of the drawers scattered across the surface. He was a happy, relaxed man whose untidiness irritated his wife beyond belief. When her parents finally divorced, Kate had relished the thought of spending time with Graham Brady at his tiny new flat, where she wouldn't have to worry about leaving her clothes on the floor, washing up her cup immediately after its use and making sure that every surface was clutter free and polished to a high shine. Except she had soon come to notice that once away from the family home, Graham Brady seemed almost as tidy as his wife and Kate had watched with bewildered eyes the first time she and her father returned home from a rainy afternoon walk and he put both his own and Kate's wellies neatly side by side on the mat. She had never shared this information with her mother. Kate was quite happy with the blame she had imposed on Marcia Brady and the scenario where her unrelenting tidiness had driven her husband out of the house. But the memory had stayed like a sharp little thorn in her brain.

'She's obsessive,' Kate had said dismissively as she turned away from the garden and sat on the settee. She could hear the clink of the teapot as her mother waited for the kettle to boil in the kitchen.

Alex had shrugged, examining the silver photo frames set out neatly on the sideboard, all pictures of Kate at various stages of growth. 'But it's nice isn't it?'

Kate looked at him blankly.

'Coming into a house like this. It's nice.'

The conversation had ended as Marcia arrived at the doorway and Alex had jumped to his feet to open the door a little wider and pull out the coffee table which Marcia always used for the tea tray. Kate had looked around the spotless living room with its elegant furniture, polished surfaces and plumped cushions. She had deliberately kept her own flat in a state of perpetual untidiness once she'd finally moved out from under Marcia's immaculate iron rod. She had done it mainly to annoy her mother but as Kate sipped her tea she looked around and accepted that maybe it was nice to spend time in such a pleasant room where everything was organised, coordinated and tidy. Marcia had created a room of harmony and peace. At least Alex seemed to think so and Kate watched him as he drank his tea and chatted to Marcia.

Alex's parents lived in New Zealand. They had moved there as soon as he had started his first job and although he spoke to them regularly on the phone there was no cosy family home to retreat to at the weekend. But he seemed more than happy to visit Marcia and it was Kate who would sit on the edge of the settee, watching the clock and waiting until she could reasonably say it was time to go. Alex by contrast, loved spending time in Marcia's home and would sit perfectly relaxed amongst the immaculate cushions sipping tea from his china cup with an expression of sheer contentment on his face.

When she and Alex arrived back at the flat that evening, Kate had looked at the mismatched furniture and haphazard decor with new eyes and the following day she bought two matching cushions and a new pair of curtains. She would give Alex the kind of home he wanted, even if that meant adopting some of her mother's approach to life.

Kate turned over. It must be late, the sun was starting to peep through the curtains and she could hear Millie chuntering to herself.

'Oh Alex,' she whispered, a tear rolling down her cheek. 'I tried so hard, why did you go?'

Millie's chuntering was growing louder and eventually Kate sat up and swung her legs onto the floor. It was time to start another day.

When Fiona came round that evening, a bottle of wine clutched under her arm, Kate led her through to the kitchen where her laptop sat on the table. The evidence of a day spent crying showed in her red rimmed eyes and she looked frail and deeply sad.

'I think it may be my fault Alex left,' she said in a voice that was raw with crying.

'What! Oh Kate, you can't blame yourself. Alex just isn't thinking clearly, he's having a midlife crisis or something.'

Fiona waved her hand at Kate's raised eyebrow, 'Okay he's a bit young for a midlife crisis but he's having something similar! He'll come round. But you can't blame yourself honey!'

Kate was shaking her head sadly. 'But I've spent the day reading about it Fee, and I definitely did something wrong.'

'Reading about what?'

'Husbands leaving, why they leave, why they come back, if they come back.'

Fiona looked confused. 'Where …?'

'I looked it up on Google.'

'Google?'

'The answer to everything is always on Google Fee.'

'Well, the answer to most things may be on Google but I would have thought in this instance marriage counselling would be more appropriate.'

'But marriage counselling takes two! And besides, Google was full of really interesting information. All about why men leave their wives and I really think,' Kate's voice cracked and her eyes were once again swimming with tears, 'that it's my fault.'

Fiona opened the wine, filling two glasses and thrusting one into Kate's hand. 'You stop this right now Kate Patterson. I don't care what Google says, you are not to blame! Alex has walked out, how can that possibly be your fault?'

'I think I neglected him?'

'Neglected him! Hardly Kate, I don't think I know of a less neglected husband than Alex. In fact, if anything you did far too much for him, he had an easy life you know …'

65

Kate waved her hand in the air as she interrupted. 'Yes, yes. I looked after him physically, but did I neglect him emotionally?'

'Emotionally?'

'Yes, did I look after his emotional needs as well as iron his shirts?'

'I – er, well I'm not sure…'

'You see I've been looking at what Google has to say and I think I may have left him feeling unappreciated and wondering what his role in the household was after Millie arrived.'

'His role in the household! What on earth is that supposed to mean?'

'I think he's having an affair.'

'Oh Kate we've been through all this. I'm sorry I ever mentioned Sandra Maddison. I'm certain that Alex would never have an affair with her, it's madness to even think such a thing.'

'Then why did he go Fee? If we were so happy and so in love – why did he go?'

There was silence as Fee looked helpless and Kate dried the tears sliding down her cheeks.

'Oh Kate, I wish I knew what to say!'

But Kate was tapping away at her laptop, turning the screen round so Fiona could see. 'All these husbands told their wives they needed space. They were feeling trapped and tied down or just not sure what they wanted out of life and needed some time to think.'

'Don't tell me,' interrupted Fiona caustically,' they needed to find themselves!'

'Yes, but most of them turned out to be having affairs – or about to have affairs or wanting to have affairs.'

Fiona shook her head.

'This lot,' Kate flicked frantically through a few more pages, 'they were all honest enough to tell their wives there was someone else.'

'Well thank goodness for honesty,' remarked Fiona taking a large glug of wine.

'Now this section,' Kate paused, her lip trembling slightly. 'These are different. Because these men all said there was no-one else, they just didn't want to be with their wives anymore. They no longer loved them, they didn't want to spend any more time with them.'

Kate turned to Fiona. 'I couldn't bear it if Alex was in this group Fee. I just couldn't cope with the thought that he'd left because he couldn't stand being in the same house as me anymore.'

Fiona put down her glass and reached a hand out to her friend. 'Don't be ridiculous Kate, it was obvious to anyone who saw you two together that he adored you!'

'Then why did he leave?' whispered Kate. 'Why did he go if there was nothing wrong with our marriage?'

'I don't know honey, I only wish I had an answer for you.'

'If he's having an affair...'

'Kate stop ...'

'If he's having an affair,' continued Kate, 'then I have to ask myself why.'

'Surely you should ask him that?'

'I have to ask myself what went wrong in our marriage that made him turn to someone else. And according to this ...'

'According to Google?'

'Yes, according to Google, one of the reasons why husbands have affairs isn't because they've fallen in love with someone else, it's because they feeling lost and quite lonely even though they're married. They feel their wives are neglecting them.'

'Oh Kate! Alex is the least neglected person I've ever known. You cook him a cordon bleu meal every night of the week, you keep this home immaculate, you clean, wash, iron. You iron his underwear for God's sake! And you think he's feeling neglected?'

Kate nodded her head sadly. 'I must have forgotten something Fee. Because that's what it says here,' Kate pointed at the laptop. 'Men have affairs because they feel abandoned, not important to their wives anymore. Especially when a new baby comes along.'

'Then those men need to grow up!' declared Fiona, ignoring Kate's admonishing look as she slammed her wine glass onto the table without using a coaster. 'They need to thank their lucky stars that they've got a lovely new baby and a wife and a tidy house and stop sulking about how little attention they're getting.'

'No,' insisted Kate stubbornly. 'I think I neglected Alex emotionally, I think maybe I didn't give him enough of my time and he ended up looking elsewhere.'

'And maybe you were the perfect wife and he isn't having an affair and he's left because … because of something ese.'

'That's why I need to find out why he left Fee. Because if he is having an affair, then I'll be able to deal with it.'

'Deal with it! And how exactly are you going to do that?'

Kate nibbled her lip. 'Well,' she started, turning the laptop back to face her. 'Google says that I need to make him want to come home. He needs to realise he's made a mistake but that he can come back.'

She carried on tapping, 'I need to remind him of the person he fell in love with.'

'How?'

'Well I'm not entirely sure yet. But Google says that I need to accept I played a part in his actions and it wasn't all his fault,' she quoted, ignoring Fiona's snort of derision.

'And I need to …'

'You need to stop reading Google! This isn't down to you Kate, this is all entirely Alex's fault.'

Kate stuck out her chin stubbornly. 'Apportioning blame isn't the answer Fee,' she insisted. 'I need to forgive Alex and leave the way open for him to come back.'

'Forgive him! You'd forgive him if it turned out he was having an affair?'

Kate slammed the laptop closed. 'I want him back Fee! I just want Alex back and if I have to forgive him to make that happen then I will!'

'Oh Kate honey, I'm sorry. Of course you want him home. But you don't even know he is having an affair yet so let's not get too carried away. I still can't believe that he would have left you for someone else and certainly not Sandra

Maddison! I think he's just having a bit of a wobble over something. It's nothing you've done wrong.'

'But it is,' whispered Kate. 'I must have done something wrong because why else would he have left us Fee, why would he have walked out of the house and left me and his beautiful daughter?

Chapter 7

Kate had asked Fiona if she would look after Millie for a couple of hours and also if Kate could borrow her car.

'Borrow the car?' Fiona looked puzzled. 'Well of course you can. Why do you need it, anything I can help with?'

Kate had shaken her head and said that she just needed to get a few things, sort out a few bits and pieces and when Fiona cheerfully offered to come along and help, Kate had smiled and said it was really kind of Fiona to offer but actually she could do with a little break, without Millie, without anybody.

Mortified that she hadn't thought of that earlier Fiona took Millie from Kate's arms and passed the keys back in return.

'Take your time,' she urged. 'Have a little 'me' time.'

So now Kate was in Fiona's car, driving towards town with her heart beating frantically and her hands trembling slightly on the wheel.

Part of the cost cutting exercise the previous year had been the disposal of Kate's beloved little car. She'd had it for years and there was barely an inch that didn't have a scratch or a dent and its own story to tell. But two cars went way beyond their budget and with local shops within walking range, Kate had offered her little car in sacrifice. It meant that the supermarket was only possible once Alex was home and his car was on the drive and if Kate wanted to go further afield during the day it was a trip on the bus with a baby and a pushchair, something she had only braved a handful of times.

Driving slowly, being careful not to treat Fiona's car in the same slightly haphazard way she used to treat her own, Kate hit the outskirts of Leeds at 17:20. The rush hour was already in full flow but the majority of cars were travelling out of town and Kate was hopeful that she'd get a parking place without too much trouble.

It took a couple of circles around the block but eventually Kate found the perfect spot and parked the car, tucking it behind a large 4X4. It was already dark. The weak sun that had struggled throughout the day had given up and slipped away and the only light came from the street lamps and the office windows that lined the road. Kate sat back and waited. She was early but she hadn't wanted to risk being unable to park and missing the moment, seeing everybody walk away and not be able to find who she was looking for.

Thirty minutes later the first straggle of people emerged from the door Kate was watching. One ran down the street and hopped into a car that was waiting, the rest spread out in different directions as they cleared the doorway. A crowd came out together, all shouting goodbye and waving before turning in their own direction. More came out, some alone walking swiftly on their chosen path, others in pairs or groups.

Kate waited. The straggle became a stream and it was harder now to check everyone that appeared. Some stood in the doorway enjoying a cigarette before heading home, some set off at a sprint while others loitered, chatting to colleagues as they ambled down the street. Very few came to get in any of the cars that were parked near Kate, street parking was too expensive, but many disappeared into the underground parking whose entrance was a little further down the street, behind where Kate was parked.

Suddenly Kate sat up straight. There was a clutch of people gathered in the doorway and it was hard to isolate them but Kate was sure that the blonde head bobbing around near the steps was the one she had been looking for. Kate leaned around the 4X4 to get a better look, still keeping herself fairly low so as not to be seen and then shrank back into her seat as Sandra Maddison broke free of the group and set off down the street, walking within inches of Kate's car as she headed towards the underground entrance. Kate's mouth was so dry she could hardly swallow. Her breathing was fast and shallow as her eyes followed Sandra's progress from the door of the office to the entrance of the car park.

She was wearing very high shoes and they clipped their way past Kate's car like a military tattoo. Her skirt was short, a coat pulled tight at the front hiding its detail. The blonde hair was down, curling onto her shoulders. This time Kate could see her face. She could see red lips, a small nose and outlined eyes. Not exactly pretty, thought Kate in satisfaction and yet there was something about her, something that drew the eye.

Sandra disappeared into the car park and Kate fastened her seatbelt and started the car. She waited, her eyes peeled on the entrance to the car park. There was a momentary distraction when someone jumped into the car in front of her and pulled away but it made it easier for Kate when a minute later a car pulled out onto the street, a blonde head at the wheel. Kate waited until it passed her, then she pulled smoothly out into the traffic following the blue Peugeot.

Twenty-five minutes later Kate was drenched in sweat with the effort of keeping the blue car in her sights when finally it pulled into a residential street and parked. Kate followed, pulling into the first parking space she saw and quickly dimming her lights. The blue Peugeot had stopped halfway down the street and Kate watched as Sandra jumped out, locked the door behind her then turned and walked directly towards Kate's car. Kate panicked. Wildly she looked around for something to disguise herself with, sliding down in her seat and bracing herself for the knock on the window. But still several feet away Sandra turned left and walked towards the large glass door of a small block of flats leaving Kate weak kneed with relief. She watched as Sandra let herself into the well-lit entrance and walked towards the staircase before disappearing from sight. Breathing deeply, trying to restore her heart beat to its normal rhythm, Kate sat up again, wiping the sweat from her forehead as she peered up at the building. If Sandra was heading towards the back then Kate wouldn't be able to see her. But if she was at the front of the three story block then Kate might be able to see where she went. She watched, her eyes flitting along the front of the building, moving rapidly from one floor to another, shooting along its length. Suddenly she saw it, a light had flickered in one of the rooms on the second floor. Holding her breath Kate leaned forward, straining to see over the tops of the cars parked along the street. But then another light came on in the same window, bright and clear and there was Sandra Maddison, outlined clearly as she gazed briefly down onto the street below before turning away and disappearing into the shadows at the back of the room.

Kate had thought long and hard about the reason why Alex had left her. She still found it almost physically impossible to think of Alex with another woman, the pain left her gasping for breath and she had doubled over holding her heart like an aching limb. But an exhaustive search of Google had made her realise that there were actually few reasons why husbands suddenly left wives. And after she had discounted volatile relationships, drug dependency and gender confusion – none of which described Kate and Alex's perfect marriage, she was left with the unpalatable truth that Alex was almost certainly having an affair. It had hurt Kate to the core to even contemplate that Alex would turn to someone else and she had spent a restless night trying to justify his actions.

Perhaps Alex had suddenly become quite weary of working hard and not going out. Maybe Kate had been correct and he was feeling emotionally neglected and more than a little left out since Millie's arrival. And maybe when Sandra Maddison with her too short dress and her desperate ways had trailed her fingers down his arm at the Christmas Party, Alex feeling momentarily weak willed and miserable, had allowed himself to feel that tingle of attraction. And maybe, just maybe, when the music was blaring and everyone was occupied on the dance floor they had slipped outside to refresh their lungs with cold night air and she had moved in closer, pretending to shiver and he had put his arm around her. Perhaps at that moment she had tilted her face up to meet his so that all he had to do was move an inch, just a minuscule little inch, and their lips were touching. And then of course, in the thrill of a new romance, when all it took was for someone to walk into a room to set your heart beating quicker, maybe she had suggested that he could move in with her so he could forget about Kate and Millie, forget about a life that was all work and no play. He could be with Sandra instead and she would have convinced him that they could have fun, just like Alex and Kate used to have fun. They could laugh and dance and kiss and talk, just like Alex and Kate once did. And Sandra could have trailed her long red tipped nails along his arm and whispered in his ear that he should leave Kate straight away, while he still remembered what fun was like and move in with her. And Alex – well of course Alex would agree because she would be there, in his face, laughing, seductive, pouting, trailing those fingers and Alex was tired and sad and miserable and feeling neglected so of course he would give in, what man wouldn't?

The thoughts had kept Kate awake most off the night. She had laid in bed staring into the dark and she could see Sandra Maddison leaning towards Kate's husband, leaning into him, whispering words Kate couldn't hear, drawing him away from Kate's side as she whispered and giggled and held his attention so that he forgot to look back and see his wife standing there, waiting for him.

But despite the pain, this situation was one Kate was certain she could overcome because it meant she was right when she'd suggested that Alex may have been feeling neglected. Her husband had fallen victim to the charms of someone who was promising him something more, something better. But Kate could whisper and giggle just as well as Sandra Maddison. She had once been fun, she had enjoyed dancing and laughing and had looked round eagerly when Alex came home each evening and fallen into his arms with a sigh. Kate may spend most of her time plumping cushions and ironing these days but she could be everything that Sandra Maddison was. Especially if it meant getting Alex back where he belonged with his wife and daughter.

Kate waited for over an hour and cold and cramped, she was just pondering the stupidity of her actions when another car turned into the

77

street. This one didn't shoot past Kate like the rest had, in a hurry to reach its destination. This one slowed down, crawling along looking for somewhere to park. Kate held her breath as it drew alongside, and this car made the last hour worthwhile because this car was Alex's shining, silver car and the person in the driving seat was none other than her errant husband. Sliding down into her seat Kate watched as he parked a little further down the street. Like Sandra he turned and walked in the direction of Kate's car. She held her breath. It was dark but his outline was clear as he walked briskly along the pavement and Kate didn't need to see his face to know every detail there; to imagine the fringe flopping on his forehead, the eyes slightly screwed with concentration, the lips set firm and a little stern which was his natural look – until of course he smiled and then Kate's heart would skip a beat as the lips curved upwards and his eyes would send a warm glow along her spine.

He was almost at the doorway to the flats and was it Kate's imagination, she wondered, or was there a definite spring in his step. He took a key out of his pocket and Kate wondered if he could hear her moan of despair from inside the car. A key! He already had his own key. Pushing the door open, he turned in the direction of the steps and Kate's eyes immediately flew to the window she knew hid Sandra Maddison. Kate had known someone was expected. Sandra had left her curtains open and had looked out to check the street every ten minutes since she'd arrived home. Kate knew that she was waiting for someone and her heart knew that it must be Alex. But she had still wondered, hoped. Until now, until Alex had turned up with his own key. Kate's eyes were glued to the window and she saw Sandra check the street once more, only to turn quickly around. And then they were together. Alex had arrived even as Sandra had been gazing out of the window, searching for his shadow on the street below.

He had let himself in as she stood there looking to see if he was perhaps driving down the street and Kate watched and wept as he moved towards Sandra and the two stood in the window, arms around each other as they kissed.

Chapter 8

When Kate returned the car to Fiona, her pale face and ravaged eyes told Fiona immediately that something had occurred.

'Kate, come in. Why don't you stay for tea? Millie is hard and fast asleep upstairs.'

Kate stood uncertainly on the doorstep, part of her just wanted to go home and curl up in her own bed. Part of her needed to share her discovery.

'He's living with Sandra Maddison.'

Kate was still on the doorstep, still standing in the cold night air as she delivered the information and Fiona's eyes widened with shock, her mouth falling open in surprise.

'Kate please come in. Come in, stay with us, eat something. Stuart will take you and Millie home later.'

Kate remained on the doorstep, her teeth chattering.

'I followed her, Sandra Maddison. I followed her home and waited and then Alex came and he had a key …' Kate's voice cracked. 'He had a key Fiona. And she was waiting for him and he was there and …'

Stuart appeared in the hallway, surprisingly light on his feet despite his size. He exchanged a look with Fiona then reached out and took hold of Kate's elbow, gently but firmly drawing her into the hallway.

'You'll have to come in Kate love,' he said, 'it's bloody freezing out there.'

Kate allowed herself to be pushed in the direction of the living room, Fiona taking over at her side as Stuart disappeared into the kitchen.

'Come on, sit down,' and she pushed Kate into one of the comfy armchairs by the fire. This was a designated no children zone and although there was an absence of toys and children related chaos, it was far from a pristine room. Fiona didn't believe in show houses. She declared that when she and Stuart sank onto the settee at the end of the evening, they wanted warmth and comfort, not immaculate cream carpets and accessories all chosen for their ability to blend in with the colour scheme. Fiona felt that Kate spent far too much time tidying and told her so frequently and Kate had to admit that the large messy room with its blazing fire and book laden shelves certainly gave the welcome that Fiona wanted.

Stuart reappeared with a large glass of wine for each of the women. He set one beside Kate and then crouched down to look into her eyes.

'I'm going to leave you two to talk, Kate love. Fee's got one of her fantastic beef casseroles in the oven and in about 15 minutes I'm going serve it up and you're going to stay and have some with us.' He held up his hand to stop Kate from interrupting. 'There's always plenty, you know Fee she cooks for the five thousand every night and to be honest you look as though you haven't had a square meal in weeks.'

81

He noticed the tremor of Kate's hand and he leant nearer to give it a squeeze. 'And when you've eaten you can either stay here tonight or I'll drive you and Millie back.'

Kate lifted grateful eyes. For some reason his solicitude was almost more than she could bear. Perhaps it was just the feeling of someone taking charge, of making the decisions and looking after her. The last few days had left Kate feeling totally alone.

He smiled and dropping a kiss on the top of his wife's head he walked back into the kitchen and Kate could hear the muted sounds of the table being laid and smell the intoxicating aroma of a casserole drifting down the hallway.

'What happened?' asked Fiona.

Kate lent back in the chair, feeling the warmth of the fire begin to defrost her toes and the comfort of the room start to envelop her.

She closed her eyes for a moment, trying to bring herself back into the present.

'I decided to follow Sandra home, see if there was any sign of Alex and her being together.'

She laughed humorlessly at Fiona's expression. 'Yes I know it was a bit mad but I just wanted to know Fee. Well I think I already knew but I just wanted to be certain.'

'And?'

'And he turned up. He had his own key and he let himself in and then I saw them just for a few seconds before they pulled the curtains. Saw them in the window … kissing.'

Fiona closed her eyes in distress. 'Oh Kate I'm so sorry.'

Kate nodded. It had been a little like watching a drama unfold on TV. She had been fairly certain of the path it was taking but then came the reveal, the moment when accompanied by dramatic music all suspicions were confirmed and even though in her heart she already knew what would happen, it was still a shock to see it all laid bare before her eyes.

They sat in silence for a couple of minutes as Kate sipped at her wine and enjoyed the warmth.

'Kate?'

'Mm.'

'Are you okay?'

Kate looked at her anxious friend, sitting on the edge of the seat, ready to catch Kate if she swooned in grief, or pass her the tissues if the tears came streaming down again.

'I'm fine,' assured Kate in an almost dreamy voice. 'At least I know why he left.'

Kate swirled the wine in her glass, looking at its golden colour as it reflected the light from the fire.

'You seem very – calm,' offered Fiona still ready for the total breakdown of her friend.

'Calm? Mm, maybe not calm. But I do feel more settled.'

'Settled? Knowing your husband has left you for another woman has made you feel settled?' asked Fiona in disbelief.

Kate smiled. 'But I know exactly what's happened now Fee, I know what he's done and why and now I know what I have to do.'

'And what do you have to do?'

Kate raised her eyebrows in surprise. 'Get him back of course!'

Fiona snorted. 'I'm not sure I would want Stuart back after something like that. To be honest if that were Stuart and I'd just found out he'd left me for another woman I don't think I'd be in the slightest bit settled or calm. I'd be debating between getting a kitchen knife and hunting him down or throwing myself off a bridge!' and patting her friend on the shoulder she slipped out to see how Stuart was doing serving the casserole into three huge bowls.

Kate could hear the sounds of the oven opening, the flavor of the casserole wafting through the room and she stared into the fire watching the light shift as a log suddenly gave way and moved the flames.

The first dinner party Alex and Kate gave as a couple was in their tiny flat. They had invited four of Kate's friends around and although Kate had been very blasé about it when the invitations were issued, as the date approached she started to feel very nervous. Alex had delivered the invitation one Sunday afternoon in the pub and the reaction had been one of hilarity.

'Oh God Alex, you do realise how legendary Kate's lack of culinary skills are don't you? She can't make toast without burning it!'

Kate had tried to look offended but then the giggles broke through.

'I try!' she defended herself. 'And yes, Alex is aware. There is no suggestion that I've tricked him into thinking I'm a wonderful cook and he'll be coming home to coq au vin every night!'

'He'll be lucky if he comes home to a kitchen that's still intact! Alex, you do know that she once set fire to Sarah's kitchen trying to fry an egg?'

Gales of laughter flooded the table and Kate waved them away with her hand, refusing to let their comments from discouraging her. Alex sat by her side, his head in his hands in mock despair but through the tangle of his fingers he caught Kate's eye and winked at her.

But Kate's confidence had lessened as the great event drew near and on the day itself she was of the opinion they should just forget the whole thing and get in a take away.

'Absolutely not!' insisted Alex. 'If I have to put up with your cooking why shouldn't they?'

Of course he had apologized for his remark but that took place in the bedroom and put Kate even further behind schedule. But she had soldiered on and when the doorbell rang she was in the kitchen, her hair standing on end, flour smeared across her face something, she couldn't identify in her hair but with a three course meal ready to be served.

The starter was creamy cauliflower soup and although Kate had followed the recipe to the letter, the result was lumps of rather soggy cauliflower sitting in a bowl of something that looked and tasted like greasy washing up water. She watched as each person bravely attempted to empty their bowl but when Sarah eventually threw in the towel and said 'I'm sorry, I just can't, really I just can't' they had all exchanged a look and Alex was the first one to break, his shoulders heaving as he tried to quell his laughter.

Kate graciously took away the bowls so no-one felt obliged to eat any more and to a drum roll from Alex she produced her next offering which was lasagna. It looked promising, it looked exactly as a lasagna should look. Unfortunately, it tasted nothing like a lasagna should taste. The filling was a grey mince with large swathes of still crisp onion, the sauce was thin and watery a little like curdled milk and the lasagna itself was chewy and raw in the middle and crisp and burnt on the edges. Again everyone battled their way through as much as possible amid many sniggers and calls for Kate to resign but several bottles of wine helped some of the dish to disappear. The desert was perfect. As Kate brought the cheesecake to the table the occupants fell silent. There it sat on the plate, shining and delicious. Kate cut deep into the centre and even the most amateur cook could tell the texture was perfect. She slid a large serving onto each plate and as she sat back waiting for them to take a bite, all she could hear were soft appreciative murmurings.

'Bloody hell, Kate – this is gorgeous!'

'Oh Kate, it's lovely!'

Kate sat at the head of the tiny table wedged up against the kitchen door and smiled regally, accepting the praise heaped on her shoulders.

'Did you really make this yourself Kate? '

Everyone looked in her direction.

'Of course not!' exclaimed Kate. 'We had to have something we could eat. This came from the bakery down the road. Cheers everyone!'

The night was a huge success, their friends departed happy and full of cheesecake and Alex and Kate looked at the piles of washing in the sink.

'Let's do it tomorrow,' whispered Alex in Kate's ear. 'Right now I think I should take my little cook to bed.'

Kate giggled and turned round in his arms to view the left over piles of food.

'I'm not a natural am I?' she asked a little despondently.

'No,' agreed Alex 'but there are other things you are very good at which is why I'm going to take you into the bedroom right now so you can show me your skills'

Kate let him move her out of the kitchen and into the equally tiny bedroom. 'Maybe I need to practice more?' she mused as Alex began to unbutton her blouse.

'I wouldn't worry about it,' he mumbled into her neck, 'let's think of other things instead.'

But Kate did think about it and even as Alex pushed her down onto the bed she couldn't help worrying that in a couple of years when Alex came home from work he would want more than washing up water cauliflower soup and grey lasagna for tea.

The very next day Kate enrolled on a cookery course.

Another log shifted, causing the fire to flare and Kate to return to the moment. And now Alex had gone. It wasn't Kate's cooking, she was sure of that. She'd become quite a superb cook and Alex had walked into the kitchen every night to delicious aromas and a superb meal, with lasagna now one of her signature dishes. And he hadn't left because she didn't keep the house tidy. She had followed Marcia's example and their house had become a shrine to all things fashionable and neat and she could put her own mother to shame for highly polished surfaces. But Kate had done something wrong and Alex had left.

Now she had to persuade him to come home and then she would address whatever flaws she had, whatever mistakes she had made and she would make absolutely certain that he never felt the urge to leave again. She could change. She'd changed already into what she had believed was the perfect wife. She could change again. If Alex needed high heels and whispered dalliances then Kate would make sure he had them- in his own house, in his own bedroom. If he needed laughter and partying and more fun, then Kate could provide all those things. Maybe she'd taken her eye off the ball, overlooked Alex's needs but it was nothing that she couldn't address.

She could put it all right, she just had to make Alex come home.

Chapter 9

The wind was blowing and icy sheets of rain were hitting the windows as Kate sat at the kitchen table.

She was still writhing with shame at her lack of control the previous evening. Her calmness at discovering her husband was now with another woman had remained as she shared the news with Fiona and Stuart. It had remained as Stuart drove her home and helped her carry Millie indoors. It had remained as Kate climbed into bed and let her exhausted body sink into the mattress. But at two o'clock in the morning, when Kate had woken up sobbing at the image of Alex and Sandra Maddison framed in the window with their arms wrapped around each other, the calm had disappeared and in its place was a frantic and heartbroken Kate.

She had dialed Alex's mobile number with shaking hands and when his bleary voice answered she had been unable to restrain herself as she screamed at him.

'How could you Alex,' she had sobbed uncontrollably down the phone. 'How could you do that to me, to Millie.'

Alex had been shocked to hear his wife's voice, shocked at the raw emotion she had poured down the phone and shocked that she seemed to know so much when he had told her so little.

'Kate I don't know what you think …'

'I know where you are Alex,' Kate had screamed. 'I know where you are and who you're with. I know!'

Kate thought she had detected the soft murmur of another voice in the background. 'She's there isn't she, next to you? In bed with you!'

'Kate it's two in the morning. I don't think this is the time or place to be having this conversation. I think …'

'When were you going to tell me?'

'Tell you what?' Alex had asked warily.

'Tell me about Sandra Maddison,' Kate had screamed. 'When were you going to tell me about her Alex?'

There had been silence, more whispered asides in the background.

'Kate there isn't…'

'Don't lie to me! Don't make it worse by lying to me.'

'Kate please, we'll talk but not right now. Let's talk later.'

His voice had been desperate and it occurred to Kate that he was feeling disapproval at both ends of the phone.

'I know you're with her,' she had whispered, her voice suddenly soft, almost enticing. 'I know what you've done but it's okay Alex. Just come home and we'll sort it all out. Come home and it'll be okay.'

'Kate I can't…'

'Come home Alex!' Kate had shouted, 'come home!'

In the end Alex had promised to contact her later so they could talk.

'When?' Kate had demanded.

'Soon,'

'Tomorrow?'

'I don't know. Maybe we should take a little bit of time away from each other first …'

'No! phone me tomorrow, I need to speak to you Alex.'

'Look Kate please stop. We'll talk, soon okay. We'll talk.'

'Tomorrow?'

'Oh God Kate, I don't know.'

Again the whispered voices.

'Alex I need …'

'I'll phone soon,' and then he was gone leaving Kate holding the phone and sobbing for the rest of the night. She had been out of bed and downstairs before six o'clock in the morning, staring at the phone and waiting for Alex to call. At 8.30 she had sent him a text saying that now was a convenient time to speak. Her phone remained silent. At 8.35 she decided the message obviously hadn't gone through so she sent another, and another and another. When Fiona called in after taking her children to school she found Kate sitting at the kitchen table, sobbing frantically and sending the nineteenth message to Alex saying she was waiting for his call. Fiona had taken her phone away from her and listened to how Kate had lost control and phoned Alex the previous night.

Kate had cried and cried and Fiona had said nothing, just held her friend closely. Eventually Kate had calmed down and taken several deep breaths.

'Why isn't he phoning me Fee? He promised he would. He said he'd phone me so we could talk.'

'But he didn't say he would phone today Kate.'

'Well he said he would try.'

'Maybe he'll phone tomorrow honey. Or the day after. Maybe it is best if you have a few days to get your thoughts in order. Maybe...'

'No! He'll phone today, I know he will. He knows I want to speak to him.'

'Well he's probably busy at work, or in a meeting - or something.' Fiona dried Kate's tear sodden face for the umpteenth time.

'He's probably just waiting for the right time, this isn't a conversation he wants to have in front of the office Kate.'

'Or in front of Sandra Maddison,' Kate responded bitterly.

'Exactly. So he's just got to find the right time.'

'And when will that be? A five minute slot between finishing work and going back to her? Is that what I've become, an inconvenient conversation he needs to make in the car park!' and the tears were back as Kate lay her head on the kitchen table and sobbed.

'I shouldn't have phoned him Fee.'

Fee had shrugged. 'Well maybe it did him good to realise you know what he's up to. A dose of reality.'

Kate lifted waterlogged eyes to her friend. 'Do you think so?'

'Well it can't hurt, can it.'

'I don't know. I was reading on Google yesterday ...'

'Oh let's not go back there Kate!'

Kate ignored her. 'I was reading on Google yesterday about what you should do when your husband leaves and it said that one thing you definitely shouldn't do was phone him constantly and scream at him. It will just make him relieved to be out of the relationship.'

'But it is a perfectly natural reaction Kate.'

But Kate has sighed and shaken her head. 'No, I need to think carefully about how to get him back and I don't think that phone call helped.'

Eventually Fiona had gone home and Kate had put Millie down for a nap and flicked open her computer.

She phoned Fiona later that afternoon.

'Oh God Fee, do you think we were in a zombie marriage and I just didn't notice?'

'A what!'

'A zombie marriage. On Google it says that some couples get stuck in zombie marriages, it seems to be working okay on the outside but it's quite dead on the inside.'

'A zombie? You think Alex was a zombie?'

'No not Alex,' said Kate impatiently. 'Our marriage, maybe it had turned into a zombie marriage and I was too stupid to realise.'

'Well was your marriage dead on the inside?' queried Fiona.

Kate thought. 'Well I didn't think it was. I mean, I still loved Alex and he still loved me and we did still talk and enjoy spending time together so …'

'So maybe neither of you were zombies Kate. Stop looking for excuses for Alex. He is having an affair and he left you.'

Kate cried out in pain and Fiona carried on hastily. 'Oh - I'm so sorry honey I didn't mean it to sound like that. It's just that you're looking for a reason Alex left but you already know the reason. He was having an affair. Stop trying to find something you did wrong.'

'But the affair is the effect not the cause Fee,' said Kate seriously, ignoring her friend's deep sigh. 'Yes he had an affair but why?'

'Because he's a tosser?' suggested Fiona.

'Be serious ...'

'I am being serious Kate! The man left you with a nine month old baby because he wanted to sleep with another woman. Maybe he should start reading Google and work out just why he's such a waste of space.'

The conversation finished.

An hour later Kate phoned Fiona again.

'Oh my God Fee,' she wailed down the phone. 'I devitalized him!'

Fiona stopped chewing her sandwich. 'You did what to him?'

'I devitalized him. Our marriage had become devitalized. No wonder he had to find someone else.'

'Deviralised?'

'No! Devitalised! It's when the passion goes and you become two units instead of one. I put Millie and the house and the ironing and everything else first you see, our focus had become about our daily tasks and not our love.'

'Right,' said Fiona faintly.

'I drained the love from him.'

'Hold on a minute Kate. What were you supposed to do with Millie. Put her on the back burner so Alex could keep his vitality? Stop cleaning so he feels better about himself?'

'Well no, obviously I needed to care for Millie as well but I let the passion disappear from my relationship with Alex ....'

'So you still look after Millie, you still clean and cook and iron but as soon as Alex arrives home from work you turn on the passion. Never mind making him something to eat, washing his clothes, looking after his daughter – you should have just had him right there and then in the kitchen?'

'Well no ...'

'So what are you on about Kate? You'd just had a baby for crying out loud. If he felt things had got a bit routine and mundane he could have just helped out a bit more so you had the energy to seduce him again.'

The conversation ended.

'Fee – we lost our emotional connection. I forgot to appreciate him and I stopped making time for him in my ...'

'For the love of God Kate if you don't stop reading all this twaddle I will come round there and take your computer away!'

'But it's important that I …'

'No, it is not at all important. Alex has left because he is miserable excuse of a man who is having an affair and has walked out on his wife and baby! And if he did all that because he was in a sulk and feeling left out because his wife was actually daring to pour love and attention on her daughter – on his daughter, that just makes it much worse! Are you getting the picture yet Kate?'

'But I didn't …'

'No Kate, this isn't about what you didn't do it's about Alex behaving very badly.'

'But Fee, you said yourself that life shouldn't stop just because you have children.'

There was a pause. 'Well yes,' admitted Fiona reluctantly. 'I did say that you should still go out occasionally …'

'You said it was important to carry on enjoying each other's company.'

Fiona ground her teeth. 'Well yes, I did say that but …'

'So I did neglect him?'

'No! You didn't neglect him.'

'I think I did Fee. I think I looked after his physical needs but I forgot about his emotional needs. I stopped appreciating him as my husband and my lover and he felt alone and unwanted.' Kate's voice was unsteady as she choked back tears.

'No! Kate no. You decided not to go to the Christmas party – that hardly constitutes neglect!'

'Well it was enough for Alex to start an affair with Sandra Maddison. You see Fee I should have

97

made sure he knew that I still needed him. It says right here that men have to feel wanted, they have to feel that someone needs them and I think I forgot to do that.'

The conversation ended.

'Kate?'

'Mm?'

'I've been thinking. What did Alex want you to do that you weren't doing?'

She could hear Kate tapping on her computer.

'Er – fulfill his emotional needs as well as his physical needs.'

'Yes – but what does that actually mean Kate?'

'Well it means that although I still looked after him, did his washing and cooked for him, I wasn't er fulfilling his emotional needs.'

'I'm hearing you Kate but what exactly were his emotional needs?'

More tapping.

'Well he needs to feel wanted, appreciated, admired, er … as though he still has an important place in the household…

'Okay. So what should you have been doing?'

'Fulfilling his emotional needs …'

'Stop saying that! What I'm asking is what were these emotional needs he was having so much trouble with?'

'Well I'm not entirely sure exactly which ones …'

'So it's just words, isn't it? It's just an excuse for a man that's feeling a bit fed up because he's not first in the pecking order any more. He can claim that his emotional needs aren't being fulfilled and you take all the blame and feel dreadful for letting him down. And what about your emotional needs Kate? If you're busy looking after Alex's overwhelming need to be appreciated, who is supposed to be making sure your emotional connection is still thriving and your vitality is still – vital?'

The conversation ended.

'He needed to feel desire Fee. He needed to feel that I couldn't wait for him to get home - simply because I missed him, not because I needed a hand with the cooking. He needed to feel that I thought about him during the day and looked forward to seeing him every night. You see that's all emotional stuff. Nothing physical.'

'He needs to grow up and remember that you've got a baby on your hip and a house to look after!'

'But he's right Fee,' said Kate wistfully. 'Because I did used to think about him during the day. I used to think about him all the time and I couldn't wait to get home from work just so I could see him.'

'We all feel like that at the beginning honey. And I'm not saying you shouldn't feel it now but not necessarily every minute of the day. Life gets in the way, children come along. It's called being grown up Kate.'

A sob drifted down the line.

'I still look forward to Stuart coming home but I must admit a lot of the time it's so I have another pair of hands in the kitchen. But that doesn't mean I don't love him Kate. I'm honest with him, I tell him I need some help and he helps. It doesn't mean we're not emotionally connected. I get tired, lay in bed and cuddle him and tell him I love him but that sex is simply not an option that night and he doesn't sulk or have an affair with someone.'

'Maybe I just didn't tell him I loved him enough Fee,' whispered Kate. 'But I thought he knew. I thought he knew that I loved him with all my heart. I thought I knew he loved me. I thought we were happy. I thought that life would get easier when Millie got older and I went back to work. I thought that we'd always be together and that we'd be old and grey but still holding hands on the settee.'

Fiona's voice was as unsteady as Kate's own. 'I know honey, I know.'

'And if he's gone because of something I did or didn't do then I need a chance to put it all right.'

Tears were rolling down Kate's cheeks as she carried on. 'I just want him to come home Fee, I just want Alex home.'

And the conversation ended.

Chapter 10

Kate was staring listlessly into the fridge and wondering if she could summon enough energy to make herself something to eat when Fiona arrived.

'Stuart's taken the kids to his mother's for Sunday lunch,' she announced holding out a pizza box and a bottle of wine. 'He said he'd look after the kids for the day and I should come and spend some time with you. Because we're a partnership,' she continued pointedly, 'and because we support each other when necessary even though our attention may be elsewhere.'

Fiona grinned and Kate couldn't help smiling back although the muscles in her cheeks felt weak from lack of use.

They sat in the kitchen with the pizza on the table and when Kate started to get out plates, knives forks, serviettes, Fiona had put a hand on her arm.

'Really not necessary Kate, it's just you, me and a pizza!'

And Kate had stared at the greasy box and Fiona with a piece already in her fingers and shrugged. She gave Millie a little corner to gum on and opened the wine.

'Glasses or shall we just drink from the bottle?'

Fiona grinned delightedly. 'Well that's more like the Kate I know!'

For a while they munched happily, Millie finding that pizza was to her liking and Kate realising that she was in fact starving.

She licked her fingers thoughtfully, remembering how good food tasted straight from the container.

When she'd met Alex her kitchen contained two mismatched plates and an odd assortment of cutlery. Her mother had every known implement including soup spoons, fish knives and salad forks and not only were they kept in their original boxes and cleaned regularly, they were actually used. The first time she and Alex had eaten a meal at Marcia's house, Kate had started to apologise for the vast expanse of cutlery that was lined at either side of the plate.

But Alex had interrupted her with a smile. 'It's okay – I love having the full set out, don't you?'

Kate didn't. She had always found it unnecessary and another sign of her mother's unbending formality. But she swallowed her words and instead watched Alex instinctively reach for the correct fork when Marcia served a salad for starters. She couldn't fail to see the little glimpse of approval in her mother's eyes.

Later, as they drove home, Kate had asked Alex about cutlery.

'Cutlery?' he'd laughed, flicking her a glance as he drove. 'What do you mean?'

'Well not many people bother to have anything more than a knife and fork these days, except for my mother who finds it perfectly normal,' complained Kate.

'Oh my grandma used to have the most amazing collection, it was my job to clean them when I went to visit. I used to love having three or four different knives lined up to eat beans on toast!' he had laughed.

Kate had smiled and nodded. And some months later, she had included on her wedding list a full set of cutlery including desert spoons, salad forks and fish knives so whenever they ate there was always more than one knife and fork beside Alex's plate.

'So,' began Fiona, taking a sip of wine and sitting back. 'Do you still want Alex back?'

Kate stared at her. 'Of course!'

'Even though you know he's left you and moved in with Sandra Maddison?'

Kate closed her eyes. Hearing the words out loud was like a knife plunging through her heart.

'Yes,' she whispered.

'And you think you could forgive him?'

Another knife, more pain. Actually, she didn't think she would ever really be able to forgive Alex. He had shattered her life and broken her dreams of the perfect marriage.

'Yes,' she said and when Fiona raised an eyebrow Kate continued. 'I have to forgive him Fee, or at least I have to say that I forgive him, it's the only way I can get him back and we can move on.'

Fiona sighed. 'You could move on without him,' she suggested. 'Admit it didn't work and make a new life for you and Millie.'

'No! I can't Fee, I just can't! He's made a mistake that's all. He's fed up or depressed or something but he's just made a mistake. We love each other, deep down I know he still loves me and he will come home. I just need to make sure he knows he can.'

Fiona shook her head disapprovingly. 'I think you're mad to even consider letting him back Kate but if that's what you want, okay.'

Kate looked at her questioningly.

'Well let's get on with it then,' said Fiona and she pushed the pizza box out of the way and pulled Kate's laptop in front of them.

'You've told me all the reasons why Alex may have left, now let's find all the reasons he might come back!'

For the next hour Kate and Fiona trawled the internet. They looked at site after site, went onto forums that left them weeping with tales of unhappiness and betrayal, read articles on how to rescue marriages, how to rekindle the love between spouses and more to the point, what to do when the love of your life leaves you for another woman.

While Kate read longingly of accounts where common sense had won and shamefaced husbands appeared on the doorstep after a few weeks, Fiona went straight to the advice pages and started making copious notes on a pad she found in the kitchen drawer.

'Okay, we have a strategy!' declared Fiona.

Kate flicked on the kettle and then sat expectantly at the table.

'It's essential that you don't stalk him, ring him incessantly, text him non-stop or generally follow him around begging him to come back,' began Fiona sternly.

Kate blushed. 'It was just the one call,' she said defensively, 'and you said that you would have probably done the same.'

'It was one call and nineteen texts Kate but that's okay, we'll put that on the 'made a mistake but won't do again pile' just remember no more contact from you. It's essential that in future Alex is the one making the calls.'

Kate nodded. 'Okay.'

'And when you do speak you must be calm, in control and in no way desperate and weepy.'

Kate bit her lip. She wasn't entirely sure she would be able to do calm and controlled. She was even less sure that she could hide how desperate and weepy she felt. But she nodded at Fiona's querying look.

'If you stop communication with him then he'll start to wonder what you're doing and how you're managing without him. He'll start to think of you more and more and want to get in touch,' read Fiona.

Alex had made no attempt to get in touch with Kate since his departure. He hadn't seemed overly curious to know how she was getting on and he certainly hadn't asked anything at all about what she was doing during her hysterical phone call to him.

'How long does that take?' she demanded.

'Er, well it doesn't say exactly how long to wait, just to be patient.'

Kate chewed her lip. She would have preferred an exact time frame but she nodded at Fiona to continue.

'You must not obsess about the other woman – it's hours of your life you won't ever get back,' quoted Fiona, 'forget about her and concentrate on yourself.'

Now that was an impossible task, decided Kate. Every time she closed her eyes she relived the moment she saw her husband's arms slide round Sandra's waist and the way she had turned round to meet his lips. Every time she thought of Alex, which was every minute of every day since he had left, she also thought about Sandra Maddison. Every time she wept and wondered why he had left, she wondered what Sandra had promised that made him prepared to turn his back on his wife and child. She constantly wondered how and when the affair had started, where they had met, what they had done – oh that was a particularly painful thought, the ever present vision of her husband and another woman in bed together.

Fiona was watching her carefully.

'Kate?'

'Sorry, yes, no obsessing about Sandra Maddison,' repeated Kate obediently, wondering what Sandra was doing at that precise moment in time, whether she was sitting on her settee with Alex by her side, feeling quite smug that she had managed to ensnare Kate's husband.

Fiona stroked the back of her friend's hand in sympathy then carried on.

'Next, you need to go out and make new friends,' instructed Fiona.

'New friends?' asked Kate startled. 'Can't I just make do with the ones I have?

Fiona frowned. 'Well, I would rather I stayed your friend and I do want to help but it does say you should have new friends.'

'Why?'

Fiona flicked through the notes in front of her. 'So Alex can see that you are not lost without him. That you're moving on. Apparently they don't like it when they see their wives getting on with life. You move on and he'll want to move on with you. I think.'

They both stayed silent.

'Maybe this advice is for women who don't already have a good friend?' suggested Kate.

'Yes! I think you're probably right.'

A little happier Fiona continued.

'You need to have some fun.'

'Fun!'

Kate stared. How on earth was it possible to have fun when your husband had just walked out on your marriage.

'What kind of fun?'

'Well any kind really but you should go out and look happy and relaxed so that – well so that you feel happy and relaxed but also so that Alex sees you having fun and starts to wonder what it would be like to be back with you – having fun together.'

Kate frowned. 'I don't really feel like going anywhere,' she confessed. 'To be honest it's a struggle getting out of bed in the morning without having to go out and have fun.'

Fiona looked sympathetic, 'I can imagine honey.'

'And how would Alex know if I was having fun anyway? If I'm not speaking to him, not communicating in any way. How on earth is he going to know I've just been out and had two hours of solid fun?'

'Mm, that's a good point,' mused Fiona going back to the laptop. 'It doesn't specify exactly what fun or where or how.'

She fell silent, her brow furrowed. 'I suppose at some point it will just become obvious. I mean he phones up and asks to see Millie and you say - oh great because I wanted to go salsa dancing tonight.'

'Salsa dancing?'

'Well it doesn't have to be salsa dancing as such, it could be yoga if you prefer. Although I think you naturally have slightly less fun at yoga than salsa.'

Kate stared out of the window dreamily. 'I used to go salsa dancing you know.'

Fiona's eyebrows shot upwards. 'You did?'

'Mm. I loved it. I stopped when I started going out with Alex because he's not a fan. He liked line dancing.'

'So did you go line dancing together?'

'No because...'

Kate stopped. Actually she couldn't really remember why they hadn't gone. She had happily stopped her salsa evenings because Alex suggested line dancing as an alternative, but it had just never happened.

'Then maybe salsa dancing is something you should do now.'

Kate looked at Fiona as though she were mad.

'Alex had just left me for another women and you think that's the ideal time to start salsa dancing?'

But Fiona was looking quite excited. 'Yes! Oh Kate yes that's exactly what you should do!'

She grinned at her baffled friend. 'And I know exactly the class you should go to!'

Kate looked blank.

'It's on a Friday night at the wine bar by the library. Starts 7.00 I think, before the bar gets too busy.

'What on earth …'

'It's the perfect opportunity Kate. I'll look after Millie.'

'Fiona I am not going to salsa. I have much more important things to worry about …'

'It's all part of the plan Kate. You can go out, make new friends, have fun and let Alex know that you are moving on without him - all in one hour a week. Perfect!'

'But I…'

'Because that's where Olivia has started going! A few weeks ago. She loves it and has persuaded Helen in Sales to go with her as well. Don't you see Kate, it'll be all round the office in no time at all if you join them. Alex is bound to find out.

'I don't know Fee, I can't see why Alex would come back just because I've started going to salsa.'

'You were the one who said Google had the answers Kate. Google is telling you how to put it right. You have to follow the advice. You have to go to salsa!'

'Google doesn't say I have to go to salsa.'

'It says you have to go somewhere and have fun and unless you've got a better idea, salsa it is!'

'But …'

'No buts. Do you want him back?'

''Yes,' whispered Kate. 'I do.'

'Then while I don't agree that you should even think of letting him back into your life, I accept that you want to try and this is a good place to start.'

'I just don't see how going to salsa is going to make Alex come back,' wailed Kate.

'Because,' Fiona frowned reading the screen in front of her, 'it will hurt his ego that you don't seem devastated. It will make him wonder why you're out there having fun when he assumed you'd be at home crying.' Kate grimaced at the thought of all the crying she had done since Alex left. 'And it will make him want to initiate contact again because he probably isn't ready for you to move on without him, even though he's with Sandra.'

'And then he'll come back?'

'Yes! Well, maybe. But not straight away, we have to make him realise what he's lost, establish that Sandra is a poor substitute, that he behaved impulsively and remind him of all the reasons he fell in love with you in the first place.'

Kate flinched. It was a long list.

'But then he'll come back,' continued Fiona hurriedly. 'For now we just need to get Alex's attention. And salsa is the start!'

Chapter 11

Kate had changed her mind several times about going to the salsa class. She had begged Fiona to go with her but her friend refused.

'If I go then he'll think I'm taking you out because you're desperately sad and need distracting.'

'I am desperately sad,' Kate had wailed.

'But remember what it said on Google, you have to look as though you're out there making new friends, starting a new life, without Alex.'

'But I don't want to make a new life without him Fee, I just want him to come home!'

'I know darling, I know, but this is a means to that end. Remember what Google said - engage his interest, make him intrigued, make him start thinking about you again.'

Kate had given in and packed a few things for Millie who was going to stay with Fiona and Stuart. If nothing else, she reasoned, it would get her out of the house for a brief time. She had spent the last week staring out of the window for hours on end, her phone clutched in her hand waiting for Alex's call - which never came. The tears still rolled down her cheeks constantly, she spent every night sobbing and every day searching her memories for the moment Alex stopped loving her.

'And don't think you have to come straight back!' Fiona had said, 'stay out a little bit, enjoy yourself.'

'I'm going to salsa,' Kate replied firmly. 'There's only so much enjoyment I can cope with at the moment and I think that will do.'

'Well please don't worry about rushing back.'

Kate had reluctantly looked through her wardrobe for something to wear, eventually pulling out a dress from the back that almost made her smile. It was plain black, cut on the bias with a deep ruffly asymmetric skirt and she'd worn it when she and Alex had gone to a Latin American themed party three years ago. They'd had such fun that night, thought Kate dreamily. Well come to think of it, she'd had fun, Alex had become a little tetchy as the night wore on. Kate hadn't stopped dancing from the moment they'd arrived, catching up with old friends and having a great time. Alex had declared after a few hours that he had a headache and was tired after a hard week at work. Kate had felt mildly irritated, she'd had a hard week at work as well and that was in part why she was having such a good time now, relaxing with friends and enjoying the throb of good music. But it was a momentary irritation and she had obligingly left much earlier than she might have done otherwise. She'd kissed Alex's aching head and said that they really must go dancing more often. Alex had agreed and thanked her for being so understanding and they'd gone home, where Alex's headache had disappeared so they made love and Kate had fallen into a deep, contented sleep, thankful she was so happily married to such a wonderful person.

Kate sighed, but surprisingly the tears didn't fall this time. She had spent most of the week with a face so waterlogged that she was amazed she hadn't developed scales. Maybe she was simply empty of tears, maybe there would come a day when she just couldn't cry any more.

She shook the creases from the dress and hung it on the outside of the wardrobe. In fact, as she looked at it with her head tipped to one side, did she detect the faint feeling of anticipation at the thought of going out that night? She shook her head, of course not. It was just nerves, or dread. It wouldn't be at all the same without Alex and she wandered downstairs to answer Millie's strident call for attention.

Kate put the dress back in the wardrobe twice during the course of the afternoon and phoned Fiona to tell her she wasn't going to salsa. She would much rather stay at home and feel sorry for herself. And, she had said, what if that was the evening that Alex phoned her? The fact that Kate's phone had remained silent after her late night call hurt almost as much as Alex walking out. Kate had been forced to accept that Alex had been prepared to say anything to end the call, and the fact that Sandra had been a witness to Kate's distress brought yet another stab of pain to Kate's already battered heart.

But both times she phoned, Fiona reminded her of the plan and pointed out how wonderful it would be if Alex did phone whilst Kate was breathless from salsa and so clearly out enjoying herself and both times Kate acquiesced and took the dress back out.

When she finally turned up on her friend's doorstep, Stuart gave a low wolf whistle that caused Kate to blush deeply.

'Wow,' offered Fiona. 'You look great! Absolutely perfect!'

Kate had been tempted to throw on a pair of jeans, go to salsa for the prescribed hour and return home where she could report that she had at least followed the plan. But of course the whole purpose was to get Alex's attention, to reach out to that part of him that had turned away from Kate and to remind him of the girl he had fallen in love with. And Olivia and Helen reporting back to the office that Alex's abandoned wife had turned up to salsa with red rimmed eyes and blotchy skin was more than she could bear.

So Kate had spent the afternoon in preparation, chatting away to Millie who watched as her mother had a long soak in a scented bath, lathered on half a pot of cream to soothe her dry and cracked skin worn away from days of crying and generally did everything possible to look like someone who had left the house for the sole purpose of having fun.

Her legs had been shaved and moisturized, her hair washed and conditioned until it gleamed and hung down her back in a radiance of strawberry blonde waves. She had steadied her hand long enough to hide the violet shadows under her eyes. She had outlined her lips in a soft pink and her eyes with dark gray. She had curled her lashes and swept them with mascara and finally she had slipped on the black ruffled dress that to her delight was a little loose around the hips and showed more than a glimpse of long slim legs.

'Really?' asked Kate, tugging at the dress which she had suddenly decided was a little too short.

'Really!' confirmed Fiona, her eyes shining at the sight of Kate looking back to her normal self.

'Right Stuart will drop you off at the wine bar.'

'Oh no,' exclaimed Kate. 'I'll catch a bus, I can't have you looking after Millie and driving me and …'

'Stuart will drop you at the wine bar,' repeated Fiona firmly. 'It's never easy looking your best when you've just had an encounter with public transport. You just make sure you look drop dead gorgeous when it all starts.'

Kate nodded, butterflies dancing their own salsa in her stomach and followed Stuart to the car.

'Do you want me to come in with you?' he asked after they'd been sitting outside the wine bar for five minutes without Kate moving.

Kate shook her head. 'Sorry Stuart, I am going in. I just need to – get ready.'

Stuart nodded. He'd left the engine running so the heating kept the cold night air at bay and he sat back in his seat. 'Take your time Kate love, take your time.'

Eventually Kate straightened her shoulders. 'Okay, wish me luck,' and she was gone, slipping out of the car and dashing across the already frosted pavement to the welcome heat of the wine bar.

Kate's heart was hammering and she headed straight for the ladies as instructed by Fiona. She took off her coat, straightened her dress and smoothed down her hair. Another coat of lip gloss and she went back into the wine bar, already containing a surprising number of people.

Music played softly in the background and there was a hum of voices and an air of suppressed excitement. Kate's palms were slightly damp and she wiped them discreetly along her dress.

It felt so strange walking into the room without Alex by her side, as though she had forgotten something important. She closed her eyes, perhaps it was too soon to do the whole fun thing. Google didn't know everything, perhaps she just wasn't ready to show Alex what a good time she could have without him.

'Salsa?' asked a bright voice to her left and Kate swung round to see a young woman in a cat suit that left nothing to the imagination.

'Er yes.'

'Been before?' asked the sultry young thing.

'No, er yes. I mean,' said Kate in confusion, 'first time here but I have done some salsa before.'

'Excellent! Name?'

'Kate'

'My name is Chantelle and I give the class with my colleague Victor - enjoy yourself!' and off she wandered, calling out to a small group who had just opened the door and let in a blast of Artic air.

Kate hung her coat in the corner with the others and tugging at her skirt again she stood hugging her arms around herself for comfort.

116

'Hi, you new?' asked another voice.

Kate turned to see a plump young woman standing by her side, a friendly face smiling at her under a mop of curly brown hair.

'Er - yes I am,' Kate replied, trying for a friendly casual tone which sounded more like a frightened squeak.

'Don't worry,' grinned the woman, 'we're a friendly lot!'

Kate stretched her face into a smile. 'Good.'

She remembered Fiona's instructions that she was to make new friends and was about to ask the young woman her name when there was a clap of hands.

'Oaky!' shouted Chantelle. 'Everybody ready?'

A small cheer went through the group and Kate looked round. It was mainly women with a smattering of men and they all stood in small groups ready to begin.

'We'll go through the basics, get everybody up to speed. Everyone got a partner? Kate wasn't it, do you have a partner?'

Everybody in the room turned to look at Kate whose cheeks burned with embarrassment. She wondered if it was obvious to everyone that she was clearly without a partner in every sense of the word, abandoned and unwanted.

She shook her head, not trusting herself to speak.

'No problem,' shouted Chantelle across the music, 'we often get people coming on their own.'

And yet she still hadn't learnt the art of diplomacy thought Kate.

'Come to the front and join Victor. Maybe you can persuade a friend to come next time?'

Horrified Kate stayed were she was. She had allowed herself to be talked into an hour of fun, not to stand in front of a large group of people and be humiliated.

'Actually I'm on my own this week.'

It was the plump woman who had spoken to Kate. 'Perhaps Kate and I could pair up?'

'Excellent Sophie,' shouted Chantelle. 'Now let's go.'

An hour later Kate's cheeks were flushed with colour, her hair was flying round her shoulders and her hips were wriggling as she and Sophie counted … one, two, three … and … one, two, three … and … one, two, three … and … one, two, three -over and over again.

Then the music stopped, a round of applause broke out and to Kate's disappointment the class was over.

'Hey you were really good!' congratulated Sophie. 'I thought you said you'd only been a few times before.'

'I had, but I did used to love it.'

'Coming again?' grinned Sophie.

'You bet,' said Kate without any hesitation as she joined in with the clapping.

The bar was starting to fill up and even the area to the back where the group had been dancing was now ringed with evening revelers, all watching the salsa.

It had taken Kate a matter of minutes to remember how much she had enjoyed dancing and only a few minutes more to remember how much she loved going out and being part of a happy throng of people. As she and Sophie made their way towards the rest of the dance group, now having a well-deserved drink, she caught the eye of a tall, dark haired man who had been leaning against a pillar watching them dance.

'Hey well done you two,' he offered as Sophie and Kate walked by. 'It's almost making me want to join in.'

'Then brush off the dancing shoes,' joked Sophie, 'the more the merrier.'

'I might take you up on that,' he murmured holding Kate's eye briefly and she gave him a quick smile before hurrying after Sophie.

'Wine?' asked Sophie having elbowed her way to the bar.

''Oh I wasn't going to stay,' started Kate, 'I just came for the class. I've left my daughter with friends you see and …'

Sophie tilted her head to one side. 'But everyone has at least one quick drink before they leave. Sure I can't tempt you?'

Kate thought back to Fiona as she had closed the door behind Kate and Stuart. 'Remember, stay as long as you want honey. Millie is quite safe here with us.'

Kate chewed on her lip. She was, against the odds actually enjoying herself.

'Okay, I'll have white please,' and smiling, Sophie called out their order.

Five minutes later Kate was stood with a group of salsa dancers as they laughed about the mistakes they'd made when she felt a hand on her arm.

Swinging round she saw a face she recognized.

'Kate isn't it, Alex Patterson's wife?'

Kate nodded.

'I'm Olivia, we've met a couple of times.'

Kate didn't mention that only recently she had stared at Olivia's photograph and wondered if she was the women her husband was now in bed with.

'Hi Olivia, were you doing the salsa as well?' asked Kate innocently.

Olivia nodded enthusiastically. 'Oh yes, I've been coming for a few weeks and now I've persuaded Helen to join me.' She grabbed her friend's arm and turned her round so she could see Kate.

'Look who I've found, it's Alex's wife, Kate.'

Helen was a wiry little thing with masses of frizzy hair and more energy than Battersea power station.

'Oh wasn't it fun!' she demanded. 'Is it your first week as well? Will you be coming again? I can't wait for next week!'

Both Kate and Olivia laughed and Kate agreed that she would indeed be joining them the following week.

'So,' twinkled Olivia, 'any chance of seeing Alex here next Friday? Is he a salsa man?'

Kate felt the blood pounding in her head. She felt her hand shake, a tiny little shake as she held onto her wine glass.

'Alex?' she laughed. It was a little tinny but at least it wasn't a sob. 'Oh I don't think so. Not unless Sandra comes as well.'

Olivia and Helen looked at Kate with blank expressions.

'Alex has left me,' explained Kate carefully, wanting to get the facts out and keep the emotion in. 'He left me for Sandra Maddison - last week. You probably know her, doesn't she work in accounts with you Olivia?'

The effort was almost too much for Kate and she felt her legs go slightly weak. It was the first time she had said the words out loud. The first time she had acknowledged Alex's betrayal to anyone other than Fiona – excluding of course the queue at the butcher's shop.

She had expected it to be difficult and it was. But also ever so slightly liberating.

'Left you?' echoed Olivia in shock.

'For Sandra Maddison!' added Helen.

Kate nodded, blinking rapidly so the tears were kept at bay.

'Oh my God,' exclaimed Olivia looking pale. 'I'm so sorry Kate, I really had no idea.'

'For Sandra Maddison!' screeched Helen again. 'Is he mad? He let you for Sandra Maddison?'

Kate could have kissed her. Whether Helen was being honest or supportive, it was the boost Kate needed and she wanted to fling her arms around Helen's neck and give her a big kiss. Instead she just nodded, not entirely trusting her voice.

The two women shook their heads in disbelief. 'Well he's kept that quiet,' said Helen grimly. 'They both have.'

'Haven't you got a baby?' asked Olivia.

'Millie. Nine months old, well going on for ten months now.'

There was another gasp as Olivia and Helen looked at each other in shock.

'And he's with Sandra Maddison, now?' asked Helen as though she still felt she may have misunderstood what Kate had been saying.

Another nod from Kate.

'Well he's a fool,' announced Olivia fervently, laying a comforting hand on Kate's arm. 'An absolute fool.'

'And good for you,' added Helen. 'You do absolutely right, getting out and enjoying yourself. No point staying at home crying for that waste of space.'

Oh if only they knew thought Kate sadly, if only they knew.

'And you obviously enjoyed it,' declared Olivia, 'I was watching you!'

Kate smiled. 'Well I tried salsa years ago,' she confided, 'but I stopped when I met Alex. He didn't like it much.'

'Well, maybe he should have carried on dancing. Might have kept his mind off Sandra Maddison!' declared Olivia then held up her glass, 'Welcome to salsa Kate! We're going to have a wonderful time!'

Chapter 12

It was four days after the salsa and Kate was as despondent as ever. There had been no contact from Alex and the promised call had never arrived. Fiona was countenancing patience although Kate had pointed out that Alex should surely have been in touch to check on Millie even if he didn't want to speak to Kate. The silence hurt.

And although she had enjoyed her prescribed hour of fun at salsa, it had left her feeling worse than ever. It had been such a long time since she and Alex had been out and enjoyed themselves. She'd told Fiona that it made her realise how much she had neglected Alex, letting their social life fall by the wayside after Millie had arrived.

'Kate I know I said that you should still make an effort to get out after having a baby but I didn't mean that you should have carried on as though she weren't there! Of course your social life is going to suffer. Alex needs to be a grown up and realise that. Millie is his daughter as well.'

But Kate had descended into a swamp of guilt and despair, convinced that her reluctance to go out in general and to the Christmas party in particular had made her husband turn to another woman.

She fed Millie and cleaned the house, although her enthusiasm for a gleaming home seemed to be deteriorating the longer Alex stayed away. Her interest in tidiness and a perfectly matched décor had been entirely for the benefit of Alex who clearly hadn't appreciated any of it enough to make him want to stay. She stared at her phone a lot and willed it to ring and of course she spent hours torturing herself with images of Alex and Sandra Maddison. She wondered if they now left the office together, letting everyone see that they were a couple. She wondered if they ate out like Kate and Alex had before Millie's arrival, deciding on the spur of the moment to go to their favourite Italian or grab a Chinese and take it home. And she thought of them in bed. Despite the unbelievable pain it caused, she could not stop thinking of them in bed, wondering if Alex whispered the same words into Sandra's ear that he used to whisper into Kate's own. Wondering if he wrapped his arms around her before drifting off to sleep, if he woke in the morning and reached out for her.

She knew how destructive it was to obsess about her husband's other woman, how self-defeating and hurtful. But although Google provided her with plenty of reasons why she shouldn't spend every minute of every day thinking about Sandra, it had failed to advise her just how she was meant to stop doing exactly that.

So Kate's days continued, Alex's silence was deafening and the brief escape of Friday night and salsa seemed as though it had never happened.

But, decided Kate with a sigh, even if Alex was not prepared to communicate it had come to the point where Kate was going to have to let Marcia Brady know that her long held suspicions that her daughter was too wayward to hold down a husband seemed to be true.

Marcia's brisk tone answered the phone and Kate arranged to call round that afternoon with Millie.

'During the week?' queried Marcia. 'Do you have the car?'

'No,' admitted Kate, 'we'll be coming on the bus.'

'Then why not wait until the weekend when Alex can bring you?' asked Marcia in a reasonable tone.

'Because,' sighed Kate, 'I need to see you now and … well Alex won't be here at the weekend.'

'And what's so important that it won't wait?'

Kate gritted her teeth. It was her own fault, she and Millie weren't exactly regular visitors at Marcia's door but when she finally decided to include her mother in her life the least she could at was co-operate.

'Anyone would think you didn't want to see us!' she tried a deliberately light tone.

'Don't be ridiculous. I'm just curious why you suddenly need to see me midweek when you don't have the car.'

'Well I can tell you when I get there can't I! Do I take it you'll be in?'

'Well if I know you're coming I'll change my plans and I'll be here.'

Why was it Kate wondered, that even when her mother was agreeing with her she made it sound as though Kate was so very wrong in everything she did.

'That'll be lovely. See you later,' and Kate put the phone down quickly

Millie was dressed, had eaten her breakfast and her eyelashes were drifting down ready for her morning nap. Kate examined herself in the mirror. She had washed her hair, piling on the conditioner in an attempt to banish the dry lifeless look and it gleamed and shone. She had been very careful with her makeup, making an attempt to cover the dark circles underneath the sad grey eyes. She didn't want to appear defeated; she didn't want anyone to look at her and say that they could understand why Alex had left his wife for another woman. And she especially didn't want Marcia to look at her with admonishment in her eyes and say briskly that a good wife always made sure she looked presentable

She took a deep breath. 'Come on then Millie, let's get going.'

Kate had two buses to catch before she was within a twenty-minute walk of her mother's house and as she pushed the buggy down the street her fingers were almost numb with cold. But eventually they arrived and turning into her mother's drive Kate straightened her spine and took a deep breath.

Marcia must have been looking out for her daughter because the door swung open before Kate had time to reach out to grab the highly polished brass knocker and her mother welcomed them with a smile then busied herself helping Millie out of the buggy and taking them both through to the warmth of the immaculate living room.

Not for Marcia a casual cup of tea around the kitchen table. If guests came they were always treated properly, even if the guest was her daughter.

'Your fingers are like ice,' she chastised Kate. 'why on earth didn't you put on some gloves? Warm yourself and I'll make some tea,' and off she bustled leaving Kate sitting on the edge of the settee a sleepy Millie in her arms.

A few minutes later Marcia returned with the tea tray, the teapot, milk jug and china cups and for a moment the little dose of normality was almost more than Kate could bear. She bit her lip, fussing with Millie whose eyes had flown open at the clink of cups and was looking round to see if anything was coming her way.

Marcia gave her a few moments and then having poured the tea she sat down opposite Kate and looked her in the eye.

'What's happened?'

For a moment Kate considered turning this into a visit, a normal visit from a daughter to a mother complete with beautiful granddaughter in tow. Did she really have the strength to lay herself open to her mother's disapproval?

'Alex has left me, she announced in a steady voice. 'He's moved in with another woman, someone he met at work.'

For a moment there was a flash of something in Marcia's eye that Kate couldn't quite pin down. Was it anger, sympathy, resignation? But then it was gone and there was a moment of silence as Marcia registered what had been said

'And is this a … fling or does he intend to stay with this woman?'

Kate shrugged. 'I don't know. We haven't really spoken.'

'When did he leave?'

'A couple of weeks ago.'

Marcia's eyebrows raised.

'He hasn't been in touch?'

Kate shook her head, her cheeks flushing. She couldn't bring herself to discuss the hysterical phone call she had made to her husband the night she'd found out he had indeed left her for another woman.

'No,' said Kate looking at her fingers instead of her mother.

'And in the meantime?'

Kate looked at her mother.

'Are you okay in the meantime Kate, do you have money, are you happy in the house by yourself, can you cope with Millie … are you okay?'

Kate thought for a moment. Was she okay? Did she have money? She hadn't actually given the financial side of things a second thought, the bills seemed to be getting paid as normal and she spent her days sitting at home feeling miserable not out spending money. As for the house, she had to admit that having the house to herself was actually quite pleasant. She hadn't felt any of the usual pressure to have a meal ready the moment Alex walked through the door, to have the crisp white shirts he wore for work washed, ironed and hanging in his wardrobe. She had even left a couple of towels on the bathroom floor the day before and been almost surprised to find that it had no effect on the rest of her day.

Marcia was waiting for a reply.

'I'm okay Mum. It was just a bit of a shock.'

'Why didn't you tell me when it happened?'

Kate had been waiting for the question.

'I think,' she began slowly, 'I think I didn't want you to be disappointed in me.'

Marcia placed her cup carefully back on the saucer.

'Why would Alex leaving make me disappointed in you?'

Kate closed her eyes briefly. 'I remember you telling me that I needed to grow up. When I told you that Alex and I were getting married you told me that I had to be more responsible, more grown up. That I had to look after him and behave like a proper wife and keep the kitchen clean and wash the sheets and make him a meal every night.'

Marcia looked a little startled but only briefly before her familiar detached expression settled once more.

'And I tried Mum, I really tried,' cried Kate. 'But it obviously wasn't enough because he left me. So I failed and I knew you would be disappointed.'

There was a long, long silence as Kate looked down at Millie scrunched up in her arms, not wanting to meet her mother's eyes and read how let down she was in her daughter's failure to grow up and look after her husband.

'Kate, you surely can't think that this is your fault?'

'Of course it is. He wouldn't have left me if he'd been happy! I didn't make him happy. I didn't keep the house tidy enough, I let him down, I …'

'Kate! Marriages don't end because one of them is untidy.'

Kate blinked. 'Yours did.'

Marcia looked shocked. 'Of course it didn't! Were on earth did you get that idea from?'

'You told me,' answered Kate, 'I asked where dad had gone and you said to somewhere he could make all the mess he liked.'

Kate had not been unaware of the tension in her parent's marriage. But it had been that way for as long as she could remember so she had thought it to be the normal way of married life. Her mother's constant remonstrations about her father's inability to put anything away, that fact that he left his plates piled in the sink, crumbs on the table, the butter left with the lid off - these were all rebukes heard constantly. And her father's tired response, that there was more to life than washing up, that a little bit of untidiness was good for the soul, that mess could be cleaned up in a flash, pleas for her to leave him be and give him some peace. Kate had been left in no doubt that the main reason for the eventual parting of their ways was entirely due to her father's inability to tidy up after himself and her mother's overwhelming need to keep an orderly house

'Kate, you can't really think that your father and I divorced because he wasn't tidy enough?'

'Yes,' answered Kate simply.

'But that's ridiculous!'

'Then why did you make him leave?'

Marcia shook her head, the cool demeanor slipping ever so slightly.

'We weren't happy Kate. That's the long and the short of it. We just weren't happy together. We tried to be, we worked at it for a long time but we were never suited to each other and as a result we were never happy.'

'You didn't love him?'

For a brief, very brief moment Kate saw a look of such intense pain in her mother's eyes that she almost cried out.

'Oh we loved each other Kate. I loved your father with my entire soul and I know he loved me, at least to begin with. But sometimes love just isn't enough. Your father was carefree and outgoing, full of life and vigour. He wanted to pack a bag and explore another continent, he wanted to wake up each morning and go wherever his heart took him, not to be tied down by everyday chores and the grind of daily life. We wanted entirely different things from life but we loved each other and we were both quite convinced that we could make it work.'

Kate sat very still as Marcia stared out of the window, almost lost in her own thoughts.

'But in the end we had to admit that we were two very different people and it was better that he left.'

'But you said he was untidy, you were always complaining, you said ...' Kate trailed off in bewilderment

'A symptom, not the cause, said Marcia with a smile. 'The more I felt him drift away from me the more I became the very person he would object to the most I suppose.'

Kat shook her head in bewilderment. 'I never realised, I just always thought … but why did you tell me to grow up, to become the perfect wife for Alex?'

'Just down to earth motherly advice Kate. You were dreadfully disorganised before you met Alex and that may be sweet when the first flush of love is still in the air but believe me it loses its sparkle when you come home after a hard day at work to a flat looking like yours used to.'

Kate's mother had always been horrified whenever she visited her wayward daughter and found a week's worth of clothes littering the floor, a sink piled high with unwashed plates and nothing in the fridge but left overs covered in mould.

Kate would watch Marcia's reaction with something approaching satisfaction, proud that she had not succumbed to her mother's ways. And all this time Kate had been wrong. Her father hadn't left because he was too untidy, he had left simply because he didn't love her mother enough to stay.

'Was there another woman?' asked Kate suddenly.

'No. He met Eileen of course but that was years later.'

'Why did you never find anyone else?'

Marcia smiled. 'Because your father was the love of my life Kate. I never wanted anyone else,' she said simply.

For some reason Kate felt quite humbled. And ashamed. She had never really spoken to her mother about the departure of her father, she had been quite happy to lay the blame at the feet of Marcia's obsessive need for order. Graham Brady had died suddenly five years after the divorce and all that was left of him now were Kate's memories.

'Bu we should be talking about you and Alex,' said Marcia briskly, checking the pot. 'I'm going to boil some more water and then you must tell me your plans for the future.'

Kate was deep in thought when Marcia arrived back in the room with a fresh pot of tea.

'I tried really hard Mum,' she repeated. 'I did everything I thought I should. I learned how to cook, I tried to be tidy - I did everything properly. And I loved him, we loved each other. Why would he go? I tried so hard to be a perfect wife.'

Marcia Brady sighed. She put the teapot full of hot fresh tea on the tray and sighed as she looked at her daughter's heartbroken face.

'Who knows my dear. But maybe perfection wasn't what Alex was looking for?' and she poured another cup of tea which they drank in silence, both staring out into the frost covered garden.

Chapter 13

It was Friday again and Fiona phoned Kate to check that she was bringing Millie around and going to salsa.

'Actually,' started Kate, 'I really don't know if…'

'No!' shrieked Fiona. 'Do not give up already Kate. You're doing this for a reason, remember. And even if you weren't– you enjoyed it last week, didn't you?'

Kate thought back to the previous week. She had loved every minute of salsa, she had enjoyed chatting to new people and she had actually stopped thinking about Alex for almost a full hour as she and Sophie wriggled their hips and giggled their way through the class.

'But I don't think it's working Fee.'

'Google didn't say it would work overnight honey. You need to carry on until Alex realises that you're getting on with your life and he'll soon want to get in touch.'

'But …'

'No buts. This is good for you Kate, regardless of whether Alex comes back or not,' Fiona continued. 'You need something, even if it's only an hour or so a week, something that you do for yourself.'

Kate hesitated.

'And just imagine if Olivia and Helen go back to work on Monday and tell everyone that you didn't turn up this week. Alex will think that you couldn't cope with a night out without him, that you're at home crying again.'

'I'm beginning to think that Alex doesn't care in the slightest whether I'm out or not Fee. Still not so much as a text from him.'

'Well all the more reason you should carry on going to salsa,' insisted Fiona.

Kate sighed. It all seemed like too much effort but she nodded her head.

'Okay, I'll go,' she agreed and couldn't help smiling at Fiona's whoop of delight.

Kate didn't spend quite so much time getting ready this week and she told Millie, who watched as her mother dried her hair and brushed it until it shone, that despite anything Fiona might say, this was going to be the last week.

'Not much point Millie darling, if daddy doesn't care what I do I might as well stay at home with you.'

Millie had laughed and thrown her donkey on the floor for Kate to retrieve and for a moment she had a memory of getting ready on a Friday night when she was seeing Alex. She would leave work as early as possible and within an hour her small cramped flat would look like a scene from an earthquake as she pulled item after item from her wardrobe to find just the right outfit. There would be flutters of anticipation dancing in her stomach and when she was finally happy with her appearance she would hang out of the window waiting to see Alex's car drive down the street.

135

Kate had lots of friends. She was a sociable person who loved to party and during the early part of their relationship she'd had a wonderful time introducing Alex to everyone she knew. They would meet a crowd of friends for a meal, or at the cinema and there were constant parties and impromptu drinks. But it had only taken a few months for Kate to realise that Alex was a lot less outgoing than Kate. Although her carefree, sunny disposition was one of the main reasons Alex had fallen in love with Kate, once their relationship was established he had always looked for ways to slow down their social life and Kate, madly in love with the young blond man by her side, had seen less and less of her friends and their weekends had become more intimate, quieter with Kate's party days a thing of the past. She sighed deeply, what had she done to drive him away, she thought sadly; she had tried so hard to be what Alex wanted, to be a perfect wife.

Pushing aside the memories, she followed Fiona's advice and got ready for an evening at salsa. This week she wore a pair of trousers that hugged her hips and narrowed to finish slightly above the ankle. The weight Kate had lost was evident as she fastened the zip and even Kate had to admit that she looked good. She pulled on a silver top that sparkled and shimmered and swung around Kate's hips as she moved and then took out her make up brush to attack her pale cheeks and the violet shadows underneath her eyes.

Wrapping up warmly she took Millie to Fiona's and this time didn't waste her breath arguing when Stuart said he was driving her to the wine bar. And when he pulled the car to a halt outside the front door, Kate only sat for thirty seconds biting her lip before jumping out and dashing through the rain to the front door.

She smiled at several people she recognized from the week before, looking around for Sophie and hoping that she would be able to partner Kate again.

'Kate, this is my friend Alan.'

That was Kate's plan ruined. She smiled at the shy young man at Sophie's side.

'I've been trying to persuade him to join me and he's kept promising to think about it. I told him that I had a great new partner last week and if he didn't want to come that was okay -but he decided to join us this week.'

Kate hid her smile at the twinkle in Sophie's eye and shook Alan's hand. 'Pleased to meet you,' she offered although she was anything but; no Sophie meant that Kate was probably going to have to join Victor at the front of the class.

She saw Olivia and Helen walk through the door and they smiled and waved as they walked towards her.

'Hello!' shouted Helen excitedly. 'I'm so glad you came again. We were telling everyone last week how lovely you looked and how well you did the salsa.'

Kate's heat did a little flip. She wondered if any of the news had reached Alex's ear.

Helen's eyes were shining. 'I was talking to Susanne from customer services and telling her how amazing you'd been and who should be stood behind me?'

She paused theatrically and Kate's heart literally stood still. Was it Alex, she wondered desperately? Please say it was Alex.

'Sandra Maddison!' crowed Helen. 'She heard everything I said and she did not look pleased at all!'

Was that a good thing wondered Kate? Was Sandra likely to go home and tell Alex that she'd heard his ex-wife, the one he'd recently abandoned, was enjoying herself at salsa and looking amazing? No, decided Kate, she would probably keep that information to herself. But it gave Kate a little boost that at least Sandra wouldn't be viewing Kate as a sad left over, sitting at home and weeping while Sandra gazed into Alex's eyes and held on tightly to his arm.

'Hi there.'

Kate turned, frowning at the figure standing in front of her.

He held his hand out. 'Josh,' he said, smiling at Kate.

Kate looked blank taking the proffered hand. 'Er, Kate.'

Sophie was watching them grinning.

'We met last week,' Josh explained. 'You and your friend were so good I said I might join in.'

'Oh,' started Kate, for some reason blushing furiously, 'I remember, you were standing at the back watching.'

Out of the corner of her eye she could see Olivia and Helen nudging each other and Sophie's grin stretching even wider.

'You were so impressive,' said Josh gravely. 'I decided I had to give it a go myself.'

Kate was aware of the flush still on her cheeks.

'Well I hope you enjoy it,' she offered lamely.

'Of course I haven't got a partner.'

The flush deepened as Sophie jumped in. 'Oh that's actually really good because Kate doesn't have one this week either.'

She ignored Kate's wide eyes and disapproving mouth.

'My friend has come this week you see,' she said pushing Kate a little nearer to Josh.

'And we've come together,' chorused Olivia and Helen, taking a step back so there was a clear space around Kate.

'So you can be Kate's partner!' finished Sophie happily.

'Well that would be wonderful!' Josh was looking directly at Kate. 'As long as you don't mind Kate?'

Ambushed Kate shook her head. 'Of course not,' she said politely, trying to ignore the delighted glances that were winging between Sophie, Olivia and Helen.

Just then Chantelle began clapping her hands to call everyone's attention and salsa music burst into the room.

Josh took Kate's hand and pulled her gently sideways into a space. 'Thank you for being my partner,' he said gravely.

Kate nibbled her lip. 'It's okay.'

'I've been looking forward to this all week,' Josh said in a low voice, stepping closer to Kate as Chantelle began her count -one two three and one two three.

'Salsa?'

'Well, that as well,' answered Josh with a twinkle in his eye that brought the colour flooding back into Kate's face and then there was no more time for talk as the rhythm took over and Kate and Josh counted and stepped and shimmied with the rest of the room.

An hour later when they finally stopped, breathless and laughing, Kate had become used to the feel of Josh's hand holding hers. She no longer flinched when their hips bumped together or when they took a wrong step and crashed into each other. His face with its strong jaw, slightly dimpled chin and very blue eyes had become quite familiar as was his chuckle when they lost the beat or turned the wrong way. But the minute the lights were turned up, the music stopped and the dance was over, Kate's cheeks began to flush again and her eyes remained staring at the ground as Josh leaned over to speak to her.

'Well?' he asked. 'Do you think there's any hope for me?'

Kate shrugged. 'Did you enjoy it?'

Josh laughed. 'I must admit I did. I'm not much of a dancer, I usually sit at the side watching others.'

'So why did you decide to try salsa?' asked Kate, only to drop her eyes at his grin.

'Oh, it has its attractions!'

Olivia and Helen appeared at their side both looking smug.

'You two looked really good,' said Helen, not bothering with any subtlety. 'Are you coming again next week Josh?'

Kate found herself standing very still.

'Oh I think so, it's quite addictive isn't it?' smiled Josh

Sophie was peering round Josh's broad shoulders grinning.

'Good, I'm sure Kate will be happy to be your partner again. Right shall we all have a drink before we go, Kate, white wine isn't it?' and not leaving Kate chance to turn down the offer she marched to the bar.

'Sorry,' mumbled Kate. 'They're a bit obvious.'

Josh threw back his head and laughed. 'Saves time though,' he suggested. 'Otherwise it could have taken me hours to summon the courage to ask if you'd join me again next week.'

Kate met his eyes. They were kind, smiling, interested.

'I have a daughter,' she announced watching him blink with surprise.

'Okay.'

'And a husband,' added Kate, seeing a quick look of disappointment flash across his face.

'Oh I see…'

'Well, I suppose at the moment he's a sort of ex-husband. He left me a couple of weeks ago. My friend said I had to come to salsa so he knows I'm getting on with life.'

Josh looked curious. 'And are you?'

Kate thought for a moment. She had a feeling that the answer was no, but in the interests of trying to get on with her life she lied.

'Yes. I am.'

'That's good,' nodded Josh. 'And are you getting on with life enough to come to salsa next week and be my partner again?'

Kate felt that again the answer should be no. After all it wasn't quite two weeks since Alex had walked out on her. She was still devastated and certainly wasn't ready for assignations with men at salsa class.

'Yes, I think so.'

Josh smiled and nodded his head. Reaching out he squeezed Kate's hand slightly. 'Good. I'm glad for you, that you're moving on with your life, and I'm very glad for me,' and then he took the beer that Alan was holding out to him and stepped slightly away from Kate so that Olivia, Helen and Sophie could join them as they drank wine, grinned at each other and watched Josh smile at Kate and Kate smile shyly back.

Chapter 14

Kate told Fiona she'd had a lovely time at salsa and then let Stuart drive her and Millie home. On Saturday, when she spoke to Fiona on the phone, she admitted that her partner had not been Sophie but a pleasant man called Josh but refused to answer of any of Fiona's highly excited questions about just how pleasant and did she actually mean pleasant or good looking.

On Sunday when Fiona phoned and invited Kate to come over for lunch, Kate told Fiona that Josh had asked if she would go to salsa the following week and be his partner again. After a piercing shriek from Fiona, Kate had declined lunch and also any further conversation regarding

Josh's suitability as a replacement husband, reminding Fiona that the salsa was purely a strategy as advised by Google, a means to redirect her husband's attention in Kate's direction.

On Monday Fiona phoned Kate and asked if she had any more to add to the story and laughing Kate had said no, Fiona was up to date with it all.

'But Fee, the plan isn't working is it? I don't think Alex cares that I'm out enjoying myself, making new friends and getting on with life. It's probably just a relief to him that I'm moving on.'

Fiona had clucked with sympathy.

'Keep at it Kate honey. At the very worst if Alex doesn't come back you'll have something to do on a Friday night!'

Kate had not been impressed by any suggestion that Alex wouldn't be returning but sighing she said goodbye to Fiona and put the phone down.

It was a depressing thought that maybe Alex would not come home. She had spent the weekend on Google crying at the many sad stories she read about women whose husband's simply never came back despite everything they said and tried. Closing her laptop Kate had refused to believe that could happen to her. She loved Alex too much to let him disappear from her life.

Kate looked at the kitchen. She had cleaned it as she did every morning, but the shiny new sparkle that she always put on the surfaces wasn't there and a couple of mugs still sat in the sink from the coffee Kate had drunk that morning. Somehow, the need to have a house that looked so very clean and bright on a daily basis didn't seem quite so important now there was only Kate and Millie to appreciate it. Kate couldn't help but wonder if the hours she had spent on domestic chores in the past hadn't all been a waste of time, it certainly hadn't kept Alex at home. She looked at the mugs then shrugged and turned her back, walking into the living room instead.

She sat in her favourite chair by the fire and thought back to Friday night. Once the embarrassment of having Josh thrown at her had worn off she'd thoroughly enjoyed the salsa. She smiled to herself, Josh had been far from perfect and there were several times when his face had been tense and full of concentration as he counted out loud and tried to keep the rhythm going.

He'd apologised to Kate as they sipped their drinks, for the number of times he'd stood on her toes, going forwards instead of backwards or lurching to the side as Kate stood still.

Kate had smiled and said it really hadn't mattered. She remembered when Alex had gone with her. He had been the same, finding the rhythm hard to keep. But he hadn't laughed like Josh, Alex had become quite frustrated and after only a couple of classes said it really wasn't for him.

'You should still go,' he had said to Kate when she'd looked disappointed, 'no reason why you shouldn't go if you enjoy it so much but I'll give it a miss.'

And so the following week Kate had put on her dancing shoes and stood in the doorway to say goodbye.

'Where are you going?' Alex had asked in surprise.

Kate stared at him 'Salsa of course! Have you forgotten it's Wednesday?'

There had been the tiniest of little pauses but it was long enough for her to realise that Alex may have said that Kate should go dancing without him but he hadn't expected that she would.

'Don't you want me to go?' Kate had asked.

Alex had shrugged, appearing nonchalant. 'Of course you should go,' he'd said. 'If you enjoy it you should carry on.'

But it didn't seem to Kate that the words were meant and although she went to salsa that week and the next, the disappointment in Alex's eyes had led to her declaring on the third week that she would stay at home with Alex instead. He had grabbed her by the waist and swung her round and buried his face in her hair telling her how much he loved her. He said that he knew Kate loved dancing and why didn't they go to line dancing instead, he much preferred it to salsa. And Kate had been so delighted with his response that she soon forgot about salsa and although she realised several weeks later that the line dancing had never materialized, by now they had a whole new routine on a Wednesday evening which revolved around a bottle of wine and a DVD and the two of them snuggled on the settee.

Her Thursday evenings had also fallen by the wayside. They had been wonderful evenings when she would meet up with a couple of girlfriends at a local restaurant and they would drink wine and eat pizza and compare their weeks and their jobs and their outfits and their partners.

'I feel as though I'm being judged,' Alex had said trying to pass it off as a light hearted comment.

'Don't be silly!' Kate had exclaimed laughing. 'I only say the nicest things about you. They all get bored with how all my comments start with 'Alex says...'

She had found Alex's concern amusing but as the weeks went by and his demeanor each Thursday became increasingly stiff, she had reduced the weekly event to a monthly event. It was surprising how many times Alex declared that he hadn't realised that this was the Thursday Kate was meeting her friends and he had organised a meal out for the two of them or bought tickets to the theatre.

And although Kate could never put her finger on when it had happened, suddenly she realised she had gone months without taking part in the get together and that most of her Thursdays were now spent with Alex.

The phone rang and with a sigh Kate grabbed the handset. Her mother had phoned several times to make sure Kate was okay and although every call left Kate feeling tense, waiting for the criticism she felt Marcia was about to dole her way, her mother had actually been nothing but supportive and pleasant.

'Kate?'

Kate almost dropped the phone. It was the voice she'd been waiting to hear for two weeks. Two weeks to the day in fact since Alex had stood in the doorway and told Kate that her perfect marriage had failed and he was leaving her.

'Alex?' she whispered.

'Kate are you there?'

Kate gathered her wild thoughts and tried again. 'Alex – hello.'

There was a pause, a long pause as neither seemed to know what should happen next.

Kate waited.

'Kate, I'm sorry I haven't phoned earlier.' Alex gave her a chance to say it was okay but Kate remained silent. 'I had a lot of thinking to do as you can imagine.'

Kate could imagine. She had been doing a lot of thinking herself over the last two weeks.

Her hands started shaking and all she could hear for a moment was her heartbeat drumming against her rib cage. Oh God he had phoned, Alex had finally phoned.

There was another pause.

'Have you been okay?'

Was he mad, wondered Kate? He had walked out on her with no warning and no explanation and then ignored her for two weeks.

'I'm okay,' she answered.

Alex gave her a chance to ask if he was okay but Kate was silent again.

'Right, well that's good.'

When did talking to each other become so difficult wondered Kate? Had it been like this before Alex left and she just hadn't noticed? Had their easy banter and interest in each other disappeared to be left with a stilted conversation about how well they both were?

'Kate I think we need to sit down and discuss – well you know, things.'

Kate held her breath. Was this the moment she had been waiting for, the moment when Alex told her he had made a mistake and wanted to come back? Was this the Google moment she'd been working towards?

'I realise that my leaving must have come as a shock to you.'

Kate let out a breath of disappointment. Maybe not.

'Yes,' she said bravely, holding back the tears. 'It was.'

She heard a soft sigh echo down the phone. 'I had tried to tell you Kate, I had tried to talk to you about how unhappy I was.'

'Yes, strange I don't remember that conversation Alex,' she snapped.

'Oh er … well it's difficult isn't it?'

Which part wondered Kate? Having an affair and making sure your wife was none the wiser, walking out on her and your baby daughter, explaining why you felt the need to leap into bed with Sandra Maddison?

Kate resorted to silence. Her eyes fell on her laptop sitting on the sofa and she desperately tried to remember all the advice she and Fiona had read. It's essential you are calm when speaking to your husband, accusations and anger will not help your new relationship progress.

Kate bit her lip. 'I imagine it is Alex,' she said calmly.

'Right, okay well, perhaps we should meet then. Have a chat and talk about – you know.'

Kate allowed herself a tiny flutter of excitement. It was all going as planned. She and Alex would start communicating and he would remember the girl he'd fallen in love with, he would regret Sandra Maddison and her come to bed eyes and his heart would return to Kate. At least according to Google that's what would happen.

'I think that would be very sensible Alex.' Kate kept her tone neutral, no glimmer of excitement or triumph. 'When were you thinking?'

'Er how about Friday night? I could meet you after work?' Maybe we could get a bite of something to eat and talk.'

Kate's heart beat a tattoo as she felt her lips stretching outwards into a huge smile. 'Friday night?' she queried.

'If that's okay with you? Will Fiona look after Millie do you think?'

Suddenly the smile faltered. Friday night, that would mean missing salsa. Of course, reasoned Kate, the whole reason she was going to salsa was so she could wave a red flag in Alex's direction, capture his attention without resorting to hysterical phone calls and demands. Of course she would miss salsa if it meant moving a step closer to Alex returning home.

But Kate was enjoying salsa. She was actually doing something she enjoyed. Something she had previously given up for Alex. Something she had given up so she could concentrate on becoming a perfect wife. The sort that had a perfect marriage. The sort whose husbands remained faithful.

'Friday?' she said. 'Actually, Friday isn't good for me Alex, can we make it another night?'

The silence was overwhelming. It stretched on for several seconds.

'You're busy on Friday?' he asked disbelievingly.

A trickle of something travelled down Kate's backbone.

'Yes.'

'And it's not something that you can put off?'

Of course it was thought Kate, she just didn't want to.

'Not really.'

'Oh is it the salsa class thing you've started doing?' he asked casually.

Kate's eyes widened. He knew. He had heard about her going to salsa. Maybe not from Sandra but he'd heard from someone at the office that his wife, his abandoned wife, was not at home crying but was out dancing the salsa and looking good. And not just dancing, but dancing with a good looking man. That's why he had phoned.

Kate punched the air with delight.

'It is,' she said calmly.

'And you can't miss a night of salsa to talk to me?'

'Of course I could,' said Kate thoughtfully, 'but I would prefer not to.'

'Another long pause.

'Right,' Alex started in a huff. 'Well what night are you free?'

Should she suggest he wait while she checked her diary, thought Kate. It was unsurprisingly very empty, apart from one hour on Friday night.

'No point waiting until Friday is there? What about ton - tomorrow?' suggested Kate.

It had been on the tip of her tongue to suggest they meet that night but her brain immediately thought of all the work that was needed, the research into which outfit would bring her husband back to her, what she should and shouldn't say, what phrases would make him realise his mistake.

'Okay,' replied Alex gruffly, 'tomorrow then. I'll meet you in town after work, around half six?'

'No,' said Kate before he could put down the phone. 'Collect me from the house. You may not recall Alex that you have taken the only car we have and I don't fancy catching two buses into town,' and happy that she had at least given him something to think about, Kate hung up before feverishly dialing Fiona's number and tapping the keys of her keyboard to see what advice Google had for someone who was about to meet their unfaithful husband for the first time since he had abandoned her.

Chapter 15

The next morning, only minutes after the school bell had rung, Fiona was at Kate's door, blowing on her cold hands and dancing around with excitement.

'I knew it would work,' she declared, pulling off her coat and following Kate through to the kitchen. 'I knew as soon as he heard you were okay and going out he'd be in touch. I knew he'd want to know what was going on in your life. He may have moved on to someone else but the plan was never that you would! I knew …'

Kate held her hand up laughing. 'Okay, okay,' she said giggling. 'I agree the plan worked. He even tried to arrange a meeting for Friday so I wouldn't go to salsa!'

'Bastard!' ground out Fiona. 'How dare he!'

Kate shrugged her shoulders. Today wasn't the day to hate Alex. Today was the day to take the first step forward with her plan to get her husband back.

'Right,' said Fiona grinning. 'Let's get started.'

They had spoken to each other nonstop on the phone the day before, both investigating every lead offered by Google and reading every article and piece of advice they could find about how to treat the husband who left you for another woman when you want him back.

Fiona produced a large piece of yellow card covered in bullet pints in green felt tip.

'All I could find,' she said at Kate's raised eyebrows.

She placed the card on the table and pointed to the first line.

'He's made contact – that's good.'

Kate grinned.

'He's heard you've been out enjoying yourself. I bet he wants to know more about what you're doing.'

Kate nodded happily.

'It's probably a fact finding mission, but you've got his attention. So let's stick with the plan.'

'Okay.'

'You have to play it cool Kate. No tears, no pleading, no begging. Apparently nothing puts unfaithful husbands off quite so much as a desperate, weeping wife.'

Kate nodded again. Hadn't she been calm when Alex had finally phoned her and she heard his voice for the first time in over two weeks? Okay she had cried for two hours after she'd hung up the phone but she'd been calm at the time.

She took a deep breath and agreed. 'Calm,' she agreed.

'He needs to see that you've been hurt but that you're not devastated and lost without him. That will fuel his belief that he was right to leave you in the first place,' quoted Fiona.

'Why?'

Fiona bit her lip. 'Something to do with feeling that he's trapped and needing air and space.'

'Right,' nodded Kate. 'So I'm going to be quietly hurt but …?'

'Er – just a minute. Hurt but resigned and ready to start your life again without him,' read Fiona.

Kate frowned. 'But don't I want him to know I miss him and want him home?'

'No,' began Fiona quickly checking her notes, 'well yes, but in a controlled way. He needs to know that you're strong enough to cope without him. That will dent his ego and make him want you again.'

'Really?' queried Kate doubtfully.

'Yes.'

Kate nodded.

'You need to make him accept what he's done Kate,' said Fiona firmly. 'That means none of this blaming yourself and making excuses why he cheated on you.'

Kate hung her head and nodded.

'You need to remind him in a clear and unemotional way that he has been unfaithful. He walked out on his wife and daughter and that in your opinion, that was a bad thing to do.'

Kate nodded harder.

'You do not for a moment suggest that you were in any way to blame,' continued Fiona in her sternest voice.

Kate bit her lip.

'Kate!' warned Fiona.

'Okay, okay,' Kate sighed. 'But I need to accept that some of it may have been my fault.'

'It wasn't your fault Kate.'

'Some of it may have been. Google said he was feeling neglected and if that's because I didn't pay him enough attention then it was partly my fault.

Fiona gritted her teeth. 'It was not your fault. But,' she sighed in resignation, 'you can listen to his excuses …'

'His reasons.'

'His excuses, and be prepared to consider any claims he makes regarding your own behavior.'

'Isn't that the same as saying it's my fault?' asked Kate.

'No, it is not. You will listen to his excuses and ponder them. You will not throw yourself across the table and tell him it's all your fault, you made him have an affair and you forgive him.'

'But forgivingness is essential to move on' insisted Kate. 'Google definitely said that I would have to forgive Alex before he could come home.'

'Well Google also says make him pay!'

Kate sighed, her head was beginning to ache.

'Okay, calm, rational, make him admit he behaved badly, let him give his excuses, think about them but hold off on the forgiveness for now,' she repeated rubbing at the furrow on her forehead.

'Good!'

Kate wondered if she could write all this on the back of her hand, it seemed a lot to remember during the pressure of her first meeting with Alex.

'What if he says he wants to come back?' she asked happily.

'He won't'

'But what if he does?'

'Well he won't, not just yet. He'll want to test the water and see just how accommodating you're likely to be.'

Kate nodded but couldn't help the little shiver of excitement that chased down her spine. Google didn't know everything, maybe Alex had been distraught at the tales of his wife dressed to impress and dancing the salsa with a strange man.

'Kate,' said Fiona gently,' he won't ask to come back. It's too soon.'

Kate nodded agreement even as she started to imagine coming back with Alex after the meeting, saying casually to Fiona that Alex had come home.

Fiona sighed as she saw the dreamy expression on Kate's face.

'It's a long journey Kate, this is just the first step. Alex will have to face up to what he's done first of all, then he'll have to accept that he's made a mistake and then decide that he wants to come back home …' she relented at the disappointment in her friend's face. 'He'll come home Kate, I just don't think it will be tonight.'

Fiona continued working through her bullet points giving Kate instructions for any eventuality that might occur, making her practice responses to possible questions and rehearse a cool, faintly disinterested smile designed to make Alex slightly crazy with curiosity until Kate could not take in any more information.

'Okay, well I think we've done all we can for now' accepted Fiona eventually. 'Now I need to go and collect my brood from school but Stuart is coming home early to feed them so I'll be back shortly for the fun part.'

156

Kate looked questioningly as Fiona stood up. 'We've got to make you look so drop dead gorgeous he won't be able to believe he made the mistake of ever leaving you!'

Kate spent a few hours nervously pacing around the house, her mind bubbling with hope and excitement as well as worry and anxiety. Fiona soon returned and she and Millie watched as Kate spent the next two hours making herself look better than she had in years, in a way that indicated that she had made no effort at all.

Her hair was brushed and teased until it hung down her back in rippling waves, the way Alex loved. She sat, her face almost immobile from the face pack Fiona had brought with her and watched Millie eat her tea. Millie was fascinated by her mother's suddenly green face but Kate couldn't smile, her cheeks held rigid by the paste that claimed it would invigorate her skin and provide the equivalent glow of a great night's sleep. Privately Kate thought that it would take a good deal more than a face pack to make her look as though she'd had anything remotely resembling a decent night's sleep but she was willing to give it a try so she sat, unspeaking with a face held rigid for fifteen minutes until Fiona declared it was time to peel it away.

Peering in the mirror, Kate felt that although it hadn't quite lived up to its claims she did look a little more alert, as though she'd had a decent nap at least.

There was a great deal of debate over the outfit. Taking the laptop upstairs, Fiona flicked through page upon page of advice while Kate pulled out outfit after outfit.

'This is a really important bit,' declared Fiona. 'You can't afford to look as though you've gone to too much effort, he'll think you're desperate.'

Kate refrained from saying she was very desperate and if it resulted in Alex coming back home she was happy to go out wearing hot pants and little else.

'But obviously you need to look fabulous, so he remembers how much he loved you, starts to regret not being with you.'

Kate nodded.

'So you need to look sexy in a disinterested kind of a way. Alluring, but not as though you've gone to any effort.'

Kate frowned. 'All that in one outfit?'

'We can do it!' declared Fiona trying to sound confident.

The next half hour Kate tried on almost everything in her wardrobe.

'Too formal,' announced Fiona as Kate took out a skirt and cashmere top.

'Too desperate,' she declared as Kate replaced it with a tight red dress that left nothing to the imagination.

'Too casual,' she insisted as Kate tried for the everyday approach in jeans and a silk blouse.

After much debate which included emptying Kate's wardrobe and covering her bed with discarded outfits that reminded Kate of her old flat, they stood side by side looking at Kate's reflection in the mirror

Neither of them said anything then Fiona broke into a grin. 'I think we've done it honey, that's the outfit.'

Kate was dressed in black silk trousers which grazed her ankle and a top in a soft copper hue that clung to Kate's figure, showed off the strawberry blonde hair to perfection and even brought a slight glow to Kate's skin. The top was cut low enough to provide an enchanting peak of cleavage but was not so low as to suggest that Kate was seeking attention. The stone that Kate had lost since Alex had left meant the trousers hugged her hips and the top showed her shrinking waist.

'Exactly right,' breathed Fiona. 'Exactly right.'

Kate hung the outfit on the front of the wardrobe until nearer the time and turned her attention to her makeup. A good hour before Alex was due to arrive Fiona ran into the bathroom to spray Kate with her favourite perfume.

'It mustn't appear too fresh when Alex arrives,' she explained. 'He needs to be able to smell a familiar smell which will remind him of you, but it mustn't be too strong or too obvious. We don't want him thinking you're put it on solely for his benefit.'

Kate stood still while Fiona sent a soft spray towards Kate's curls before directing her hand downwards towards her breasts, winking at Kate as she sprayed.

Then she took Millie away to have a bath while Kate concentrated on her face. She covered the shadows under her eyes, already slightly depleted from her face mask, she brought some colour back to her pale cheeks, she outlined her eyes and applied just enough mascara to make sure her lashes were curling upwards and she rubbed soft pink gloss into lips dry with constant crying.

Stepping back to look in the mirror, she nodded. To the untrained eye it was understated, minimal effort for a face that was naturally pretty and had a golden glow. Only Kate knew how much effort it had required.

Fiona put Millie into her cutest pyjamas and fluffed up her blonde baby curls. She smelt of baby and soap suds and Kate felt her heart contract as she imagined Millie growing up without Alex in their lives. She kissed the blonde head and thanked Fiona for all her help before going back to the outfit hanging on the wardrobe door.

When she walked downstairs Fiona looked at her from every angle before smiling and giving her a hug.

'You look amazing,' she whispered. 'Absolutely amazing. He'll be hard pressed to think why on earth he left you!'

Kate nodded, too nervous to speak as she put her coat and bag on the kitchen table ready to grab when Alex came.

'I'll get the door,' announced Fiona. 'You'll be on the phone when he arrives.'

Kate looked at her blankly. 'I will?'

'Yes, you'll just be saying goodbye and the last thing you'll say is - see you on Friday night.'

'But who am I phoning?'

Fiona tutted. 'You won't be phoning anybody! But it will look as though someone has just phoned you.'

She shook her head at Kate's continued confusion and carried on slowly. 'You will pretend you are speaking to someone, imagine that it's Josh.'

Kate blushed and Fiona continued. 'And as Alex comes through the door you'll say that you have to go but you're looking forward to Friday.'

Kate's mouthed dropped open. 'Ah!'

'And when Alex asks who you were speaking to, and he will, you will look at him as though it's none of his business and then with a little smile you'll say it was just your salsa partner.'

Kate's eyes were now huge. 'What if he asks me more?'

'Then you'll be casual, shrug your shoulders and don't give him any info.'

'But what if …'

'Kate! Alex is the one who left you and shacked up with Sandra Maddison! He's the one answering the questions tonight!'

Kate nibbled at her finger only to have it slapped by Fiona. She looked down at the immaculate nails painted a soft pearly pink.

'I really don't think that lying is going to help things at all Fiona.'

'Lying, who's lying? Did you partner Josh at salsa last week?'

'Well yes but …'

'Did Josh ask you to partner him at salsa again this week?'

'Yes but …'

161

'Then there is no lying Kate, other than the lying Alex has been doing of course. You are simply letting him believe what he wants.'

Kate still looked uncertain but at that moment the doorbell rang out into the house making both Kate and Fiona jump.

'Oh God Fee, he's here!'

Kate had started to shake and for a moment the glamorous facade she'd spent all afternoon erecting looked under threat of falling down around her ears.

Fiona grabbed her friends hand. 'Keep calm Kate. Deep breaths, remember everything we've said. Alex is going to fall in love with you again tonight and everything will work out fine.'

Kate thought about dashing to the bathroom, she could feel the bile rising in her stomach. Her mind was blank, all the research she and Fiona had done was now a thing of the past. She couldn't remember a single piece of advice.

'Kate!' Fiona was shaking her arm, looking at her friend in consternation. 'Come on Kate, it's time.'

Slowly Kate nodded, trying to control the frantic beating of her heart. Alex was here, the first part of her plan had worked and now it was stage two. She looked at Millie sitting on Fiona's hip and felt a little control flow back. She needed to do this for Millie as much as herself. She needed to re-unite the family Alex had ripped apart.

Another peal of the doorbell erupted into the room and Fiona picked up Kate's phone and thrust it into her hand.

'Remember what we said Kate!' she warned and then made her way to the front door.

'Hello Alex,' Kate heard her say, followed by a mumble that she imagined was Alex answering.

Fiona's voice was pitched loud and clear so Kate could hear everything from the living room.

'Kate's on the phone, I'm sure she won't be a minute.'

For a moment Kate was thankful that she wasn't the one facing Fiona in the small hallway, her words may have been pleasant enough but the disapproving tone had made Kate wince and she could imagine the look she was casting Alex.

Taking a deep breath Kate clutched the phone to her ear and walked towards the doorway.

'I'll have to go,' she mumbled quietly, too quietly.

She cleared her throat and tried again as she took a step into the hall. 'I really have to go,' she said again, this time no tremor in her voice.

She glanced up in time to see Alex turn to look at her, his eyes widening as she stood framed by the light from the living room.

She managed a little giggle, more in response to the appreciation in her husband's eye than to her acting ability. 'I'll see you on Friday,' she carried on a little breathlessly as she watched Alex's eyes follow the long slim line of her legs and then zoom back to her face and the cloud of soft waves sliding over her shoulders. She caught Fiona's eye and added hastily, 'I'm looking forward to it,' before pressing a few buttons and pretending to finish her call

'Hello Alex.'

She couldn't believe how calm her voice was, unlike the mass of hysterical butterflies leaping around in her stomach. She saw Fiona give a slight smile of approval.

'Hello Kate. You look – well.'

She waited for him to ask who she'd been speaking to but Alex had already turned away and was stroking Millie's head and cooing.

'Hello Millie darling. Oh I've missed my little girl.'

'Well whose fault is that,' snapped Fiona glaring at Alex who withdrew his hand as though stung.

Kate sent her friend an admonishing glance which she deflected with a shrug. It was clear Fiona did not see herself as part of the Alex charm campaign.

'Ready?' asked Alex nervously.

Kate inclined her head gracefully, not daring herself to speak and collecting her coat from the kitchen she came back into the hallway to find Alex already in the street and getting into the car in his haste to remove himself from Fiona's deadly glare.

'Fee!' whispered Kate as she stood in the doorway, pulling on her coat and kissing Millie.

'Look, you be as nice as you need to be Kate, you want him to fall back in love with you. Personally I don't care what he thinks of me.'

Then in a show of remorse and support she grasped her friend's hand.

'Oh Kate, you look stunning, did you see the way he looked at you? Remember everything we

said. Go out there and make Alex Patterson fall
back in love with you.'

Chapter 16

Kate shivered as she climbed into the car and Alex obligingly turned up the heating.

'Alfredo's okay for you?' he asked.

Kate wasn't sure whether to laugh or cry. Alfredo's was a tiny restaurant only a few minutes away and a regular haunt of Alex and Kate's over the years.

Was he already reminiscing over the good times they'd had together wondered Kate? Had he been thinking about the nights they'd spent there, hands held across the table as they discussed the day's events, the weekend to come, the holiday they'd just had, their future. Was it a good sign that he wanted to visit such an important part of their past?

'It should be quiet and it's cheap,' added Alex and Kate bit her lip and stared out of the window.

'Who were you talking to, on the phone?'

Kate's heart thudded against her ribcage. 'Oh er, no-one,' she offered lamely.

'No-one?'

Alex laughed, but it wasn't a very sincere laugh. 'Do you often speak to no-one on the phone?'

Yes, Kate wanted to snap. Since you left me alone with our daughter, yes I am left speaking to no-one!

'It was just my Salsa partner.'

Belatedly she remembered she was meant to smile and look casual so she stretched her mouth into a grin that looked more like a snarl then quickly looked out of the window, relieved it was too dark for Alex to see her face.

He didn't answer and they pulled up outside Alfredo's with Kate none the wiser as to whether Alex actually cared what she was doing on a Friday night.

Sitting inside in the warmth, a glass of wine in front of her, Kate tried hard not to dwell on the last time she and Alex had been here. It was a few days before Millie had arrived. Alex had come home and announced that they'd better make the most of their last few days of freedom and why didn't they share a pizza. Kate's stomach had been huge and she had loved the attention she'd received the moment she walked through the door. Everyone had asked when their baby was due, asked about names and wished them good luck and Kate had gone home happy in the knowledge that the next time they visited they would have an extra member of the household.

'Who is it?'

She stared at Alex. She'd been lost in her thoughts. 'What?'

'Who is it, your Salsa partner? Olivia mentioned she'd seen you at the dance, just wondered who you were going with?'

Alex was swirling his beer round his glass, looking disinterested and Kate watched him for a moment across the table.

'Oh, no-one you know,' she answered eventually.

Was that a little frown between Alex's eyebrows wondered Kate? A tiny touch of truculence.

'Right. Just wondered.'

Kate looked at her husband across the table and her heart ached. She had missed him beyond words and after two long weeks he was now so close she could actually feel him. She wanted to reach out and stroke his cheek, run her fingers through his hair, kiss him as she had done a thousand times before. She wanted to tell him how much she loved him, how much she wanted him back. She wanted to tell him she was sorry for anything and everything, if only he would forgive her and come home. Never mind the advice on Google, Kate didn't want to play games. She simply wanted Alex back.

'Alex …' she whispered.

'How long have you been going to salsa?'

Kate stared at the familiar face. 'Oh, a couple of weeks. Alex …'

'Really? I didn't realise you missed it so much, you must have started going the minute I walked out of the door.'

Kate's head snapped up. He was still swirling his beer, his eyes sliding between the table and Kate's face.

'And what did you expect I would do Alex – when you walked out of the door? Did you actually give a moment's thought to what I would do, how I would feel?' she hissed across the table.

Alex's eyes widened in shock. 'Well of course I did! I was really worried about you Kate, I was desperately worried …'

'And that's why you phoned so often? To make sure I was okay?'

'Well … we, I mean I didn't think it would help if I was constantly checking up on you, phoning you. You needed time to get used to me not being there.'

Alex was sweating, his top lip had a tiny bead of moisture sitting on the skin and his eyes were swiveling in the direction of the doorway. Kate reined in her anger. This was not going to plan. It was not going to plan at all. She took a deep breath and a large sip of wine.

Confrontation won't help, a husband needs to feel regret that he has left his wife, not relief that the relationship has ended.

'Sorry,' she said lightly.

Alex refused to meet her eyes, his lips were set in a straight line, stubborn and defensive and his shoulders were rigid. Kate watched him for a moment.

'His name is Josh.'

Alex's head swiveled in her direction. 'What?'

'My salsa partner, the one you seem so interested in. His name is Josh.'

Kate took another sip of wine and realised she had emptied her glass. Fiona had warned her not to drink too much. 'You'll get all teary and start saying things you shouldn't,' she had advised.

Kate refilled her glass to the brim.

'Oh, right. Josh.'

His shoulders were still tense but he had shifted slightly in his seat to face Kate and she frowned as she tried to read the expression on his face. Could it be? Was that a tiny hint of jealousy in his eyes, the tiniest touch of disapproval?

Men may leave their wives to start a new relationship but often still feel a sense of ownership towards their spouse.

'Did you meet him at salsa?'

Kate raised an eyebrow and Alex continued. 'I mean did you already know him, is he a friend or did you meet there or …'

A few weeks ago Kate would have laughed and said that Alex would know if she had a friend called Josh, he knew every friend she had. But then a few weeks ago Kate believed she knew all Alex's friends.

'I met him there,' answered Kate casually.

'Right. Just wondered.' Alex shrugged, still swirling his beer.

They sat in silence for a moment.

'But we're not here to talk about my salsa class Alex.'

More silence. More wine.

The husband must take responsibility for his actions, he has to accept what he has done and what the repercussions may be.

'Alex.'

He looked up, meeting her eyes and her breath caught. Oh how she loved him! Even after the last two weeks she still loved him with all her heart. She took a deep breath.

'Alex, please tell me why you left,' she said softly.

There was a long pause and she watched as her husband struggled to find an answer.

'I just need to know why,' Kate pleaded. 'why did you stop loving me, why did you decide to leave me and Millie?'

Her voice was uneven, catching as she spoke and she clenched her fists in an effort to stop herself from holding out her hand, reaching out to him.

'Kate, I … I …'

'I know about you and Sandra, I don't need a confession Alex. I know you had an affair, are having an affair. But why Alex, why?'

The room seemed to go quiet, the steady background chatter dropped for a moment and Kate felt as though she were suspended in time. She stared at the table behind Alex, a young couple leaning across to hold hands between the salt and pepper and the small vase of flowers that blocked their way. Young, in love, happy.

There was a resigned expression on Alex's face and the faintest suggestion of a sigh as though he had been hoping they could have a conversation about him leaving without actually discussing why he had left.

'I wasn't happy Kate,' he said bluntly as his eyes came back to hers. 'It just wasn't working anymore.'

'It? You mean me, our marriage?'

'Yes.' He fiddled with the salt and pepper pot.

'I thought it was working. I love you. You loved me – or I thought you still loved me,' she took a short, sharp breath quelling the tears.

'I suppose what I mean is, well things had changed. I – I felt our marriage had reached the end of the line.'

Kate had often wondered at the term a broken heart, she thought it would be better explained as an aching heart. But in the seconds after Alex spoke she agreed that a broken heart was indeed very apt. Her own had just broken, she'd heard it crack as it fell apart.

'In what way?' she asked in a shaky voice.

'It's hard to say exactly. We'd just grown apart I suppose. We used to be such a great team, always together, having fun, sharing our lives, me and you, you and me.'

'And now?'

Alex had the grace to look a little apologetic as he watched his wife struggle for control.

'Well there is no us anymore. There's a Kate and an Alex but it's as though you have your own life now and I'm not really a part of it anymore. The fun had gone, everything had gone. Now it's all about Millie and the house and things we need to do, not necessarily about things we want to do.'

'Millie?'

Alex shifted in his seat. 'Well I'm not saying it's Millie's fault,' he said.

Kate lifted an eyebrow. 'I should hope not!'

'No! Of course not,' he agreed. 'It's just that it made it all a little worse. Brought it all home so to speak.'

'Made it worse?' echoed Kate.

'Well what I mean is, well you don't really seem to need me anymore Kate. I feel as though I'm at the end of a long line of things that need your attention, I think you'd stopped actually seeing me as someone who was important in your life and our marriage was – empty.'

Kate looked down at her fingers.

Men often begin an affair in an attempt to boost their self- esteem. They feel unhappy, they feel unappreciated, they turn to someone else.

'And you felt – left out?' she suggested.

Alex nodded eagerly, glad she understood. 'Yes!'

Kate looked up. 'And you don't think that's a little immature?'

She could see Alex bristling. 'No!'

Accept what your husband is trying to say, you may need to compromise to get him back but this should not be viewed as a defeat

Kate held up her hand. 'No, I'm sorry, it's the way you feel.'

She twisted her fingers together, choosing her words carefully.

'Life does change you know Alex. We have a baby in the house, we can't be impulsive and carefree any more. Going out takes time and planning.'

'I know that. But Millie does seem to come first, all the time.'

Kate stared at him in disbelief. 'Of course she comes first! She's a baby!'

His lips tightened at the criticism. 'You didn't even come to the Christmas party,' he accused.

'Millie was unwell and I was so tired …'

'But that sums it up Kate. You didn't want to go with me to my Christmas party.'

'So you decided to teach me a lesson and sleep with Sandra Maddison?' snapped Kate, her eyes flashing.

Alex stopped. 'No of course not, 'he answered hastily. 'That just - happened.'

Kate took her hand away from her glass in case she succumbed to the temptation to throw it.

'You left me because I wouldn't go to the Christmas Party?'

'Of course not!' Alex shifted in his seat. 'Look I knew you wouldn't understand, that's why it was so hard to explain things before I left. I knew you'd be like this!'

Like what wondered Kate, upset because her husband had walked out on his wife and baby daughter over a Christmas party?

'Of course I didn't leave over the party. But it was the final straw. It just made it clear that it was over between you and me, that you didn't have anything left to give me. But I knew you wouldn't understand.'

Reconciliation is only possible if you accept he believed he was left with no choice but to leave and that part of the fault was your own.

'No -I'm sorry, of course I understand,' said Kate with a calmness she didn't feel. She tried a smile but it didn't quite work.

Alex looked at her suspiciously. 'You do?'

No, thought Kate. Not in the slightest. She gritted her teeth to stop herself telling him he was behaving like a spoiled child. 'I understand that you were feeling – neglected since Millie arrived and wanted us to have more of a social life, spend more time together.'

Alex nodded. 'Yes! That's just how I felt Kate. Like I didn't need to be there anymore because I

174

wasn't part of your life, or at least an important part of your life.'

Kate finished the wine in her glass and looked over at the young couple in the restaurant. Less than a year ago she and Alex had sat there, full of hope and love.

'You think I'm being selfish don't you?'

Alex's face had closed again, his lips tightening as he waited for Kate to reply.

Kate held up her hand. 'No, I understand. Really, I do.'

They sat for a moment, both looking anywhere but at each other.

'Alex, are you in love with Sandra?'

He could have no idea how much effort that question had cost her and although it appeared that Kate was leaving him time to answer, she was in fact desperately trying to control her emotions. Asking your husband if he was in love with another woman must be one of the hardest questions that could occur within a marriage she thought struggling not to cry.

'Well,' he blustered, 'well I think it's a bit early to say that I love her.'

'But you left me to be with her, surely that was because you loved her? More than you loved me.'

Alex was sweating again. 'I just needed something more Kate,' he said defensively. 'I felt like our marriage was over and I needed more.'

'The more being Sandra?'

'No, well yes, I suppose so.'

Kate frowned. 'So you had an affair and left me but not because you fell in love with Sandra, just because you felt – fed up.'

'It was more than being fed up Kate! You're not the person I married, I was unhappy and I met someone who made me feel better, much better.'

Kate pressed a hand to her chest, wondering if there was an actual knife piercing her heart the pain was so great.

'Right, sorry. But what I mean Alex, what I suppose I'm asking is are you with Sandra now? You and Sandra, is this a permanent arrangement? Is our marriage over?'

It was the longest ten seconds of Kate's life. She sat and watched the emotions drifting across the face of the man she loved. She sat, holding her breath, waiting for the answer on which her entire future rested.

Alex moved restlessly in his seat. 'I ... I don't know Kate!'

He pushed a hand through his hair and met her eyes and suddenly his movements stopped, his face filling with an expression Kate found hard to understand.

'I didn't stop loving you Kate,' he said softly. 'I just wasn't happy, our relationship had changed, it wasn't the same, you had changed and it wasn't enough anymore.'

'I see.' Kate's hands were trembling so much she pushed them under the table, out of sight.

'Oh God I'm sorry Kate. I know this must hurt, I know it probably doesn't make sense to you, I just can't really explain what went wrong, I just know it did.'

Kate stared at her glass. She desperately wanted another sip of wine but she didn't trust her hand to carry out the motion. The table was slightly misty from the tears she was trying so desperately to keep back, but she could see Alex across the table, watching her.

'You must be very angry with me Kate. I can see why you would be. I never set out with the intention of having an affair, I never wanted to hurt you Kate.'

Many men have affairs as a cry for attention. They need to feel desired, they need to feel appreciated and needed. Many soon realise they've made a mistake.

'Of course I'm hurt Alex. And angry I suppose.' And heartbroken and desperate and unable to stop crying and in such torment and pain I can hardly breath. 'But I understand what you're saying.'

Alex looked at her with such an intense expression it was almost her undoing. It was almost as though nothing had happened, as though the last two weeks had melted away and they were sitting in a restaurant having a meal, two people in love.

'Thank you Kate.'

'I suppose what matters now is what we do next Alex. Is this it? Do we both carry on with our own lives now, our separate lives?'

Fiona had instructed Kate to make sure Alex knew she could cope without him, if need be she would shrug her shoulders and start a whole new life without the man she loved. But at this precise moment Kate was very certain that she couldn't manage another day without Alex, let alone a whole new life time.

Kate waited. She was still hoping beyond hope that this was the moment when Alex would say he wanted to come home. He'd made his point and Kate had said all the things she should, been understanding, allowed him to place the blame for his actions partly on her shoulders. Now he just had to accept it had been a mistake, take Kate by the hand and say he wanted to come home. She realised she was holding her breath, willing him to say the words.

He ran his hand through his hair, sitting back in his chair looking bewildered, lost.

'I don't know what to say Kate.'

Say you'll come home. Say you want to come home. Please, please say you want to come home thought Kate.

'It's so hard, knowing what to do for the best.'

Come home, that's for the best. Come home Alex, come home.

'I just feel so confused right now.'

Kate clenched her teeth, was he looking for sympathy? Did he want her to reach out a hand and say how hard it must be for him, deciding whether to carry on breaking his wife's heart or telling Sandra that their moment of madness was over? Her calm exterior was in danger of collapsing. Just say you want to come home, she thought in frustration, let's get this madness over with and just go home.

'Kate,' her heart literally stood still, her entire body absolutely motionless as she waited. 'I really don't know what I want.'

Her heart thumped back into action, a big, heavy, disappointed thump.

'Sitting opposite you right now, I can't believe I left you, it feels almost like it used to – just the two of us. But I have to remember why I went Kate, I wasn't happy that's why I - Sandra – well that's why things didn't work. Maybe things can change ...' he gave her a quick look from under his eyelashes.

'Maybe we can get things back on track, I don't really know Kate. I just don't really know,' and he sat back in his chair with a sigh and finished his now warm beer.

Chapter 17

'The bastard!' breathed Fiona when Kate recounted the evening to her friend.

Kate sighed. She had spent weeks reading all the reasons why Alex might have left. She had told Fiona she was ready to accept some of the blame but to actually hear the words come from the man she loved had caused her heart to bleed.

'It was what I was expecting Fee,' she admitted in a slightly wobbly voice. After Alex had dropped her back at the house the previous night her control had vanished and she had spent most of the night crying. Her eyes were still red and puffy, but she had climbed out of bed with a new determination to make things work.

'I thought I was ready to hear him say I'd neglected him or not paid enough attention to him or whatever. I really thought I was ready to hear it.' Her lips trembled slightly and Fee placed a comforting hand on her friend's arm. 'But it hurt so much to hear him say he thought our marriage was over.'

'Oh Kate, you poor thing. But at least you know exactly why he left now, no more wondering or reading Google. Time to let him go and move on.'

Kate stared at Fiona's sympathetic face. 'Move on?'

'Yes, surely that's an end to it Kate? You can't still want him back after last night?'

'Of course I do!'

'Are you mad?' Fiona looked so outraged that for a moment Kate almost laughed. Almost.

'Of course I want him back Fee, that's what this is all about.'

'Yes but Kate, the things he said, the things he …'

'It doesn't matter, in fact it's quite good really.'

'Good? Good! How can any of this possibly be
good?'

'It's good because he didn't fall out of love with me. He …'

'He said you didn't pay him enough attention, he got a bit fed up so he had an affair. Are you saying that's okay?'

Kate patted Fiona's hand soothingly. 'Calm down Fee. What I mean is it is actually quite good …'

'Good!'

'Stop interrupting! Yes, it's good because it means he hasn't fallen in love with someone else. It was exactly what Google had suggested, he was feeling neglected, left out …'

'Because you had a baby! His baby!'

'Fee, shut up and listen! I'm not saying it's good that he felt like that in the first place but it does mean that I can get him back.'

'I still can't believe you would let him come back, after everything he said!'

Kate looked at her friend in amazement. 'Of course I would. I love him, he loves me. We've just lost our way a little but it's nothing we can't rescue and then Alex will come home and we'll carry on. Only this time I'll know that he needs a little more from me and I'll have to make sure he never feels like this again.'

Fiona was staring at Kate with an open mouth. 'How can you still love him Kate? How can you even think about letting him come home and carry on as though nothing has happened?'

'But Fee, you don't stop loving someone overnight just because they've done something stupid. Of course I still love him, I always have and I always will. And,' she continued stubbornly, 'he is coming home. He is coming home and we will be happy again!'

'I don't think I would ever forgive Stuart if he'd had an affair and then said it was my fault for ignoring him.'

'But it was partly my fault ...' Kate held up her hand to stop Fiona's outraged reply. 'He felt neglected Fee. I can't pretend that isn't partly my fault. Maybe I did give too much of my time to other things. You're always telling me I spend too much time cleaning the house and you said I should have made more of an effort to go out after Millie was born.'

'Yes,' grumbled Fiona, 'but at least I told you, I didn't go have an affair with someone!'

Kate grinned. 'That wouldn't really have worked would it?'

Fiona refused to smile but her shoulders relaxed a little. 'I just don't think you ...'

'Fee,' said Kate sternly. 'I am going to get my husband back. He doesn't love Sandra, he loves me, he is confused but he's already wondering if he did the right thing leaving. It was very painful to hear what he had to say last night,' she paused, the pain was in fact unbearable. 'But it means that I can rescue my marriage.'

Fiona pulled a face. 'Well I still don't agree but if it's what you want …'

'It is.'

Kate put on the kettle and sat Millie in her highchair ready for her lunch while a disgruntled Fiona failed to stop arguing.

'Just because someone admits they've made a mistake, doesn't make it okay. He's behaved really badly Kate, you're not obliged to forgive him, even if he admits he was wrong.'

'But I want to,' replied Kate serenely, sitting next to an eager Millie and feeding her mashed carrots and chicken.

'You should at the very least tell him what a waste of space he is, how angry you are with him, how you'll never forget what he did even if you do let him come home.'

'That won't help.'

'According to Google?'

'According to Google.'

Fiona sighed, a big gusty sigh that swept across the table.

'How about just one little outburst? A quick bash over the head with a vase so he knows how much he's hurt you and then you can be all calm and forgiving again?'

Kate giggled. 'No Fee. No bashing, no accusations. I have to be realistic about my part in it all.'

Fiona pulled a face. 'Okay, how about a fling with Josh? Some amazing sex, preferably on the salsa floor where everybody will see and tell Alex. That has to be okay? After all, it's only what he's done with Sandra.'

Kate didn't answer straight away. She pretended to be engrossed in feeding Millie but in actual fact her cheeks had flooded with colour at the suggestion. The thought had done strange things to her stomach and when she finally found her voice it was a little breathless.

'Don't be silly. Revenge sex never works.'

'According to Google?'

'According to Google.'

Fiona sniffed. 'Well it might not work but I still think it's a good idea.'

'There's no point getting angry about it Fee. It's exactly as we read on Google, some men just can't cope with having to share the attention after a baby comes along.'

'Yeah – I suppose I can see why they would feel unappreciated and neglected after their wives have just gone through a nine-month pregnancy, twenty-six hours of labour and are trying to stay sane looking after a baby and making their tea! Must be dreadful for them!' grumbled Fiona.

Kate shrugged. 'It is the way it is Fee, I just need to concentrate on getting Alex back. I'll carry on doing all the things that Google has suggested. It's worked so far, I'll carry on with the plan and Alex will come back. I know he will. And then it's up to me to make sure he never wants to leave again.'

Eventually Fiona had to admit defeat, having been totally unable to sway Kate from her chosen course and saying goodbye, she disappeared to collect her own family from school and go home to make Stuart some tea and tell him of the unutterable consequences that would follow should he ever even think of being unfaithful.

So on Friday night, unbidden by Fiona, Kate got ready for salsa and found herself humming, actually humming a little tune as she flicked through her wardrobe deciding what to wear. Was she happy, she wondered? She tipped her head to one side and thought very hard. No, of course she wasn't happy. Maybe she was hopeful? Maybe there was a tiny little kernel of hope that had grown during the last few days. Not enough to sprout into happiness but enough to bring a small smile to her face as she thought about going out and enough to make her carry on humming softly with the tiniest of little smiles on her lips as she carried on searching for something to wear, looking forward to a night out with friends at salsa.

Kate dropped Millie at Fiona's house as arranged.

'I might be back a little bit later tonight,' she said casually as she was handing over Millie's bag.

Fiona was stroking the top of Millie's blonde curls and cooing. 'That's okay. I've told you, this isn't just about Alex, you need some time to yourself. Try and actually enjoy the evening!'

Kate smiled and nodded, kissing Millie goodbye.

'Why?'

Kate blinked.

'Why will you be late? Not that it matters,' added Fiona hastily, 'just wondered – why?'

'Sophie wants me to stay and have a few drinks after salsa,' she explained. 'We always have one but she wants me to stay a bit longer tonight. She's asked Olivia and Helen as well.'

'And Josh?' asked Fiona with an impish smile on her face.

'I don't really know,' answered Kate with supreme indifference.

Fiona gave a big sigh. 'I suppose I should feel dreadfully left out, you out on the town with your new friends, me left at home with the baby.'

'Oh no Fee, please don't …'

'I'm kidding! I think it's lovely that you've got someone else to talk to – and dance with. Have a wonderful time and come home as late as you like,' and Fiona had shoved Kate out of the door and into Stuart's waiting car.

The air was still bitterly cold and as Kate walked into the wine bar she glanced round the room, no longer nervous and worried but happy and ready to salsa!

'Hi,' said Sophie slightly breathlessly as she took off her padded coat. 'Still on for drinks tonight?'

Kate nodded. 'Yes! I'm looking forward to it. I see Alan's come again,' she said looking over Sophie's shoulder.

Sophie couldn't help the smirk. 'Mm. He enjoyed himself last week. Wanted me to point out who the partner was I'd had so much fun with the week before.'

Kate giggled. Sophie was obviously very keen on Alan and she had a feeling Alan was very keen on Sophie. He was also clearly very shy.

'Staying for a few drinks tonight Alan?' asked Kate as he approached, shuffling his feet.

'Oh er, yes, I mean I'd like to, but only if Sophie doesn't... if she thinks it's ...'

'That's excellent,' beamed Kate. 'I know Sophie was hoping you'd join us.'

She ignored Sophie's raised eyebrows and instead smiled at the flush of delight on Alan's face. After all, there was no point anyone else being unhappy. Kate had cornered that department.

She waved as she saw Olivia and Helen walk through the door and then jumped as a hand slid round her shoulders and pulled her in for a hug.

'Hello salsa partner,' said Josh, letting her go and watching with amusement the deep blush that spread across her face.

'Oh, hello.'

'I was hoping you'd be here,' he said still watching her.

'Did you think I wouldn't come?'

'Oh I don't really know what to think where you're concerned Kate. But I hoped my dancing hadn't scared you away!'

'Josh, are you staying for a few drinks after dancing tonight?'

It was Sophie, relishing her revenge.

Josh looked at Kate. 'That would be great,' he said, 'just great.'

Kate blushed more and Sophie clapped her hands in delight. 'Wonderful,' she said turning to cast a wink at Kate. 'Just wonderful.'

The dancing started and this time Kate didn't flinch every time she and Josh were thrown together, she let herself enjoy the music and the dance. She found herself pressed against Josh's long lean body on several occasions and far from feeling uncomfortable, it started to feel very normal to have his hand on hers, his hips close to her own. He concentrated hard on the steps but occasionally Kate would turn and find him looking at her, watching her hair fly over her shoulders and her eyes sparkle with energy. And she realised that even when he was unsure about the steps and turning in the wrong direction he held her so firmly and securely that she didn't really mind at all. Eventually the hour finished on a round of applause and smiling widely Kate turned to Josh impulsively.

'Oh that was lovely, don't you think?'

Josh laughed, pulling a slightly rueful face. 'Well I don't think my skills quite match up to yours and I'm so sorry about all the times I stamped on your foot, but yes,' he smiled, tucking a curl behind Kate's ear. 'I did think it was lovely.'

Kate stepped back as though shot. 'Josh, I did tell you I was married didn't I?'

Josh shrugged his broad shoulders. 'Actually you told me that your husband had just left you and your baby daughter to live with someone else.'

'Yes, well he did. But I'm still married and the thing is he will come home.'

'And you'd have him back?'

'Oh yes,' nodded Kate firmly. 'You see we love each other and Alex has just made a mistake. He'll come home and we'll be married again – well we already are married but you know what I mean.'

Josh didn't say anything and Kate continued in a hurry.

'It's just that I don't want you to think that – well I don't want you to feel that …'

'What I think,' interrupted Josh firmly, 'is that if your husband comes back and you want to forgive him, then that will be wonderful for you.'

Kate nodded her agreement.

'But in the meantime you can have some fun and go to salsa and have drinks with friends and enjoy yourself, can't you?'

Kate frowned. 'Well yes but …'

'There's nothing wrong with any of this Kate. I won't deny I'm very attracted to you,' he watched with amusement as Kate's blush spread across her cheeks again, 'but I understand the situation perfectly. It doesn't stop me wanting to be friends with you. We can be friends can't we?'

Kate thought for a moment. Wasn't that exactly what Google had advised? Make new friends, go out, enjoy yourself, let your husband see that if he doesn't come back to you quickly you are capable of making a new life for yourself. She didn't remember reading anything on Google that advised doing all of those things with a 6' foot hunk who had the most amazing blue eyes, dark hair and a very strong jaw. But perhaps she'd just missed that bit.

'Well yes,' she agreed. 'We could be friends. I think that would be okay.'

'Friends that salsa together, meet up for a drink every now and then, have Sunday lunch together?'

'I suppose so – Sunday lunch?'

'Yes, I thought it would be nice. There's a fantastic little restaurant I know, does the most amazing lunches. I thought we could go this Sunday.'

'But I can't …'

'As friends of course, because that's what friends do isn't it?'

Kate shook her head in frustration. ''I can't go for Sunday lunch with you!' she exclaimed. 'Of course I can't!'

'Why not?'

'Because I have a baby, remember? I'm fairly certain I told you that as well.'

'You did,' agreed Josh. 'Millie. 9 months old, actually probably 10 months old now, blonde curls, very cute, a bit loud, loves bananas.'

Kate stopped, he really had been listening.

'Well, you should understand why I can't go with you,' she said huffily.

'Millie also enjoys chicken and potatoes and loves sprouts!'

Kate stared at him. Had she really told him all that?

'That's why I thought lunch would be better than dinner and why I chose this restaurant. They do the most amazing roast chicken.'

Kate continued to stare.

'Millie will love it,' he said, 'I'm sure she'll enjoy the chicken and we can ask if they've got any bananas.'

'You want to take Millie with us?'

Now it was Josh's turn to stare. 'Of course! Not going to leave her at home are we? I'm taking you both out – only as friends of course,' and he smiled a great big smile before clapping Alan on the back and telling him that he really had got the making of a salsa dancer.

Chapter 18

Kate told Millie several times on Sunday that they were not going for lunch with Josh. She told Fiona that she and Millie would not be joining Josh for lunch. She picked up the phone on three occasions to tell Josh that she would not be joining him for lunch.

But each time she simply held the receiver in her hand for a few minutes contemplating what to say and on all three occasions she put the phone back down.

She couldn't deny that the idea of going out was appealing. Just getting out of the house was a treat and the idea of spending a lazy Sunday lunch letting someone else do the cooking and the washing up was very tempting. She had stopped cooking anything approaching proper meals since Alex had gone, the effort just didn't seem worth it and the very thought of a plate of roast chicken was making her stomach rumble.

Sunday lunch seemed a very good idea.

But that it was Josh taking them to the lunch had left Kate nibbling on her lip.

He wanted them to be friends and that was okay, she reasoned. She'd had lots of male friends in the past, good genuine friends who she wouldn't have hesitated to join for a drink or lunch. They had all fallen by the road side after she had met Alex. He hadn't felt comfortable with the idea and even though Kate had laughed and told him he really had nothing to worry about, he had pouted and been rather cold whenever the occasion arose. In the end Kate had stopped going, not even trying to explain the situation to her friends but just claiming that she was busy or that she had a prior engagement until the invitations inevitably stopped coming.

But this was different. Josh had told Kate that he was attracted to her. And as far as Kate was concerned that was dangerous territory.

But even as she decided again that she most definitely was not going to lunch with Josh, she remembered that the reason she was quite lonely and in desperate need of a change of scenery was because her husband had walked out on her to be with someone else. Why on earth shouldn't Kate have some fun on a Sunday that would otherwise be spent washing Millie's clothes? After all, she reminded herself, the whole point of going out was to catch Alex's attention. And it had worked so far. He had been on the phone as soon as he'd heard reports of Kate and a handsome stranger at salsa. Maybe news of her spending Sunday afternoon in a restaurant would prompt him pick up the phone again. Why shouldn't she go to lunch with a friend?

Because if she were honest, Kate thought, she'd also felt a little flutter of attraction when Josh looked at her with those lovely blue eyes. They'd all stayed behind after salsa on Friday and although Josh had behaved impeccably and made no attempt to push the boundaries of their new friendship, Kate had to admit she had enjoyed sitting next to him, feeling the warmth of his body so close to her own, watching him as he chatted and laughed. She had intercepted more than one sideways glance in her direction and he had a way of holding her eyes and smiling, a big, slow smile that stretched the corners of his mouth and drew her eyes to the dimple in his chin and did funny things to her stomach. As they had all hugged and said their goodbyes, she had felt Josh's very strong arm slide round her waist and pull her closer so he could drop a chaste kiss on her cheek as he whispered goodbye in her ear. Except for a chaste kiss it had left a surprisingly hot imprint on Kate's skin, one that lingered long after Kate had arrived home and climbed into bed.

No, she was definitely not going to let Josh take her and Millie for lunch.

When the doorbell rang Kate's heart gave a huge leap. She looked down at Millie sitting in her high chair chewing donkey's ear.

'Oh Millie darling, I don't think we should do this, I'll tell him we just can't go with him,' and then she went to open the door and let Josh enter.

He followed her to the kitchen where Millie stopped chewing briefly to give him a considered gaze.

'Hello Millie,' Josh said softly. 'How very nice to meet you.'

He kept his distance for which Kate was grateful. Millie could be funny with new people she met.

He smiled at the little girl who stared back for a long moment before giving him a big beam and then turned her attention back to donkey's ear.

Kate looked at Josh in surprise. 'She seems to like you.'

Josh grinned, 'Didn't you think she would?'

'Well not exactly but she can be a little shy with strangers.'

'My sister has three children so I'm used to them,' explained Josh easily, 'Millie can probably tell I'm a seasoned hand!'

Kate nodded slowly. 'I suppose.'

'Are you both ready?'

'Ah well, yes, about lunch…'

'Do you have a car seat?'

'Oh, er yes. It's in the hall cupboard.'

Shortly after Kate had decided not to go to lunch with Josh she had dug the car seat from the garage where it usually lived and brought it into the house.

'I'll put it in the car while you get Millie wrapped up, it's cold out there,' and he was gone leaving Kate and Millie staring at each other.

'It seems rude to say we can't go with him now Millie, don't you think?'

Millie said nothing and sighing Kate quickly checked her reflection in the mirror and tucked Millie into her pink duffle coat.

She had refused to accept any advice from Fiona about what outfit to wear.

'I'm not going Fee so you don't need to worry about what I should wear.'

But last night she had gone through her wardrobe and decided what she would wear if she were ever to go out for Sunday lunch with a friend and this morning she had dressed in a long boucle skirt that made her look positively svelte, with a pair of knee length boots and a soft knitted cardigan that was decorated with tiny pearls and clung to her shrinking figure. She told Millie that it was just because she was fed up with spending her life in jeans and slightly crusty tops and then she took care with her makeup telling Millie it was nice to make an effort occasionally, even if she were staying in all day. She had been pleased to find that the purple circles under her eyes were much reduced and her cheeks had lost some of the dreadful pallor of the last few weeks.

'Ready?'

It was Josh, back in the hallway and taking a deep breath Kate nodded and scooped Millie into her arms, conceding that maybe Sunday lunch with a friend was actually perfectly acceptable.

The restaurant wasn't too far away and Josh chatted to her on the way, asking about Millie and talking about the weather and the pretty villages they were driving through and keeping everything very comfortable.

When they pulled into the car park, Josh unbuckled the car seat while Kate rescued Millie's bag and as she turned round he had lifted Millie out and was holding her in his arms as Millie chuckled and patted the unfamiliar face.

Kate caught her breath, Millie looked so adorable in Josh's arms, so small and sweet. It made her sad that Alex had been gone so long and didn't seem to be part of Millie's life any more.

Josh passed Millie to her mother and they walked into the warm restaurant and were soon seated at a table with Millie ensconced in a high chair between them.

'This is lovely,' said Kate looking around.

'They do great food and I know they're very child friendly. I've been here before with my sister and her brood.'

Kate nodded, she was nervous although just why, she was having trouble putting her finger on.

'Kate.'

She looked up and Josh reached out to place his hand gently over her own.

'It's just lunch Kate. I'm taking my two new friends out for lunch.'

He grinned at Millie who beamed back.

'I know that you are hoping Alex comes back …'

'He will,' interrupted Kate.

'And I will be happy for you but in the meantime there's no reason for you to be sitting at home miserable. We agreed that we would be friends and this is what friends do, spend time with each other.'

Whipping out his hand he caught donkey as it flew past his ear. 'And maybe it's nice to have someone else who can spend some time with Millie, save you having to do everything?'

Kate felt the prick of tears in her eyes.

'You're a very nice man Josh,' she said softly, 'very nice,' and then the conversation halted as a waiter came to enthuse over Millie's little pink hairband and ask what they would like to drink.

The restaurant was almost full, the air heavy with the aroma of cooking and as warm as toast despite the frost gathering outside and Kate couldn't help but relax as the afternoon wore on.

Josh was good company. He didn't bat an eyelash when Millie jerked her head to one side just as Kate was feeding her a spoonful of mashed potato and it splattered onto his sleeve.

When Millie became a tiny bit fractious and her bottom lip started to tremble he carried on his conversation with Kate but retrieved donkey from under the table and enchanted Millie by having it disappear under her highchair tray only to pop back out again.

He told Kate about his sister and her three children and how her husband worked on the oil rigs in the North Sea and was away for weeks at a time.

'She goes a little stir crazy every now and then,' he said. 'It's tough for her being on her own for such long stretches so sometimes I'll go over for the day and send her off to the shops or to meet some friends.'

'I bet she really appreciates that,' said Kate with feeling. Thinking about it, Alex had never offered to take care of Millie for an entire day while Kate had some time to herself.

They talked about salsa and Josh admitted that it wasn't something that he would ever have done if he hadn't seen Kate and Sophie dancing.

'It wasn't really the salsa that attracted me,' he teased and Kate couldn't help both the blush and the smile.

'I just wish I were a little bit better,' he said mournfully. 'I can see you abandoning me for a better partner!'

Kate laughed. 'I don't think I'm quite as good as you think I am Josh. I just enjoy it.'

Josh moved some roast beef around his plate. 'Do you think you'll carry on with salsa if - when Alex comes back?'

Kate stared at her wine glass. 'I think I will,' she answered surprising herself.

'I enjoy dancing and maybe going out and doing what you enjoy is just as important as all the other things you have to do in life.'

'Do you think Alex will join you?'

Kate thought hard. Alex would say that it was a great idea, yes they should definitely go dancing. They might even go one Friday evening. Then he would suggest that maybe it wasn't quite his thing, that it was a bit noisy and hectic after a day at work, that perhaps they should go out for a meal instead, just the two of them where they could talk. Or maybe a takeaway and a film, wouldn't that be lovely and they could sit on the sofa and relax and enjoy each other's company.

'No, it's not really the sort of thing Alex likes,' Kate answered eventually. 'But I love dancing and I'll carry on going,' she smiled at Josh, 'so you won't be getting off that easily!'

They shared a grin and carried on eating, watching Millie's delight at the tiny pieces of sprout Kate had cut and mashed for her daughter.

'I don't know any other baby that loves sprouts like Millie does,' Josh had chuckled. 'Look at her tucking in!'

But he was talking to a frozen faced Kate who was sitting in her chair, ramrod straight with ashen cheeks.

'Kate? Are you alright?'

She didn't answer but carried on staring over Josh's shoulder.

'Kate! What's wrong?'

Kate's hand was trembling. She ignored her wine and took a large gulp of water. Her eyes were wide and shocked.

'It's Alex,' she whispered, putting the glass down unsteadily. 'He's just walked in with Sandra Maddison.'

Josh didn't look round, he carried on watching Kate and as her eyes followed the couple across the restaurant floor, he leant over and put his hand over hers gently.

'Do you want to leave?' he asked softly. 'I'll get the bill, we can be in the car in five minutes.'

Kate barely heard him. Her heart was drumming and the blood was rushing round her veins so loudly she could hear nothing but her own body screaming out for Alex.

She watched as Alex and Sandra sat down at a table in a corner some distance from her and Josh. She watched as Alex gallantly pulled out a chair for Sandra to sit on and carried on watching as Sandra leant across the table and blew Alex a kiss. Her heart was thudding painfully but her eyes were fixed on the couple and she didn't seem able to tear her gaze away, no matter how hard she tried.

Sandra was dressed to impress and far from the understated outfit Kate was wearing, her dress would have been more at home at a cocktail party. But she did look good, admitted Kate to herself. Her hair was gleaming and freshly styled, the dress hugged the curve of her body and her red glossy lips pouted and smiled in Alex's direction as he sat and admired her across the table.

'Kate?'

She whipped her eyes back to Josh who was still watching her anxiously. 'Kate are you okay?'

She nodded, her eyes shiny with tears. 'Sorry, just a bit of a shock,' she mumbled.

Josh smiled sympathetically. 'We can leave, just say the word.'

But Kate shook her head, straightening her shoulders and blinking away the tears.

'No,' she said calmly. 'No, we'll stay and finish our meal. I'm not leaving without trying some of that bread and butter pudding,' and she reached out for her glass, her hand almost steady as she took a sip of wine and smiled a determined smile in Josh's direction.

Chapter 19

The conversation was understandably strained following Alex's arrival and although Kate tried her best, she couldn't help her eyes from straying in the direction of her husband and the carefree laughter she could hear coming from his table.

But she was determined to see the afternoon out. Josh ate the rest of his meal while Kate pushed hers around her plate and then they ordered pudding which Kate made an admirable effort to eat and they even asked for coffee which Kate used to warm her suddenly cold fingers.

Eventually Josh suggested that it was time to go and Kate nodded her head, slightly relieved.

Standing, she asked if Josh was okay with Millie for two minutes while she visited the bathroom and thankful that the entrance was in completely the opposite direction to where Alex was seated, Kate followed the sign through a large oak door and into a long corridor. As soon as she was away from the gaze of the public room Kate stopped. Putting a hand on the wall to steady herself she took a sharp breath and almost doubled over with the pain in her heart. She could never have envisioned the day when she would be in the same restaurant as Alex but sitting at separate tables with separate people; never have imagined that Millie would be sitting next to Kate while her father sat next to another woman, none the wiser that his daughter was even in the same room.

She stood up, the effort considerable. Did Alex have any idea how much he had hurt her she wondered, did he even care?

'Kate!'

Kate didn't turn round.

'Kate!'

Kate still didn't turn round. She needed time, she needed her eyes to clear from the tears that were threatening. She needed her breathing to slow and her heart to stop hammering.

'Kate?'

Kate turned.

'Hello Alex.'

'What on earth are you doing here?'

Kate tilted her head. He sounded shocked, almost challenging.

'Having lunch, the same as you.'

'Right, of course you are -sorry.'

Kate's heart twisted. She wanted to drag Alex back to her table, remind him of the daughter he had walked away from and insist he came home with her.

He was staring at her. 'You look fantastic.'

'Oh, er thankyou.'

'Who are you with?'

'A friend,' she answered lightly.

'Yeah – who is he though?'

Kate's heart gave a little skip. Was Alex jealous?

'Just a friend.'

He pursed his lips nodding. 'It's Josh isn't it, your salsa partner?'

Kate thought briefly about telling Alex it was none of his business. Didn't Google say to keep errant husband's guessing, the less they knew about what you were doing, the more they'd want to know. But it also said to make sure the ex-husband knew that you were moving on, having a good time without them. How was she supposed to do both wondered Kate desperately?

'Yes, it is.'

Short and to the point.

'And you've moved on to lunch already?'

Kate glared at her husband. 'Let's not forget you're here with the woman you're having an affair with Alex, the woman you left me to be with,' she snapped.

'Sorry! Sorry Kate – I didn't mean, I don't know …'

Alex swept a hand through the floppy fringe, a move always guaranteed to bring a smile to Kate's lips.

She watched him unsmiling.

'It's just a surprise, seeing you here with – someone else,' he offered. 'I guess I wasn't quite ready for it.'

Kate stood ramrod straight. 'Yes it is a bit of a shock to the system,' she said politely, watching Alex's face fill with colour.

'Sorry,' he said again. 'Sorry Kate, I – sorry.'

They stood in the long hallway in silence until Alex spoke.

'Are you two together then?'

Kate blinked in surprise. 'Well hardly Alex, I only met him two weeks ago.'

'But you go to salsa with him and you're here now having lunch with him.'

Kate stretched her lips into a semblance of a smile. 'Yes,' she agreed, 'Josh is very thoughtful. He was worried about me spending so much time on my own and thought it would be nice for me – and Millie – to have a change of scenery.'

Alex had found it a chore going out with Millie. He objected to the huge volume of bits and pieces that Kate said were necessary when taking a baby out even if only for a few hours. He objected to the fact that their decision where to go, what time to go and where to sit were all dictated by Millie and when she would need to eat and sleep. He preferred to leave Millie with Fiona and take Kate out on her own.

He flushed slightly under Kate's eye.

'And it's been lovely,' enthused Kate, 'having a relaxing Sunday lunch with a friend.'

Alex's furrow deepened.

'And of course you know how I love dancing,' Kate carried on, enjoying the darkening of Alex's eyes. 'So having someone to join me on a Friday night is also wonderful.'

'Shame you never suggested going to salsa with me,' snapped Alex.

'You hated salsa,' snapped back Kate. 'We went all of twice and you found a hundred and one reasons why we shouldn't go back!'

They stood glaring at each other for a moment until Kate remembered the copious notes scattered across her kitchen table. Accusations were not the way to get your husband back.

She bit her lip and offered a smile. 'Maybe we both should have considered each other a little more?' she offered tentatively. 'Perhaps we should have gone out more – to something we both enjoyed.'

Alex nodded stiffly. 'Maybe.'

They looked at each other uncomfortably.

'Kate,' Alex began.

She waited.

'Kate – I am sorry you know.'

Kate didn't really care if Alex was sorry. She just wanted him to come back.

'I acted badly and I am so sorry I hurt you.'

Now this was progress thought Kate, feeling a sliver of excitement slide down her spine.

'I was - unhappy.'

The excitement dissipated.

'But I never meant for things to end like this,' Alex waved his hand vaguely in Kate's direction, 'for me and you to end up like this. It just all got out of control.'

'I see,' said Kate with a tremor in her voice.

Alex nodded. 'I want to see you again Kate, I want us to sit down and talk about what we can do, if we can rescue this situation.'

The excitement was back.

She nodded. 'Okay.'

'I'll phone shall I? Next week. Maybe Fiona can look after Millie again and we'll go out and spend some time together.'

Kate was holding her emotions firmly in check. It really wouldn't do to whoop and shake her fist in the air.

'That sounds good Alex. I'm sure Fee will help us out any night.' She watched as Alex let out a relieved breath.

'Of course I can't do Friday night,' she threw at him. 'Salsa remember.'

'Oh? I would have thought our future was slightly more important than Salsa.'

Kate smiled. 'Well let's wait until we work out what our future is Alex, then we'll worry about salsa!' and she turned away and carried on down the corridor to the bathroom.

Her heart was still leaping in her chest although whether from excitement, despair or nerves Kate wasn't entirely sure. She really needed to get back home and in front of her laptop. Surely Google would have some sage words of advice to offer.

Leaving the cubicle Kate had to work very hard to contain a gasp. Standing by the sink was Sandra Maddison.

Ignoring her Kate began to wash her hands. After all, the only reason she knew this was Sandra, was because she had spent a tearful evening looking at her photograph. And of course, because Kate had followed her home. Neither of these things Kate felt inclined to explain to Sandra.

'Hello Kate.'

Their eyes met in the mirror above the sink.

'I'm Sandra. Sandra Maddison.'

Kate nodded her head, rinsing her hands slowly, let the warm water run between each finger.

'I know Alex just followed you. He said he went to the bathroom but I know he wanted to speak to you.'

Alex lying to her about his whereabouts already. Kate let a flicker of a smile touch her lips and decided that her hands were as clean as they were going to get.

'I just wondered what he wanted?' said Sandra.

Kate gave her a haughty look as she walked towards the dryer. What was it to Sandra Maddison what Alex and his wife discussed?

She saw Sandra's mouth open again and she thrust her hands in the electric hand dryer, the noise filling the bathroom and blocking out whatever Sandra had to say.

Hands thoroughly dried, Kate turned round to face Sandra who had fallen silent.

They looked at each other for a moment and Kate decided that close up Sandra wasn't quite as elegant as she had first appeared. The dress was actually a little too tight and the make up a little too heavy handed. As Fiona had once told her, there was definitely more than a hint of desperation about Sandra Maddison.

'Kate I know this is really hard for you,' Kate doubted if Sandra had any comprehension just what life was like for Kate. 'And I know you probably think very badly of me.'

Kate thought for a moment. She had tortured herself thinking of Sandra and Alex together, she had sobbed most nights at the image that haunted her of her husband in bed with another woman. Why Alex had let Sandra's come to bed eyes take him to bed? What Alex had been thinking of the first time he had bent down to kiss Sandra? Why he hadn't stopped to think of Kate when he embarked on an affair with another woman? And Sandra herself, what had she felt? Was she happy, excited, triumphant that she had managed to take away Kate's husband?

'I haven't thought of you at all,' Kate lied.

Sandra's mouth tightened. 'Well whatever – but the thing is that we're in love.'

Kate took out her lipstick and reapplied some colour, watching Sandra through the mirror again.

'I know Alex finds it hard to say that to you, he's worried about your feelings.'

Kate snorted. So worried he had left her.

'I mean, he worries about how upset you might get, how lonely you are and he doesn't want you to do anything desperate or silly.'

Kate put the lipstick away. 'Do I look desperate?' she asked in surprise. She looked at her reflection, she thought she looked extremely well, under the circumstances.

Was that a flash of confusion in Sandra's eyes, wondered Kate.

'Well,' Sandra continued bravely, 'that's why he finds it hard to tell you that we love each other. He left you because he had fallen in love with me.'

Kate considered Sandra's words. She had given Alex the opportunity to say he loved Sandra and he hadn't taken it. She remembered the look in Alex's eye as they'd faced each other in the corridor only minutes earlier and Kate knew that whatever Alex's reasons for leaving it was not because he was in love with Sandra.

She smiled and gathered her handbag heading for the door.

'He doesn't love you any more, you do know that,' shouted Sandra as Kate walked past her.

'He told me all about you. He told me how you used to be such fun, how much he loved the life you had.'

Kate didn't turn round. She held onto the door handle tightly but she didn't open the door.

'But you changed,' blurted out Sandra. 'He told me how you changed, how all you think about now is tidying the house and what to have for tea and looking after your daughter.'

Kate still held on to the door handle. The words were like knives striking her in the back.

'And now he just thinks you're boring. He wanted more which is why he fell in love with me.'

Kate turned, she looked at Sandra, trembling and teary and thought that they actually had something in common after all. They were both desperately unhappy with the way Alex was treating them.

Sandra tried to look confident. 'He said you weren't the person he fell in love with and he didn't want you anymore,' she flung at Kate, her words intended to be as hurtful as she could make them.

Kate remained dry eyed. She caught a glimpse of her refection behind Sandra and was pleased that she had chosen the cardigan she was wearing. It really suited her, she decided.

She looked at Sandra. 'Alex talked about you as well Sandra,' she said with a polite smile.

'He did?' asked Sandra, the tears momentarily halting. 'what did he say?'

'He said you were available,' and with another smile and a gracious nod of her head Kate left.

Chapter 20

'So what exactly did he say?' demanded Fiona as they sat at the kitchen table later the following evening with tea and biscuits. 'Did he say he wanted to come back?'

Kate nibbled on a hobnob.

'Not exactly,' she said cheerfully. 'It was more the way he looked, the things he didn't say.'

Fiona looked doubtful. 'I always find out more when people actually speak.'

Kate grinned. 'Okay. Well he did say that he didn't know how things had got to this stage, he did say he was sorry for hurting me. He did **not** say he loved Sandra Maddison. And although he didn't say he wanted to come back he did say that he wanted to see me again and for us to sit down and talk, decide what we wanted to do next.'

Fiona looked happier. 'Okay, well that all sounds positive. And …?'

'And?' echoed Kate.

'And do you still want him back?'

Kate took another hobnob and nodded. 'Of course.'

'So when are you two getting together? I'll take Millie of course.'

Kate shrugged. 'I don't know, Alex said he'd phone me. Any day but Friday.'

'Why not Friday?'

'Salsa of course.'

Fiona stared at her friend for a moment then broke into a grin.

'And is it salsa you're looking forward to or seeing your salsa partner?'

'Fee!' Kate threw half a biscuit at her friend who caught it and dipped it in her tea. But she also noticed the flush of colour in Kate's cheeks.

'You like him don't you. Josh, I mean, you really like him?'

Kate concentrated on her tea, refusing to meet her friend's eyes.

'Of course I like him. He's a friend.'

'I'm your friend, you don't blush when someone mentions my name!'

Kate took another biscuit, swirling it in her tea until it fell in two and she watched as it drifted to the bottom of her mug.

'He's just a friend Fee,' she insisted. 'He's been incredibly nice to me – and Millie. It was lovely going out on Sunday, it's been such a long time since we had lunch out as a family.'

'But Josh isn't your family,' said Fee quietly and the flush in Kate's cheeks deepened.

'I know! What I meant was that it felt like a family type of outing and I enjoyed myself.'

Actually, thought Kate with a frown, she usually spent her Sundays cleaning the house and ironing Alex's shirts for the coming week while Alex played with Millie for approximately fifteen minutes before turning on the TV. It was occasionally broken with a visit to her mother's, something Alex enjoyed more than Kate did but which was at least was a change of scenery. So

213

Sunday with Josh, far from reminding her of what she had been missing, had actually been a whole new experience.

She looked up, Fiona was watching her from under the mop of bright red hair.

'So what happens now?' she asked.

'Well,' Kate smiled as she flipped open her laptop. 'Everything is going to plan! Alex knows I've been out making new friends,' she held up her fingers as she ticked off her list, 'he has a renewed interest in me because he is no longer aware of what is going on in my life and he is being reminded of why he loved me in the first place.' She grinned. 'Perfect!'

'But what do you do next?' asked Fiona looking longingly at the few hobnobs left in the packet.

Kate paused, 'Mm, I'm not entirely sure.' She was scrolling through the pages. 'I think he's supposed to make the next move.'

'How?' Fiona had given in and had a mouth full of biscuit.

'Well it's not really clear but I think he will need to see more of me, find out what I'm doing – that sort of thing.'

'What if he doesn't?'

Kate frowned. 'He will, it says here he will.'

'Yes, but what if he doesn't?'

The friends stared at each other for a moment.

'He will,' reiterated Kate. 'I just know he will.'

The silence fell again and both women jumped as Kate's mobile rang, vibrating along the table into her outstretched hand.

'Oh my God it's Alex,' she squealed staring at the phone in her hand.

'Well answer it,' shouted Fiona who was now sitting up straight, her hands pressed together in excitement.

Kate bit her lip. 'I don't know what to say.'

'Well you can't say anything if you don't answer it!'

'Yes but …'

'ANSWER IT KATE!'

'Hello?' Kate was trying for cool and calm but sounded breathless and unsure. 'Oh Alex,'

'Hello.'

Fiona was leaning towards her so she could hear the conversation.

'Er, hello Alex.'

'Kate, hello.'

Well that was the hellos out of the way thought Kate as she waited, holding her breath.

'I just wanted to call and say …'

Kate waited as Alex coughed and paused. Fiona had her knuckles to her mouth, pretending to gnaw on them and Kate turned away so she could concentrate on her husband's voice.

'To say how nice it was to see you yesterday.'

Kate's eyebrows shot upwards. They had both been in a restaurant with other people and had an argument in a corridor.

'Oh right – er yes, it was nice wasn't it.'

She heard Fiona groan beside her but she ignored her and hunched her shoulders over her phone.

'I mean it was a surprise seeing you and Millie there but it was – nice.'

Kate nodded. 'Yes,' she replied, 'it was nice.'

Another long pause and Fiona rolled her eyes and shook her head.

'And you looked …' both women stiffened, holding their breath. 'You looked lovely Kate.'

Fiona power punched the air and Kate let a grin spread across her face.

'Well that's n – it's lovely of you to say that Alex. Thank you.'

'I – I …'

Another long pause as Kate and Fiona waited for the revelation.

'It made me realise how much I'd missed you Kate,' Alex offered eventually. 'Seeing you sitting there with our daughter, it was hard not being a part of that.'

'Then he shouldn't have been sitting on a table with Sandra Maddison,' growled Fiona under her breath but Kate shushed her with a frown and responded shyly. 'I know what you mean Alex.'

Kate had found it unbearable, watching Alex and Sandra at their table.

'Who would have thought that would ever happen,' she said sadly. 'It made me feel strange as well.'

Another long pause. 'I meant what I said yesterday Kate, I think we need to get together and – talk.'

Kate was nodding enthusiastically. 'Me too! I mean I think it's a good idea.'

Fiona was scrabbling furiously through all the sticky notes Kate had covering her laptop and peeling one off she thrust it under Kate's nose.

RE-ESTABLISH A RELATIONSHIP it said in capital letters.

'Er yes,' carried on Kate bravely, 'I think it would be a good idea to er meet up and er …' her eyebrows were knitted together as she stared at Fiona for inspiration, 'catch up.'

Fiona rolled her eyes and Kate carried on hastily. 'Catch up with each other I mean, talk to each other about what we would like to happen and er – things.'

She closed her eyes in despair.

'Exactly what I was thinking,' said Alex softly.

Kate's eyes flew open. 'Really? I mean great.'

She grinned at Fiona who was throwing her arms in the air in a silent cheer.

'So – can I take you out one night this week?' asked Alex with mock formality and Kate couldn't help the little giggle that slipped out.

'Okay.'

'Tonight?'

Kate thought about the preparation; the waxing and moisturizing, the hours spent with the hairdryer, the trawl through her wardrobe to find an outfit that said 'suitable for first date with ex-husband' or should that be 'first date with unfaithful ex-husband who needs to be reminded of how much he used to love his wife.'

'Sorry,' she answered with just the right amount of regret in her voice. 'I know Fiona is out tonight so I won't have a babysitter.'

'I could just come round the house?' suggested Alex. 'Millie will be in bed and we can – talk.'

217

NEUTRAL TERRITORY Fiona was scribbling on a scrap of paper and waving in front of Kate's nose

'It might be better if we met somewhere else?' Kate answered quickly.

'Right, right. Yeah, you're probably right.'

'How about Wednesday?' asked Kate.

'I was hoping to see you before then,' admitted Alex and Kate's eyes suddenly filled with tears. She knew the feeling.

'Well,' she began but Fiona was writing furiously and waving her arms around.

NO! Play it cool. You are not desperate. You have moved on.

Kate didn't think a salsa class once a week constituted moving on but she collected herself and blinked away the tears.

'Wednesday's not too far away,' she laughed lightly as Fiona nodded approvingly.

'Okay,' Alex was being flatteringly forlorn. 'I suppose Wednesday will have to do. Shall we go to Alfredo's again? I know it's your favourite.'

Kate didn't answer straight away. Alfredo's was actually Alex's favourite. And it was also where Kate had sat the night Alex had told her brutal truth, that he had left her for another woman because he was no longer happy with Kate.

'Yes of course, Alfredo's is a great idea.'

And so Alex arranged to pick her up at 7.30 and Kate ended the call.

She and Fiona stared at each other across the table.

'Like I said,' Kate grinned at her friend, 'he will definitely get in touch!' and they jumped up to hug each other and squeal and laugh until they heard the sounds of Millie waking up and Kate had to dash upstairs and reassure her tiny daughter that all was well.

Fiona made another cup of tea while Kate fed Millie and then the three of them spent a happy hour in Kates bedroom, rifling through her wardrobe yet again in search of the perfect outfit that needed to say, 'I'm okay without you' at the same time as saying 'please come back' and 'look at me' while also saying 'I'm moving on'.

Fiona finally left and Kate spent the rest of the day, humming happily to herself and hugging her arms around her body in delight at the thought of having Alex back in the house.

'I knew it would all work out okay Millie,' she whispered to her daughter as she drifted to sleep in her cot that night. 'I knew daddy would come back.'

She smiled down at the sleeping baby, her cloud of soft baby curls looking like a halo around her face.

'Who could leave you and not miss you every minute of the day? Daddy just had a funny moment that's all. He's coming home Millie, he's coming back to where he belongs and we'll soon be a family again,' and smiling in delight Kate went to hang up her outfit for Wednesday and write down a beauty plan of every hair that needed plucking and every inch of skin that needed polishing.

Chapter 21

By the time Wednesday evening arrived Kate was exhausted with nerves and excitement.

She had dressed for impact in a classic black dress which clung to every part of her now enviably slim curves, allowing a promising shadow of cleavage and ending at just the right spot to show off her long slender legs. Plain, almost severe it was the perfect background for Kate's pale cheeks and the fall of strawberry blonde waves that cascaded down her back. She had sprayed Alex's favourite perfume at the hollow of her throat and across her wrists and spent hours applying her make-up.

'You look amazing,' reassured Fiona as Kate presented herself for inspection in the kitchen.

'You think so,' asked Kate nervously. 'I mean do you really think so? It's not too over the top, or not enough? Do you think I should have worn something a little bit more special? Perhaps I should have gone to a hairdresser? What about the make-up? Too understated? Maybe …'

'Kate!' Fiona a put a calming hand on her friend's shoulder.

'You look perfect Kate, believe me it's exactly right.'

Kate took a deep breath. 'Sorry,' she offered. 'I'm just a little nervous.'

Fiona nodded. She knew how important the evening was, she had spent the last 48 hours helping Kate prepare.

'Okay,' said Fiona briskly. 'Now remember, he is obviously all fired up at the thought that you've got a new friend, possibly a new love interest on the go.'

'Fee! Josh is just a friend, not a love interest! I want Alex back, I want …'

'Yes, so you keep saying Kate. But we've got to think how to get Alex don't we? And let's face it, he's showing an awful lot more interest in you since Josh came on the scene.'

'Yes but …'

'No buts Kate. I'm pretty sure if Alex had seen you out at lunch with me and Stuart on Sunday he wouldn't have bothered phoning you Monday morning! It's Josh he's interested in.'

Kate nodded thoughtfully. 'So I need to tell him all about Josh?'

'No! Absolutely not! You mustn't tell him anything about Josh.'

'But I thought …'

'Kate, remember what Google said? He probably isn't ready for you to move on with someone new, it will drive him crazy thinking about you and what you're doing. And the end result is that he'll be looking at you with new eyes, remembering the Kate he fell in love with.'

Kate bit her lip. 'So I don't tell him about Josh?' she asked in confusion.

'You let him know there is a Josh in your life, but you don't give him any more details. He will be desperate to know what you're doing. He needs to spend his days thinking about you and what might be going on.'

'But nothing is going on!'

'Precisely why you shouldn't tell Alex.'

Kate shook her head in confusion. 'Josh is a friend, we dance together at salsa and he took me out for Sunday lunch. That's it really.'

'And if Alex knew that maybe his curiosity would be eased and he'd be less interested in you.'

'Oh Fee, I feel really bad about using Josh to get Alex back. I can't pretend he's something he's not just so Alex pays me attention!'

'Of course you can honey. Do you want Alex back?'

'Well, yes …'

'Do you want him back so much you'll do anything to make it happen?'

'Well, yes but …'

'Then stop worrying about tiny little things like the truth and let Alex believe whatever he wants regarding you and Josh. Don't give him any details and Alex will make his own story up.'

Kate looked uncertain and Fiona took her hand with a sigh. 'Remember what you were like when Alex left?' she asked gently. 'You spent all day wondering what he was doing, where he was, if he was with Sandra, what they were doing together.'

Kate nodded. She still felt like that most days. She had an overwhelming need to know exactly what Alex was doing every minute of every day since he left. She'd even considered driving past Sandra's flat again to see if she could get a little glimpse into his new life.

'Well that's probably how Alex feels right now.'

Kate's eyes opened wider. 'You think so?'

'Yes! It's exactly what Google said would happen.'

Kate took a deep breath, smoothing down her skirt. 'Okay,' she said, 'I understand,' and then squealed as the doorbell rang.

Leaving Kate in the kitchen taking deep breaths, Fiona went to answer the door and glare at Alex.

Millie was admired and kissed, Fiona reassured everyone that she and Millie would be just fine and then minutes later Kate was in Alex's car as the two smiled shyly at each other before heading in the direction of Alfredo's

Small talk ensued until they were sat by the window, strangely, mused Kate, exactly where the young couple had been sat a week earlier when Kate had watched them longingly, remembering happier times between herself and Alex.

'You look amazing,' offered Alex as he poured a glass of wine for them both.

Kate inclined her head and smiled. 'Thankyou.'

'Is that a new dress?'

Kate was about to laugh and remind Alex that she'd had the dress for years but instead she took a sip of wine.

'Yes,' she said with a smile. 'I bought it last week.'

'Oh. For a special occasion?'

'Yes.'

'Right. So what was the occasion …'

The waiter appeared by their side asking if they were ready to order and the next few minutes were taken up with talk of pasta and pesto and arrabiata sauce versus gnocchi until they were alone again and Alex was staring at Kate across the table.

'Where did you go?'

Kate stared at him in confusion.

'In the dress. You said it was a special occasion. Where did you go?'

A fog suddenly entered Kate's brain. 'Oh er,' she began casting her thoughts around wildly for some amazing event that would leave Alex seething with jealousy, 'just er – just out.'

'So not a special occasion?'

Kate pulled a face, 'Well when I say out I meant out for a special – er occasion.'

Alex's eyes were glued to her face. 'Where?'

She took a deep breath. 'Well,' she said fluttering her eyelashes downwards so Alex couldn't see the desperation. 'I went out for a meal, a lovely place that Jo – my friend took me to. I just wanted to look – special.'

'Josh? You went with Josh.'

'I went with my friend.'

'You said Josh. Did you go with Josh?'

'Er, yes. I went with Josh.'

'Josh who you go to salsa with?'

'That's the one!'

'Right. It's just I thought you had only been for Sunday lunch with him. You said you went to salsa together and he'd invited you for Sunday lunch.'

Kate bit her lip and tried to recall the conversation she'd had in the hallway of the restaurant on Sunday.

'Did I?' she asked lightly.

'Yes, you said that you weren't together, you were just having lunch.'

'Well we were.'

'No, you said that's all you had done together. You never mentioned another meal.'

Kate took a glug of wine. 'Does it matter Alex? You have left me after all! Surely where I go and who I go with isn't important to you anymore?'

It was a little more direct than she would have liked but Kate was desperate for the conversation to end.

Alex blinked. He looked startled.

'Oh, yes, sorry! I didn't mean to sound as though I was questioning you. I just didn't realise that – of course you can go out with who you like!'

Silence fell and Kate hoped it wasn't a prelude to more questioning about Josh.

'I meant what I said you know.'

Kate lifted her eyebrows. 'Which part?' she asked warily.

'Seeing you in the restaurant with someone else. It was an awful feeling.'

Kate wondered if he was expecting her to apologise. Or worse, sympathise. At least he hadn't sat outside someone else's house watching her kiss the new man in her life.

She decided to say nothing and Alex sighed, reaching out his hand towards hers as it lay on the table. He stopped just short of her fingers, obviously not sure if he still had the right to cover her hand with his own.

Kate sat still, her calm exterior belying the leaping butterflies in her stomach. She watched Alex's hand creeping towards her own, his eyes fixed on her face and her heart did a little flip as she paid a silent homage to Google.

'It must have been hard for you,' Alex said, 'seeing me there with Sandra I mean, it must have been just as hard for you?'

Just as hard? Kate had been having Sunday lunch with a friend. Alex had left her for another woman. But he was taking responsibility and she made a mental note to tell Fiona that a new milestone had been reached.

'It was,' she said without adding anything further.

'I probably hurt you a great deal?'

Kate frowned. This was beginning to sound more like a who hurt who most competition.

'Of course you did Alex,' she answered politely. 'You walked out without any notice, straight into the bed of another woman.'

His hand withdrew quickly across the table. Well that makes me the winner, thought Kate.

'Yes, of course. I understand what it must have been like Kate, I do understand and I'm so sorry.'

Privately Kate thought it was highly unlikely that he would ever really understand but she accepted that he had at least reached the conclusion that he had acted badly, another tick on the list.

She took a deep breath. 'It takes two for a marriage to succeed Alex and I accept that maybe

I didn't give you all that you needed from our marriage.' She paused for a millisecond, allowing him the chance to reject her statement and admit that it was all his fault.

He said nothing.

'Maybe I concentrated too much on other things, like the house and Millie.'

She paused again, surely he would not allow that she should have restricted the attention she paid to his daughter? Again silence. Apparently he was okay with the notion that Kate should have put Alex first in the queue for her affections, ahead of their baby.

Perhaps Fiona had been right, thought Kate, perhaps she should just tell Alex to grow up and get his priorities sorted.

'So I'm sorry too,' she finished lightly, 'if I left you feeling – unhappy.'

Alex was smiling at her and the hand was sliding back across the table only this time it didn't stop when it reached Kate's fingers. He covered her hand with his own and suddenly Kate found it quite hard to breath. It was the first time he'd touched her since the morning he'd left and the feel of his oh so familiar hand on hers brought tears to her eyes. She gazed down at their hands on the table, together as they should be. Alex leaned forwards.

'Thank you Kate,' he said, sincerity etched across his forehead. 'It means a great deal that you said that.'

Kate nodded. Of course it did. Hadn't Google told her that was exactly what he needed to hear?

'Knowing that you understand why I left makes me think that perhaps we can make things work out?'

Oh my God, had he been reading Google?

'If we both accept that things need to change then it's possible we could actually make the changes?'

He had definitely been on the 'accept and move on' website, thought Kate wildly. He hadn't even changed the words!

'Because if I did – well – come back,' they both looked slightly shocked at the words, as though saying them out loud actually made them quite real and possible.

Kate gave him a small encouraging smile.

'Well, if I did come back,' continued Alex a little more bravely, 'then it wouldn't work if nothing had changed. If you hadn't changed.'

Kate's smile disappeared.

'If I don't change? Surely we both need to change Alex?'

'Oh yes of course,' he said hastily. 'Yes, what I mean is that for things to move on change has to be a part of our lives …'

'I think I understand the point,' interrupted Kate testily.

Alex nodded, a satisfied expression on his face and for a moment Kate was very tempted to turn the discussion in the direction of unfaithful husbands and atonement. But she bit her tongue; they were actually moving towards a reconciliation and now was not the time to ignore Google and let Alex know how she actually felt.

'You see Kate,' she forced herself to pay attention again as Alex continued. 'I think that maybe, well maybe I was a little hasty.'

Kate's breath was catching in her throat. She could hear the sound of her heart beating, sending the blood flowing through her body and the entire room seemed to have fallen silent.

'Hasty,' she echoed, her voice scratchy.

Alex nodded. 'I think that maybe I was unhappy and it made me act - impulsively.'

'Impulsively?' she echoed again.

'Yes. I didn't really want to leave you Kate. I didn't want to leave you and Millie.'

Kate thought he had done a very good job of something that he declared he hadn't really wanted to do. But she kept her face calm and carried on listening.

'I just seemed to run out of ideas.'

You could have talked to me, thought Kate. You could have tried talking to me before you tried an affair.

'I was unhappy and confused, I got a little bit lost Kate and things just went on from there.'

By things, Kate presumed he meant an affair with Sandra Maddison. Strangely, although Kate had been unhappy and confused of late she hadn't immediately thought to have an affair.

'But I think that – well I think I made a mistake Kate. I think I made a huge mistake and I'm beginning to regret everything that's happened.'

Kate took a huge shaky breath. He had said the words, he had actually said the words she had been waiting to hear. There should be organ music and angels singing, thought Kate wildly. This was the moment she had prayed for since the day Alex had left and a feeling of relief so huge it threatened to overwhelm her flooded into her body and left her almost dizzy.

'I want us to think about whether we can get over this Kate. I know there can't be instant forgiveness, people can't change the way they feel overnight.'

Kate wondered whether she should tell him he was wrong, that she was prepared to forgive instantly, she was prepared to change overnight. She was prepared to change now, this very minute if Alex came home. But she nodded and smiled because she knew that he had to feel comfortable taking the next step. Google had instructed her not to pressure her husband if he showed signs of wobbling back in her direction. There should be no pressure, just a calm hand held out to guide him back into the fold.

'I would like to be able to carry on seeing you Kate, I think it's important that we don't let this situation get out of hand.'

Kate wondered which situation he was talking about, the one where he thought Kate might have someone new in her life or the one where he had jumped into bed with Sandra Maddison and left Kate high and dry because she hadn't appreciated him enough. She pushed away the unkind thoughts and tried to concentrate.

'I want us to be able to sit down and talk honestly about our feelings and our life. I don't mean just every now and then but maybe we could meet up regularly and – well get to know each other again?'

He was watching her, looking for some sign of agreement and Kate nodded slowly.

She would rather he just said, Kate can I come home. She would rather he just say he loved her and ask simply if he could come back. And she really would rather he stopped talking about how she appeared to have let him down in the first place.

But it was all progress. She looked over the table at the face of the man she loved and put her hand back on the table so Alex could stroke her fingers

She smiled, the warmest smile she could summon and looking into the eyes of the man she adored, the man she thought she would spend the rest of her life alongside, she nodded.

'I think that's an excellent idea Alex, a really excellent idea.'

Chapter 22

'He wants you to get to know each other again! You've been together for eight years, which bit of you doesn't he know yet?'

'It's actually a very positive step Fee. He's admitted he made a mistake but he – we don't want to simply fall back into the same relationship if it wasn't working.'

'But you did think it was working.'

'Well I was obviously wrong,' snapped Kate. 'Because if it had been working he wouldn't have left me in the first place would he?'

Fiona bit her lip. 'Sorry honey,' she offered. 'I suppose I'm just a little bit frustrated on your behalf. I mean he's admitted he made a mistake and wants to talk about coming home – why on earth doesn't he just get on with it and come home instead of blabbering on about changes and getting to know you!'

Kate busied herself with the teapot. It was hard to answer Fiona because once the euphoria of the previous evening had worn off she'd spent an unsettled night asking herself much the same. She should be feeling relieved and confident after the hints and promise of the previous night. Instead she was feeling edgy and unsettled, no matter how much she told herself it was all working out.

'It's what Google said would happen,' she offered weakly. 'We need to put everything behind us and find the person we fell in love with again so we can carry on.'

'So basically now you've apologised and promised to change, he's thinking about forgiving you and coming home?'

'No! That's not what I said Fee.'

'No, it isn't what you said but I've a feeling that's what he meant.'

They glared at each other for a moment and then Fiona relented and reached out to hug her friend. 'I'm sorry Kate, I don't mean to spoil things for you but I really think he just needs to get on with it now, ask you to forgive him and come home to his family.'

Kate shook her head. 'He's coming back,' she said stubbornly. 'That's the main thing Fee. It may not happen today or tomorrow but he is definitely coming back.'

'And in the meantime,' Fiona pointed out gently, 'he's still living with Sandra Maddison.'

'What do you mean?'

'I mean, it's a classic case of having your cake and eating it. He wants to see you, talk about how to make things better between you, maybe start again, but he's not prepared to actually back himself by moving out of the cosy little set up with Sandra.'

Kate struggled with herself for a moment and stared out of the window.

'It's just about timing now,' she said with a shrug.

'And you're okay that he's living with another woman while he gets to know you again and tries to remember why he fell in love with you?'

Tears were blinding Kate, they gathered large and glistening in her eyes and for a few moments she could see nothing but their shimmering reflection. Kate had been shocked to discover she wasn't the perfect wife she had tried so hard to become. She had been shocked that her husband had felt alone and unhappy in their marriage. She had promised herself that she would forgive Alex his moment of weakness and she would put all thoughts of Sandra Maddison out of her head, if only he came home. And yet the thought that the two of them had woken up together this morning, in the same bed, arms wrapped around each other, was almost more than she could bear. But she couldn't let that sway her, she was so close to getting Alex back, she wouldn't let Sandra Maddison spoil it for her now.

'He's coming back Fee, that's all that matters,' Kate muttered, tears trickling slowly down her face. 'That's all I want.'

Fiona left shortly after leaving Kate to carry on with her preparations to visit her mother and with the weather suddenly much more clement, she packed Millie into her buggy and set off on the long journey.

Marcia was her usual groomed self and as Kate struggled to get the buggy through the doorway she felt as though time had suddenly lurched backwards several years. She'd made no effort to dress for the occasion, she was in jeans and a loose top with her hair scrunched on top of her head and if it hadn't been for Millie now sitting on her knee, she could have believed the last 8 years simply hadn't happened. She was the old Kate visiting her mother. Alex had always admired Marcia's slightly formal sense of dress. Whenever they visited and Marcia greeted them wearing a blue linen shift dress and pearls or a Jaeger cardigan and A line skirt, Alex would always compliment her and point out to Kate how well her mother looked. Gradually Kate took to dressing up for these visits and the first time she had left her jeans on the bedroom floor and put on a wool dress and shiny black knee length boots, Alex had smiled approvingly and made a great deal of fuss about how lovely it was sitting between two such well-presented women.

But today Kate hadn't felt the need to impress either Alex or her mother and she had simply pulled on her jeans and set off without giving her appearance another thought.

She sat in the living room with Millie on her knee and caught sight of herself in the large ornate mirror over the fireplace. Her mother would no doubt disapprove.

Marcia brought in the tea tray and set it down on the coffee table before giving Kate an assessing glance.

'You're looking better,' she said with a nod.

Kate almost dropped Millie as she stared at her mother who was now pouring the tea.'

'Much more like your old self.'

Kate didn't reply, she was staring at her reflection, at the slight hint of colour in her cheeks, at the tousled hair caught in a tortoiseshell clip and the face bare of make-up.

'I do?' she asked doubtfully.

There was a gentle pause as Marcia filled the cups and left Kate's on the table away from Millie's hands.

'How are things?'

Kate smiled. 'Actually Mum, things are going really well?'

Her mother's eyebrows raised. 'Alex is back?'

'Well not exactly, I mean no, he's not back but we're talking and he – well he said he's made a mistake and he wants us to carry on seeing each other and talking about how we move forward.'

Marcia was sipping delicately at her tea making no comment.

'With a view to getting back together, he wants us to talk about getting back together,' Kate clarified.

'I see.' Her mother smiled, putting down her tea and holding her arms out for Millie. 'Shall I take her so you can drink your tea darling? Isn't she growing, such a pretty little thing, much like you were at her age. Hello Millie, come to granny.'

Kate handed her daughter over, wondering if her mother had heard correctly.

'Yes,' she reiterated, 'so pretty soon Alex will be back. With me, back with me and Millie.'

Marcia nodded. 'Well that's good. If that's what you want.'

Kate stared at her mother. 'If that's what I want? Of course it's what I want. I mean that's been the plan all along, to get him back. Why wouldn't I want it now?'

'Plan?'

'Oh, er,' Kate had a feeling her mother had never even heard of Google let alone was aware of its all-seeing knowledge and wisdom. 'Well that's what I had hoped for and I've been trying to get Alex to see, well to see…'

'To see what Kate?'

Kate nibbled her lip. 'To see that he made a mistake leaving. But that we love each other and we could sort things out and he could come home.'

Marcia nodded. 'I see.'

'I thought you'd be pleased,' blurted Kate. 'I thought you'd be happy if Alex came home.'

Marcia looked at her daughter as she stroked the blonde curls of her granddaughter.

'Of course I'm happy Kate, but only if it makes you happy. If you don't think Alex coming home is the right thing for you then you shouldn't feel that you have to take him back.'

'Not the right thing? But Mum – of course it's the right thing. I love him and he loves me …'

'So you keep saying dear, but love isn't always enough. And love alone doesn't necessarily keep a marriage together.'

Kate stared in bewilderment. 'But if we love each other then of course it's right. It's right for us and for Millie and for – well for everyone.'

Marcia didn't answer and Kate sat in the silence of the room, a shaft of light coming in through the window and settling on the face of her now sleeping daughter.

'Don't you think we're right for each other?' Kate asked finally.

She heard the tiniest of sighs coming from her mother, the smallest sound that made Kate sit up a little straighter and lean forward.

'Mum! You love Alex, you always say what a wonderful son in law he is. Are you trying to tell me you don't think we're right for each other? After all this time!'

'Alex is a perfect son in law,' Marcia answered calmly. 'He is most helpful and courteous and quite charming company.'

'But?'

'Well if you really insist then no, I don't actually think you're right for each other.'

Kate felt as though she had been slapped. She sat, wide eyed staring at her mother sitting calmly opposite and the shock of her words was almost as great as the moment Alex said he was leaving.

'What?' whispered Kate. 'What on earth are you saying?'

Marcia sighed again, this time a heartfelt sigh that filled the room as she touched the pearls at her neck.

'I knew this conversation wasn't a good idea,' she began then broke off as Kate cried out.

'Mum! What are you talking about?'

Marcia shook her head and then took a deep breath. 'Kate my dear, your father and I loved each other very much.' Her eyes softened and she looked past Kate, the tiniest of smiles playing on her lips. 'I fell in love with him the second I saw him, I loved him madly from that very first moment. But the fact was, we were two very different people and totally unsuited to each other.'

She paused, gazing down at her sleeping grandchild. 'We knew it would be hard, we were the opposite in everything, we wanted different things from life, we wanted different lives from each other. But we were in love and so we decided that we could make it work.'

Kate held her breath. Until recently she had known almost nothing of her parent's life together other than the arguments and unhappiness of her childhood.

'We tried hard.' A cloud passed across Marcia's face. 'But in the end our differences were too great and we started to resent each other. We both found it hard to be someone we were not and eventually it became such a strain on us that it was something we couldn't recover from. Our differences became exaggerated to the point where we couldn't live in the same house without causing hurt and sorrow.'

Kate watched her mother's face, the pain in her eyes and felt a moment of sadness that she had never known the happy young couple who were so much in love.

'But that's because you were too different Mum,' Kate said softly, 'you said you wanted different things from life. That's not me and Alex. We were happy, we were in love and we were happy, until this – thing happened.'

Marcia smiled at her daughter. 'Were you dear? Were you happy?'

'Of course we were! You saw us, you saw how we lived together for years, happily, wanting the same things, being the same people!'

Maria shook her head. 'Actually my dear, I didn't see that. What I saw was my daughter fall in love with someone who was very different to herself. I saw you change to become the person you thought would make him happy, someone very different to the girl I saw grow up.'

Kate shook her head. 'No.'

'I saw you stop being the person I knew, and the person Alex had fallen in love with, and become a more subdued version of yourself, constantly adjusting yourself to make Alex happy.'

'No.'

'I saw you become an excellent wife and mother but I also saw your spark disappear, slowly extinguish as you changed into the person you thought you should be.'

'No. No! Stop it, stop it now.'

Kate was on her feet, pacing the room angrily. 'You told me to change, it wasn't Alex! You told me to change so I could keep my husband happy.'

A look of bewilderment crossed Marcia's face. 'I told you that?'

'You said I needed to be different. You said that I needed to be able to cook and keep the house clean.'

Kate's voice was raising, her fingers pointing in her mother's direction as she spoke. 'You said that no husband wanted to come home to clutter on the floor and the washing in the sink and – all that stuff. You said I had to change. You said it!'

'Kate my dear,' Marcia had laid Millie on the sofa, wedged against the back with a cushion as she stood up and tried to take her daughter in her arms. But Kate pushed her away, stepping back and holding her arms before her defensively. 'It's your fault if I changed, your fault Alex left!' she shouted

'Kate, please stop!'

Millie whimpered in her sleep and Kate's hand flew to her mouth in distress.

'Kate listen to me my darling. I told you that you needed to learn how to cook, and that you should be tidier and that you needed to be more organised. Of course I did – you were a dreadful cook Kate, you could burn a boiled egg!'

Kate had sat back down, her arms wrapped round her shaking body.

'But those are just everyday habits Kate, they don't define who we are. You were chronically untidy and chaotically disorganised. And no-one wants to share a house with someone else's mess. But you were still Kate, you were still my beautiful, happy daughter. Untidy yes, always late, always forgetting something but impulsive, carefree, full of love and - well Kate.'

'You said I had to change,' whispered Kate. 'You said it.'

Marcia touched the pearls at her throat again, her hand shaking. 'My darling girl I didn't mean that you should stop being you. You need to be true to yourself Kate, you can't be someone you're not, not indefinitely. I tried it, your father tried it and it simply didn't work. You need to be who you are. I didn't want you to change, I just wanted you to be a little bit tidier, learn how to cook so you could be as happy as you could possibly be.'

Kate was sitting on the very edge of her chair, her knees drawn upwards. 'You think Alex left me because I changed?'

'I don't know what Alex…'

'You think I changed, you think I changed and Alex doesn't love me anymore?'

'No Kate, I didn't say that …'

'Alex did. He said I wasn't the person he married, that I wasn't full of fun and laughter and – all the things I used to be.'

Kates voice was raw with grief, it had hurt so much hearing the words fall from Alex's mouth. She had refused to dwell on them, afraid of the pain and anger they would bring but now sitting in her mother's living room, they surfaced again. Hard and hurtful.

Marcia reached out her hand, her face full of distress at the sight of her daughter in so much pain.

'I don't know why Alex left you Kate. And if you love him and want him to come back then I hope it happens. But I want you to be happy my dear, I want you to be happy being you, not the person that Alex wants you to be.

Please make sure Alex coming back is what you want and make sure before he comes back or you will end up losing him twice.'

Chapter 23

Kate's mind was whirling throughout the journey home. Millie was grouchy and wriggly and Kate's head was pounding by the time she reached her own front door.

She fed Millie and sat her down with her rabbit as she sipped on a cup of tea and thought back to the conversation. Her mother's announcement had left Kate reeling with shock. She had been quietly convinced for the last eight years that given the choice Marcia would have preferred to keep Alex as a family member whilst viewing her daughter as a slight thorn in her side, a rather disquieting presence that she tolerated. Kate was now reeling at her mother's reservations regarding Kate and Alex's suitability as partners. How could her mother say such a thing, how could she think for a moment that Kate and Alex were not soul mates, meant to spend the rest of their lives together? Okay, she was right, Kate had changed. But only for the better, because it was necessary to make sure that Alex would love her even more and never want to leave. And the fact that he had left didn't mean that Kate had been wrong, it just meant she hadn't tried hard enough. She hadn't got it quite right. But she could, she just needed a second chance.

Kate shook her head, pacing the kitchen as though she could escape her thoughts. Why did she feel so restless, so disappointed? She should be feeling euphoric. Alex was coming home. He had said all the right things, he was making all the right moves. Kate was sure it was only a matter of time now. But first Fiona and now her mother, both casting doubts, both questioning whether Kate really should have Alex back in her life. Were they both blind, thought Kate? Had they not seen Alex and Kate over the last few years as they lived out their perfect marriage?

And Alex was as bad. She'd become everything he said he wanted, everything he said he loved and now he was complaining that their marriage was over, empty and barren and that she was no longer the person he'd fallen in love with. Well obviously she wasn't because that girl hadn't been able to produce cheese on toast without setting fire to the kitchen, she'd been hopeless with any household tasks and had not been able to find anything in the chaos that was her flat. Alex hadn't wanted to live like that! He may have loved Kate but he hadn't loved the way Kate lived. She'd become a woman he could both love and spend the rest of his life with. And now he was accusing her of neglecting him, of spending too much time on the daughter he adored and looking after the house he loved.

Kate threw her cup into the sink and sat back at the table to stare out into the garden. She remembered when she and Alex had moved here. The tiny flat had been left behind and the grown up Alex and Kate had moved into their lovely house. Kate had already become an excellent cook and her untidiness a thing of the past. The new house was a success story for both of them, a space that was light, bright and beautifully presented, tidy, clutter free and welcoming. A few weeks after they'd moved in Alex had suggested a dinner party and for some reason Kate had thought back to the very first time she and Alex had entertained as a couple in Kate's tiny flat. The food had been awful, the kitchen a disaster area, the flat itself untidy and chaotic. But they'd had an amazing night with their friends. They'd laughed until they cried, they'd drunk far more wine than they should have and they'd all sat up until the early hours of the morning chatting and putting the world to rights.

Kate had been thrilled at the thought of repeating the evening but in much more salubrious surroundings and with food they would actually be able to eat.

But Alex had pulled the tiniest of faces. He'd suggested that a slightly more grown up affair was called for and that some of Kate's friends were still a little immature and some of them a little loud and most of them just wouldn't appreciate what Kate and Alex had achieved.

And although Kate had wanted to defend her old friends, she wanted to make Alex happy even more so she agreed that instead Alex would invite a friend from work and an old school chum he still played squash with once a week and she tried to ignore the uneasy feeling that she had just accepted thirty pieces of silver.

Kate's cooking had been sublime and the house looked superb with its softly lit rooms and Kate's attention to detail. The evening had gone without a hitch and everyone was suitably admiring and behaved impeccably. Alex was delighted, Kate could tell from the look in his eye that he was so very happy and so Kate was too. Except that there was no raucous laughter, no telling of tales until the early hours of the morning or feelings of comradery. There was no aching of jaws from giggling and no good humoured ribbing of Kate's cooking. And whilst Alex looked relaxed and comfortable, Kate had felt ever so slightly let down and had a momentary sense of loss for times gone by when the food may be diabolical but the company was superb.

Their guests had gone and Alex had swept Kate into his arms and kissed her thoroughly.

'Wasn't that wonderful?' he had demanded. 'I bet none of them can cook as well as you can Kate. And did you see their reaction to how you'd decorated the living room? They'll all be trying to do the same, I guarantee!'

Kate had laughed, happy that Alex was happy and pushing away her sense of guilt at the absence of her old friends, she'd allowed Alex to carry her up the stairs and they had made love, Alex telling her over and over again how wonderful she was and how much he loved her.

It was getting dark and Kate couldn't see much in the garden any more. She sighed. Of course she had changed, but only for the better. Alex had been delighted with her new cooking skills and he had loved coming home every night to a house that was clean and comfortable. He used to wrap his arms round her and say how much he loved her. He would sink into the settee with its perfectly placed cushions and look around admiringly and Kate's heart would give a little skip of happiness. She'd changed because they'd all wanted her to change, it was meant to make Alex happy. So why had he left and why was everyone now telling her that she was no longer the Kate she was meant to be?

It was 10 o' clock the next morning when Alex phoned her.

Kate had gone to bed feeling quite depressed and rather than sink into a good night's sleep, happy that the trauma of the last few weeks was soon to be behind her, she had tossed and turned. Marcia's words were echoing in her head and dreams of unknown people laughing at her cooking haunted her through the night.

She had woken up and laid staring at the ceiling for a while. Alex is coming home, she whispered to herself. She ignored the little voice that said Alex hadn't actually said that he was coming home. As far as Kate was concerned it was simply a matter of time now. Soon she would wake up and he would be there, next to her where he belonged. She would rescue Millie from her cot and bring her into the bedroom where Alex could admire his small daughter's blonde hair and rosebud mouth and Millie could sit there basking in the attention from both her parents.

Kate smiled. She just needed to get through the next few days. She didn't care what her mother said, or Fiona. Kate and Alex were meant to be together. She would forgive Alex his aberration and they would resume their happy life.

Feeling a little more cheerful Kate had slipped out of bed to pick up a now chuntering Millie and was filling the washing machine when her phone rang.

'Good morning,' said Alex softly, 'how are you?'

Kate's heart melted. Alex often used to phone her up during the day, usually to complain about something at the office and it invariably left Kate juggling Millie and feeding or washing or doing something single handedly as she held the phone in the other, but she had missed the sound of his voice.

She smiled. 'I'm good.'

'I was wondering if you would like to meet up again?' There was the tiniest of pauses. 'I really enjoyed the other night. I hadn't realised just how much I'd missed you.'

Kate grinned to herself in the kitchen. Oh Google, you clever being.

'Me too, I enjoyed it as well,' she admitted.

She could tell he was smiling and for a moment all doubts and uncertainties were left way behind. She wished he was there with her, she wished she could run her hands through his wayward hair and look into the eyes she loved.

'So you'll go out with me?'

Kate giggled. 'Are you asking me on a date?'

'Well – if I was, would you come?'

Kate hugged herself in delight. 'Yes'

'Well in that case, would you go out with me Kate. On a date?'

Kate couldn't help another giggle from falling out. 'Yes, I will.'

Was it her imagination or was the sun suddenly shining much more brightly than it had earlier that morning.

'Good. I'm looking forward to seeing you again.'

His voice was low, flirtatious and Kate felt a little shiver of lust run down her spine.

'So how about tonight?'

She stiffened. She looked out into the garden where a cloud seemed to have come from nowhere.

'Can't do tonight,' she said lightly. 'Tomorrow?'

There was a silence, Kate could hear the clock ticking.

'Are you doing something else tonight?'

'Yes.'

It definitely seemed a little cooler and Kate gave another shiver but this one was entirely absent of lust.

'Oh, nothing you could put off?'

He knew she was going to Salsa. He may be pretending to have forgotten but Kate knew.

'Is tomorrow not convenient?' she asked with an edge to her voice.

'Well yes, I just wondered why not tonight?'

The clock carried on ticking.

'Oh – it's salsa isn't it?'

Kate didn't reply. Her lips were thin as she watched the rain start to fall in the garden.

'Right. So, you'd like to see me but not enough to miss salsa?' Alex laughed, though it was lacking in amusement. 'Well I suppose that puts me in my place. Is salsa more important to you than us getting back together?'

'Not really Alex. It's just part of my new life, the one I had to find for myself after you left. Tell me, is Sandra Maddison more important to you than us getting back together?'

Kate could feel his shock down the phone. She had broken one of the rules; no confrontation, no outbursts, no emotions other than pleasant ones. But she didn't really care. She had suddenly become very tired of being so accommodating, so forgiving, so perfect. Why was everybody allowed to constantly criticise Kate? Why shouldn't Kate respond with a few home truths of her own?

'What? No! Kate, no! I didn't mean that I just meant I thought you might want to give salsa a miss and spend some time with me. Discussing me coming back, us getting back together again,' he said in the tone of someone dangling a carrot. 'That's all.'

'But you don't want to commit yourself and move out of Sandra's flat,' said Kate, a statement not a question.

'What? Move out? Well of course I do. But isn't it a little sudden, we both agreed we need time to get to know each other again, we don't want to make the same mistakes again do we? Where would I go? I mean I don't have anywhere to stay if I move out right now.'

'Well I do have somewhere to go Alex, I'm going to salsa tonight,' and Kate slammed the phone down.

It was only a second before she looked down in horror at the now disconnected line, tears welling in her eyes.

Oh God what have I done, she whispered to herself, what have I done.

She picked up the phone and frantically pressed buttons trying to reconnect her call but all she heard was beeps and buzzes. Taking a deep breath she tried again this time dialing Alex's number but the tears flooding her eyes and her shaking hands led to more beeps and buzzes as she misdialed   .

Slamming the phone down Kate pressed a hand to her mouth. What was she thinking, how could she have been so stupid? Alex wanted to ask if he could come back, she'd been able to hear it in his voice, she knew it was on the tip of his tongue. She had started going to salsa to catch her husband's attention, to make his eyes turn back in her direction. It had worked, so why was Kate now being so stubborn about the whole business.

Google had been quite explicit, once your husband came knocking on the front door, don't start dithering - let him in! And she had refused because she didn't want to miss an hour of salsa.

She slumped onto one of the kitchen chairs shaking her head. She would phone him, apologise, say of course salsa didn't matter, she wanted to see Alex. She would follow the plan, she would smile and sympathise and accept she wasn't perfect and when he asked if he could come home she would take his hand and say of course he could and they would live happily ever after.

She stared at the phone nibbling on her lip. Her mother's words had been turning in Kate's mind. She had tried to ignore them but they simply wouldn't go away. The last few weeks Kate had been delving into her memories of Alex and their life together and the more she thought the more she'd come to realise just how much she'd given up to keep him happy. She was developed a sneaking suspicion that once the glow of Alex's company had been removed and she had been left looking at their relationship with clear eyes, it hadn't been quite the vision of perfection she had always believed. It had left an itch inside her that was becoming harder to ignore as each day passed and with Marcia and Fiona both questioning whether she was right to want Alex to come home, Kate had been left restless and haunted by doubt. But the undeniable truth was that she still loved Alex and the thought of not spending the rest of her life with him by her side was a very scary one. Maybe there was more that needed adjusting in their life than the amount of time Kate spent cleaning and plumping cushions. But that could come later, once Alex was home Kate was convinced she could make things work. They had for the last eight years.

She picked up the phone, staring at the numbers and then, carefully, started to dial.

'Hello?'

'Oh Fiona, I've just done something really stupid!'

In between the sobs she told Fiona about the conversation but instead of sympathy Fiona crowed with delight, stopping as Kate burst into tears again.

'Oh Kate, don't cry honey. It's going to be fine, just what he needed to hear.'

'Noo,' wailed Kate, 'it's not. He was flirting with me Fee, flirting. He wanted to meet up to talk about coming back and I said I was going to salsa.'

'Well, let's face it, how many times do you need to discuss him coming home. He could have just asked you on the phone. Not that hard really is it, 'hey Kate, I've been an absolute tosser, I'm sorry, can I come home?' Simple really.'

'But he has to feel right about it, he has to know that it will work if we try again,' insisted Kate, 'and I think I've just ruined it all.'

'Rubbish. Actually I think it was exactly the right thing to say. Sounds to me like he's suffering from a good old dose of jealousy! He's the one that left and yet you're the one out dancing and having lunch with other men. He probably can't quite get his head around what's gone wrong. Suddenly he's the one that's worried about what you're up to and not the other way round. Believe me you haven't spoiled anything, Alex will be home even sooner if you ask me!'

'Should I phone him back?'

'No! Absolutely not Kate. We stick with the plan, no contact from you. It's working honey, don't cave in now.'

'You really think so?'

'I do. Being nice and understanding can only get you so far Kate and I know Google said to share the blame and accept his actions but personally I still thing a good old battering round the head wouldn't have hurt. He needs a wakeup call honey, and I think you may have just given im one!'

Chapter 24

Kate allowed Fiona to convince her all was not lost. She stared at the phone a great deal, she even rested her hand on it for a while imagining dialing the numbers and hearing Alex's voice. She could apologise for the 'misunderstanding' and say of course she would miss salsa, she wanted to see him as much as he wanted to see her. But she resisted, mainly because Fiona said she would never speak to Kate again if she did. As the day went on the panic eased a little and Kate even started to feel encouraged by Alex's call. It may not have ended well but there had been a few moments, a few precious moments when she and Alex were talking to each other as though nothing had ever gone wrong between them. He had spoken to her in that low sexy tone that made her stomach flip with longing and she had been utterly convinced that he was coming back to her.

So Kate had dried her eyes and allowed herself to feel hopeful again. She had even ventured a little smile at the shock in Alex's voice when she had confronted him about Sandra and by the time she was getting ready for salsa she had become almost cheerful again, although she checked her phone at least every half an hour in the vain hope that Alex had left her a message of some sort.

When Kate walked into the wine bar that evening, she told herself she was looking around for her friends even though her heart knew she was looking to see if Josh was there.

He was standing by the bar talking to Sophie and Alan and as Kate caught his eye she couldn't help the blush he always seemed to bring to her cheeks.

'Hi,' he said as she walked towards him, his smile reaching his eyes.

'Hi,' responded Kate breathlessly before turning to Sophie to give her a hug.

'Everything okay?'

Kate nodded. He had called her on the Monday to make sure she was alright after her unexpected meeting with Alex and to ask if she was going to salsa on Friday.

'I was hoping you wouldn't change your mind about coming tonight,' Josh said with a grimace. 'I know one day my footwork is going to drive you away!'

They all laughed and Kate looked into his eyes briefly, wondering what they would all say if she told them she had potentially just ruined any chance of getting back with her husband for the sake of an hour of salsa.

'I can take a few broken toes,' she said lightly. 'Although I'm thinking about getting some steel capped shoes!'

They all laughed again then as the music began and people began to separate into their groups, Josh took hold of Kate's hand and led her gently to the spot they preferred, by a large stone pillar and out of view of much of the room.

'Alex been in touch again?' asked Josh casually.

Kate nodded.

'In a good way?'

Kate nodded again.

Josh smiled, 'That's good news Kate, really good news,' and then the salsa began.

Afterwards, with flushed cheeks and slightly out of breath, Kate stood at the bar with her new friends as they had a drink.

Olivia was there and she edged a little closer to Kate as the rest of them chatted.

'He's very good looking isn't he?' she asked with a sideways glance at Josh.

'Well yes but …'

'And I think he likes you,' giggled Olivia.

'Well maybe but …'

'It will do you good!'

'Well – what will?'

'A little distraction like Josh.'

Kate looked shocked. 'Oh no, we're just friends, there's nothing like that going on Olivia. Just friends,' she repeated firmly.

'Well more fool you!'

Kate stared at Olivia. 'What?'

'Oh come on Kate. I know you're hoping Alex will come back …'

'Alex is coming back!'

'Well whatever,' sniffed Olivia. 'But whichever way you cut it Kate, he's behaved very badly and I for one wouldn't blame you if you comforted yourself in the arms of a hunk like Josh!' and off she went, back to Helen's side leaving Kate wide eyed with surprise.

'She's right,' whispered a vice at her side and swinging round Kate found Sophie next to her. 'Alex may come back …'

'Alex is coming back!' insisted Kate wondering if she should have a banner made.

'Sophie shrugged, 'Well maybe he will, but in the meantime he's not here and Josh is,' and she winked at an astounded Kate who was wondering when her love life had become the main topic of conversation among the salsa dancers.

A little while later Olivia and Helen reluctantly said they had to leave and Sophie pulled on her coat, grinning like a Cheshire cat and whispering to Kate that Alan had asked her out for a meal, just the two of them, which left Kate and Josh standing at the bar.

'Can I interest you in a drink?' asked Josh politely, his head tipped to one side as he waited for Kate's reply.

'Oh no, thank you but I suppose I should go as well.'

She fidgeted with her handbag. She knew that Fiona wasn't at all worried about Kate getting back.

'Right. I just thought we could go to the little bar down the road. It's a lot quieter than this one,' he winced as a guffaw of laughter flooded the bar. 'We could chat, you can tell me how things are going.'

Kate was watching the dimple in his chin as he spoke, wondering how many other people thought she should forget her woes in Josh's rather strong arms.

'Kate?'

'Oh er sorry.' She looked away, it really was a very nice chin.

'Well I shouldn't really,' she began uncertainly.

'But …?'

She smiled. 'Okay, just one.'

The weather had improved immensely over the last week and as they walked down the road towards the tiny bar on the corner, Kate remembered how the very first night she had come to salsa she had almost frozen to the pavement.

'Weather's getting better isn't it?' Josh commented casually as though reading her mind.

It felt strange walking next to him thought Kate. With no Millie or buggy to occupy her hands it seemed almost natural for Kate to tuck her hand into the crook of Josh's arm and let him guide her over the cobbles. How would that feel she wondered, how would it feel to walk along the street arm in arm with someone who wasn't Alex? Would it feel odd or just good? Should she try it before she committed to having Alex back? Should she test out having a new man on her arm, just to see how it felt?

She realised Josh was looking at her expectantly.

'Oh, er yes,' she smiled. 'Yes it is,' and she pushed her hands deep into her pocket to avoid the temptation of his arm.

Josh opened the door for her and they slipped into the small comfortable bar where couples sat at scrubbed pine tables as they chatted and listened to melodious background music.

'So,' began Josh, stretching out his long legs and sipping at the beer in front of him. 'what happened after Sunday?'

Kate sighed. 'Well Alex phoned me the very next day,' she said sheepishly. 'Seeing me out with someone else seemed to peek his interest.'

Josh laughed. 'Well, glad I could help!'

'We went out, had a chat about – things, how they'd gone wrong, you know the kind of stuff.'

Josh had told her about his ex, Tanya whom he had been with for several years before she decided she wanted more, although under questioning from Josh had been unable to describe exactly what the 'more' was.

'Well that's good progress,' said Josh cautiously. 'And did it go well, this chat?'

Kate nodded slowly. She supposed it had gone well. It had achieved what Kate was hoping for, Alex had been reminded how much he missed her, he had realised that he had made a mistake, he was talking about trying again. All things that Kate would have sold her soul to hear a few weeks earlier. She decided now wasn't the right moment to say that a part of her husband's new interest in her was because he suspected that Kate and Josh were having a relationship.

'I suppose it did.'

'You don't sound terribly sure.'

Kate looked down at the stem of her glass which she was twiddling.

'Well, he said he thought he had made a mistake and he wanted to talk about how we could make things right.'

'But that's great news – at least for you and Alex,' added Josh softly. 'It may leave me broken hearted but I'm still pleased for you.'

Kate's eyes flew to his. 'You wouldn't be broken heated,' she denied lightly, suddenly rather breathless as she waited for his answer.

Josh leaned over the table. 'Oh I certainly would,' he said softly, watching Kate blush.

'But if it's going as well as this, why don't you look happier?'

Kate twiddled the glass some more.

'Of course I'm happy,' she started to say. But the words didn't seem very convincing.

'Well, there's a way to go yet,' she conceded. 'Alex hasn't actually said he's coming back yet and he's still with Sandra Maddison in the meantime.'

Josh frowned. 'But surely he'll move out? If he's realised he's made a mistake he'll move out of the divine Sandra's flat so he can come home to you?'

Kate shrugged. 'Well he hasn't yet.'

'And that makes you unhappy?'

Kate chewed on her nail. It actually made her deeply unhappy. She had rejected Fiona's claims that Alex was having a very large slice of cake and eating it but in fact her friend was right. That Alex seemed to be in the process of remembering the young woman he fell in love with and married was of course exactly what Kate wanted. That he remained in the arms of Sandra Maddison while he flirted with Kate on the phone was a niggling little thorn that had started to grow in Kate's heart.

'Mmm,' mumbled Kate. 'I suppose so.'

'Because now you are the other woman?'

Her eyes flew to his.

'The other woman?'

Josh shrugged. 'It's quite ironic I suppose. Alex left you for Sandra and now he's seeing you behind Sandra's back. In a strange way you've become the other woman.'

Kate didn't reply, her thoughts were like fog swirling through her mind, hard to pin down, hard to rationalise. But Josh was right, Kate was the other woman. While Alex remained with Sandra but meeting Kate, flirting with Kate, asking her out on dates, then Kate had become the other woman.

Her mouth turned down.

'Oh God, I'm sorry Kate! That was really insensitive of me.'

Josh was leaning forward, his eyes full of apologies but Kate shook her head. 'No, you're actually right. I hadn't really thought of it like that but you're right. Actually, it's what Fee said as well but I wasn't really, I mean I don't really know …'

She trailed off, deep in thought and Josh sat back, not pressing her.

'Actually,' Kate cleared her throat,' Alex wanted to meet me tonight.'

Josh sat very still. 'But you didn't go, obviously.'

They sat in silence.

'Why?' he asked quietly.

Kate shrugged. 'I enjoy salsa.'

'I see.'

'I don't want you to think that …'

Josh stopped her, putting his hand over Kate's and she stared at his fingers, remembering a few nights previously when Alex had covered her hand with his own.

'I just enjoy salsa,' she repeated. 'It wasn't for any other reason …'

'Kate, you know that I want you to be happy. If that involves taking Alex back, then I hope it happens. But make no mistake, if I thought for a moment you didn't want to be back with your husband, you'd be fighting me off.'

Kate looked down at their fingers resting together on the table. They were crammed into a small alcove with barely six inches between their bodies and as she looked up to meet Josh's eyes she found they were suddenly a whole lot closer.

'You don't have to take Alex back. You know that don't you Kate? You should decide what's best for you.'

She glanced back at their fingers now entwined on the table top. She could feel his breath on her cheek, his voice a soft whisper floating between them.

'And what's best for you might not be to stay with Alex.'

She peeped upwards and now his eyes were so close she could see the dark blue fleck on his iris.

'Josh I don't think …'

'You might be much, much happier with someone else entirely.'

'But Alex and I …'

'Much happier.'

'Josh …'

But he was so close now there was no more room between them, not even for Kate's unspoken words that faded to nothing as his lips drifted onto hers, very gentle, soft and warm and oh so delicious.

She should stop this, she thought. It was making things much more complicated than they needed to be. She should stop this straight away. But she found it surprisingly hard and instead she just let herself float into a wondrous fog of desire.

There was a sense of loss as he stopped kissing her, an empty feeling as he sat back slightly so he could look into her eyes.

'You have choices Kate, remember you have choices,' he whispered but Kate wasn't really listening because his lips were on hers again and she decided she much preferred kissing Josh to talking about her husband.

Chapter 25

Kate woke up early. She had slept very little, eventually drifting off in the early hours but as the first rays of sun started appearing in the sky she was wide awake again, lying in bed staring at the ceiling. She had spent a great deal of time inspecting her bedroom ceiling since Alex had left. She was now intimately acquainted with the tiny crack that ran in a slightly wavy line towards the central light fitting. The cobweb that hung from the lampshade had been there for over two weeks but Kate hadn't felt the need to brush it away.

She sighed. Arriving at Fiona's last night she had collected a sleeping Millie but had not mentioned why she was later than usual and she certainly hadn't mentioned anything about kissing Josh. Kate had a feeling that she didn't need to tell Fiona. Maybe it was because Kate couldn't stop smiling; maybe it was because she had drifted off and started thinking about Josh and his strong chin and the feel of his lips while Fiona was talking to her; maybe it was the look in her eyes or maybe her lips just looked kissed. Whatever it was, Kate had seen the way her friend was looking at her and she was expecting a call today from Fiona demanding an update.

And what an update it would be! Kate sighed again before giving up any pretence of sleep and sliding out of bed. She pulled on her dressing gown and crept down the stairs quietly so she didn't disturb Millie and sat at the kitchen table with a cup of tea and her phone.

The memory of Josh's lips on hers was one reason Kate had been unable to sleep. She had tossed and turned feeling alternatively guilty for allowing the contact and then shivering with delight as she relived the moment. She shouldn't be kissing Josh, she had berated herself. She shouldn't be kissing anyone, Alex excluded. She was desperately trying to save her marriage and persuade her husband to come back home, now was certainly not the time to complicate things with a little romance of her own, regardless of what Olivia and Sophie may think. And yet ….

That little trickle of delight slid down her spine again. She had looked into Josh's eyes last night and it had been so very easy to put Alex to one side for a few moments as she let herself be caught up in the pleasure of Josh's kiss.

She had smiled all the way home, she had smiled as she tucked Millie into her cot and she had smiled and hugged herself as she made a cup of tea before going to bed. She had looked in the mirror and seen her flushed face and sparkling eyes. Her mouth did look thoroughly kissed, she decided, no wonder Fiona had looked at her so searchingly. And even as Kate told herself firmly that it was a moment of madness not to be repeated, she still couldn't help the little smile that tilted her lips.

But then Kate had checked her phone, one last time before sliding into bed and her eyes had widened as she saw a message from Alex. It must have arrived when she was dancing and she just hadn't noticed. Or maybe after the dancing when she was in the pub allowing Josh to kiss her. Maybe Alex was sitting somewhere, sending a message to his wife as she sat kissing someone else. Her heart had fluttered as she read his words.

So sorry Kate. You are right, I can't be angry with you about salsa and I can't expect you to talk about me coming back home when I'm still with Sandra. Have moved out, tonight. Staying with a friend. Can we meet tomorrow? Need to talk. Alex xxx

Kate had stared at the message for what seemed like hours. She read it and reread it, then read it again. Her heart was beating loudly and her hands were shaking. Alex had moved out of Sandra's flat. He had left Sandra. He wanted to talk. Alex had left Sandra and wanted to talk to Kate – all these thoughts were tumbling through her brain where they collided with the still vivid memory of Josh and the way his lips had felt on hers until she thought her head would explode.

Alex had left Sandra and that meant only one thing. Kate had won, Alex was coming home.

She had lived this moment so many times before. She had laid in bed imagining Alex knocking on the door and telling her he missed her, saying he had made a mistake and wanted to come home. She had wandered around the shops in a daydream, a dream where Alex was waiting for her when she returned home, desperately sorry for Sandra Maddison and her come to bed eyes and her whispered enticements and just wanting Kate to forgive him. She had dreamed so many different versions, all ending the same way, Alex back at home, the family reunited. In every scenario Kate had felt unbelievable joy. She had taken his hand and smiled graciously and said yes she could forgive him and of course Alex could come home. In every dream she had felt her heart fill with relief and love as everything fell back into place.

But now the moment was so very near, Kate couldn't seem to find those feelings anywhere in her heart. She was having a great deal of difficulty pushing out the image of Josh's eyes only inches from her own and the feel of his lips on hers and replacing that memory with a picture of Alex. The relief, the happiness, they all seemed conspicuous in their absence. Instead there was a great deal of pain, more than a little anger and a whole lot of confusion.

Kate pulled her phone towards her to read the message again. Perhaps it was just the stress of the last few weeks. She wanted Alex back more than anything else in the world so the lack of excitement was purely stress she decided. Tonight when Alex came round, when she saw his face, the eyes that she had loved since the first time she looked into them, she would feel so happy. She would feel an avalanche of joy flood into her heart. She just knew she would.

Warming her hands on her mug, Kate stared out into the garden. Millie would be awake soon. If Kate were honest she didn't think that Millie had missed her father particularly. Maybe at the weekends when Millie had both parents in the house. Maybe on a Sunday morning when Kate would bring Millie into bed with them for 10 minutes before she got up to make Alex his breakfast. But generally, she didn't think Millie had really noticed the absence of her father in her life.

Kate sighed deeply. She remembered the day they had come home from the hospital with their tiny daughter. Alex had opened the door, taking hold of Kate's arm to guide her over the threshold and then into the living room to place Millie in the Moses basket waiting in the corner. They had stood side by side, holding their breath in awe as the little figure wriggled for a moment before settling down. Alex had slid his arm around Kate's waist and rested his chin on her head, his eyes not leaving Millie's scrunched up face.

'She so very small,' he had said in a whisper, holding Kate tightly. 'I'm worried I'll crush her!'

Kate giggled. 'Make the most of her Alex, everyone says they grow up so very quickly.'

Alex had smiled, his eyes still glued to his daughter. 'I can't wait,' he said, 'and then we can have another one.'

Kate winced and Alex laughed softly. 'Too soon for such talk?'

'Definitely!'

They watched Millie for a few more minutes before Alex pulled Kate round to face him. 'I love you Kate, I love you and this perfect little creature you've produced. I'll love you both for the rest of my days,' and he had kissed her, a long passionate kiss that had left tears in Kate's eyes.

Kate pressed a trembling hand to her lips. Alex may have struggled to keep his promise but she believed that he still loved her. He had lost his way a little but he had remembered how much Kate and Millie meant to him.

Kate heard Millie snuffling, heard her starting to stir. She deserved to grow up with a father. Kate deserved to spend the rest of her life with her husband. Alex deserved to come home. Kate would forgive him, they would get over this blip and spend the rest of their lives together as intended.

She tipped back her head and taking a deep breath she gently pushed aside the memory of Josh allowing Alex's face to take centre stage. Josh had been a mistake and Kate needed to take herself in hand. She would see Alex this evening and they would talk about the future and how they could recover. And Kate would be happy.

When the doorbell pealed out, Kate was in the kitchen, twisting her hands together anxiously. She had spent the afternoon on Google researching the protocol of a potential reconciliation meeting with a wayward ex. She had washed her hair and brushed it until it shone. She had dressed in a tight fitting top and slim trousers and made up her face carefully; it was essential, she read, that her husband remember the woman he fell in love with. The article had accused women of making so much effort in the early days of a relationship and not caring at all towards the end. Why would your husband stay, it had asked, if you don't even bother brushing your hair or putting on a swipe of lipstick for him when you hear his key in the door.

Then she had taken off the top, the trousers and most of the make up after reading another article that warned about false expectations, that husbands should accept the reality of wives looking after young children and the house and not expect stockings and suspenders when they walked through the door at the end of the day.

She had spent at least an hour in her dressing gown her head reeling with conflicting advice and in the end she had closed the laptop, pulled on her jeans and simply crossed her fingers.

'Hello Alex.'

'Hello Kate.'

Kate pushed the door open a little wider so Alex could come in.

'Millie in bed?'

Kate nodded. 'I thought it was probably for the best.'

They stood in uncomfortable silence for a moment until Kate waved her hand in the direction of the kitchen. 'Shall we …?'

Alex sat at the table then jumped back to his feet as Kate took a bottle of wine from the fridge.

'Shall I open it …'

'Would you like a drink …'

They both spoke at the same time and their hands collided over the bottle making Kate jump back just as Alex let go and the bottle nearly ended on the kitchen floor but for Alex's deft catch.

'Sorry!'

'Sorry!' they both echoed in unison.

Eventually the wine was poured and Kate sat down opposite Alex, both ignoring the glass in front of them.

'Kate,' he began with such a decisive tone that Kate jumped.

'Sorry,' he murmured. Then tried again, 'Kate, I'm sorry.'

Kate waited.

'I'm sorry for yesterday of course, I had no right to complain that you were going out. But I'm sorry for - well what I've done.'

She watched as Alex ran his fingers through his fringe. 'I can't actually believe I could have been so stupid, I can't believe I could have hurt you like that.'

Kate nodded, keeping quiet as Alex continued.

'I made a mistake Kate, it was foolish I know but I just felt so unappreciated, unnecessary almost. I didn't feel as though I had a place in your life anymore and I made a huge mistake.'

Ah – the unappreciated complaint. She tried to remember what her response should be.

'But Alex, we have Millie now and I have to look after her. She's so small, she relies on us totally, she has to come first.'

Kate tried not to make her voice strident or accusing, she let the words fall as gently as she could and watched Alex's face crumple as she spoke.

What else, what was the answer to the unappreciated husband?

'But,' she carried on, smiling reassuringly, 'I understand that you may feel …' she struggled for a moment. She didn't really understand at all how

273

Alex could feel left out because they now had a beautiful baby girl. But Google had said something about being accommodating to change. 'Maybe we can have a little more 'us' time, have one evening each week just for us?'

Alex couldn't have been happier. His face lit up like a puppy given a toilet roll.

'Really? That would be great Kate, just great. I don't want you to think I resent Millie,' he leaned forward earnestly, 'it's not that at all Kate.'

Kate tried to look as though she understood.

'I love Millie, I just felt quite alone.'

'I understand,' she repeated.

'It's hard to put my finger on exactly how I felt but, well, abandoned I suppose.'

Kate gritted her teeth. For some reason she had a sudden memory of Josh entertaining Millie in the restaurant the previous week. He hadn't started to sulk when Kate's attention was distracted, he hadn't sighed when Millie started to grumble. He had put down his knife and fork and simply played at peek a boo for a few minutes until her good humour was restored.

She dragged herself back to her husband.

'Yes, I understand Alex,' she said, not quite as gently as before. 'Maybe I was too preoccupied with the Millie.' The words hurt.

'Not just Millie,' suggested Alex.

'What?'

'Well it's not just Millie is it? These days you seem more interested in keeping the kitchen clean than talking to me.'

Kate's mouth hung open.

'And the cushions,' he carried on, 'why on earth do all the cushions have to be in the same order, and the pans – you polish the pans nearly every day!'

Kate felt her smile disappear. Had her marriage failed because she kept her beautiful copper pans clean? And the cushions in a straight line? Strangely she didn't recall Alex complaining in the slightest when he came home at the end of the day to a tidy house, a cooked meal and cushions all standing up straight inviting him to settle into them.

'Right,' she said shortly. 'So you want me to spend less time with housework? Because I seem to remember that you were the one who wanted copper pans and colour co-ordinated cushions!'

Alex looked a little surprised. 'No! No, I'm sorry Kate. I didn't mean it to sound like that.' He offered her a conciliatory smile but Kate was becoming less receptive.

'I just meant that you've become an amazing person, your cooking and you know all the stuff you do in the house.'

Stuff, thought Kate. Stuff!

'But it takes up a lot of your time and attention, housework and pans,' he gave a little laugh,' yeah, that's all fine but not instead of – of …'

'Instead of you? suggested Kate.

'Yes – No! Instead of us Kate. Instead of time spent on us.'

Kate chewed on her lip. This was becoming a little tiring. Sod Google.

'Do you want to come back?' she asked outright, wincing as she heard the words erupt into the room. Google had been very specific, don't ask the errant husband to return. Don't put him on the spot and make him feel pressured. Encourage him, enable him, but let him make the suggestion.

But Kate was getting a little weary of the advice she was following. She was certainly getting a little tired of accepting her part in the folly that was Alex and Sandra Maddison.

Alex stared at her, almost frozen to the table.

'I – er – I didn't think you would …'

'I would consider it.'

'You would?'

'I couldn't promise anything Alex.'

'Of course not I wouldn't expect you to …'

'But I would consider moving on -with you.'

'And – er -Sandra?'

Kate tried to stop the grimace that twitched at her lips. 'It would be hard Alex, obviously it would be hard.'

She paused and he watched her, holding his breath.

'But I think I could – forgive you.'

Alex let out a huge breath, gusting across the table.

'Oh God Kate I can't believe that you would be prepared to forgive and forget.'

Oh, thought Kate, there would be no forgetting. And there would probably wouldn't be a great deal of forgiving. Not deep down inside. But she wanted Alex back and if she had to play the part of the forgiving wife then she would do so. No matter how hard it was.

Kate frowned, she seemed to have gone completely off course. She wasn't supposed to be taking the lead in this way, she was supposed to let Alex come to the natural realisation that he wanted to come home and ask Kate if she would forgive him. She wondered what she should do next.

'Right,' she stood up.

Alex looked startled. He stood up slowly. 'Right,' he echoed uncertainly.

'Well, perhaps we both need to think about – what we've said?' Kate winced, she was acting as though she'd just given him a quote for double glazing. 'And what we need to do next?'

Alex nodded, 'Right- er – okay.'

They stood in the kitchen, the wine untouched between them.

'So – I'll go then?'

'Yes,' Kate nodded briskly,' yes, yes. You go.'

'And we'll speak soon?'

'Definitely!'

'To talk about ...'

'Yes,' Kate was still nodding furiously. 'Oh, yes to talk about ...er?'

'To talk about me coming home?'

And there it was, the moment.

Kate closed her eyes briefly, the tension suddenly leaving her shoulders.

'Yes,' she said gently, a smile lifting her lips and warming her face. 'Yes Alex, to talk about you coming home.'

She walked to the door with him and they stood in the shadows of the street light.

'Thank you Kate,' Alex whispered.

And then in a rerun of the previous night, Kate saw his face coming closer and closer. She watched as the blue of his eyes became deeper and deeper until it was only centimetres from her face.

'Thank you so much,' Alex whispered again and then his lips were on hers and it was such a familiar and well-loved feeling that she felt the tears immediately spring to her eyes and for a blissful moment it was as though the events of the last few weeks had never happened and she was exactly where she needed to be, back in the arms of her husband.

Chapter 26

It was Sunday morning and Kate was feeding Millie, spooning in the porridge that Millie loved and which invariably ended up on Kate's clothes.

'Good girl Millie darling,' she crooned as her daughter happily opened her mouth wide. 'Daddy will be home soon Millie. Won't that be wonderful?'

The porridge was finished and she showed Millie the empty dish.

'We'll be a family again, mummy, daddy and baby Millie. Just like we should be.'

Millie didn't appear at all interested as she tried to put her fingers in the bowl.

'We'll be happy again Millie, I promise. We'll forget all about what happened and daddy will love us again and we'll be back to normal. A perfect family.'

Kate's eyes strayed to the garden. A perfect family. She had been a perfect wife, or so she thought, a perfect wife looking after the perfect family. And yet Alex hadn't found that enough. He had complained about being at the back of the queue behind Millie, behind the copper pans and behind the artfully arranged cushions. Well Kate would have to work a little harder this time. The perfection had come at the cost of her husband so this time she needed to alter her tactics. She needed to revert back to the carefree, happy woman he married, full of joy and spontaneity. But, a frown creased Kate's forehead, of course he wouldn't want standards to drop. She had to be the Kate he fell in love with but still make a wonderful meal every night, clean the house, iron his shirts, look after Millie, polish the pans. How was she going to manage all that she wondered? She would just have to be even more organised. She would have to make sure she scheduled fun into her week - Wednesday afternoon – be impulsive. Friday morning – remember to have fun. Saturday afternoon – be carefree.

The phone rang and taking Millie out of her high chair and putting her on the floor where she could chew donkey's ear, she answered it.

'Kate, Hi, it's Josh.'

The room seemed to still as Kate heard his voice. Millie still sat chuntering away, the washing machine still whirled behind her but Kate could hear nothing but her own breathing as she clutched the phone to her ear.

'Hello Josh,' she answered softly.

'It's a lovely day outside,' he started cheerfully. 'I wondered if Millie might like to feed the ducks? We could take a picnic to the park and introduce her to the lake's feathered creatures?'

There was silence.

'Of course if you're busy, or if Alex …?'

'No. We're not busy.'

'And Alex?'

'Isn't here,' answered Kate truthfully.

'And the ducks?'

Kate laughed. 'I think Millie would love to meet the ducks Josh. What a lovely idea.'

They arranged that Josh would pick them up and he told Kate not to worry about the picnic, he would collect everything they needed from the shop. 'You just need to relax and have a lovely day,' he instructed, 'leave the rest to me!'

Kate couldn't help smiling. She realised that whenever she thought of Josh she smiled. Or blushed. Sometimes she smiled and blushed. She also realised that maybe she should have said no. She should have told Josh that Alex had visited the night before and they were on the verge of a reconciliation. She could tell him while they were out she decided. She could update him on her progress. He would be happy for her, even if he was sad about lost opportunities.

You should have told him on the phone, a little voice in her head remonstrated. You should have told him that Alex was coming home and that going out with Josh was inappropriate. But Kate ignored the little voice and instead carried on smiling as she dressed Millie and fluffed up her baby curls until she looked impossibly sweet and ready to meet the ducks.

It was an hour after she had spoken to Josh, as she was looking through Millie's bag to make sure she had a spare of everything that might be needed, that the phone rang again. She grinned, no doubt Josh had suddenly realised he didn't know what babies ate on picnics.

'Hello!' she sang down the phone.

'Hi Kate.'

The smile dropped. 'Oh, hello Alex.'

'I just wanted to say how happy I was that you were so – understanding last night. I mean I had hoped that we could move on, that you could forgive me but I thought it would take longer! I thought you might be too angry with me for us to move on so quickly.'

Kate stood still, the phone in her hand. She was angry but she had worked too hard to let any anger surface.

'You made a mistake Alex,' she said simply. 'You made a mistake and you want to come back to me and Millie, that's what's important.'

'You're right, I do want to come home. In fact ...'

Suddenly Kate wasn't ready. Having waited so long she just wasn't ready to hear the words.

'I'm sorry Alex,' she interrupted. 'I can't talk, I'm just on my way out.'

'Oh. Right. Well that's why I was phoning really. I wondered if you and Millie wanted to go to lunch?'

'Lunch?'

'Yes. After all, we haven't spent much time as a family lately have we so I thought it would be nice if we went out today. The weather is lovely!'

'I see. It's a lovely idea Alex, a really lovely idea.' Kate's mind was pandemonium. Of course she wanted to go with Alex. She wanted to go out with her husband and her daughter for Sunday lunch. What could be more perfect?

'I thought we could go to the restaurant. The one where we saw each other last week?'

'The restaurant?'

'Yes. It was really nice there wasn't it?'

Well, thought Kate, yes it was really nice. Apart from the fact she had been sitting on one table with Millie and Josh and Alex had been sitting on an entirely different table with the woman he was having an affair with. Had Alex always been so totally unimaginative she suddenly wondered.

'We know that Millie will be okay there, she seemed to love it last week.'

When another man took us there, thought Kate.

'So how about it Kate? A lovely lunch, me, you and Millie. A family again.'

Just what Kate had waited to hear.

'So, will you come to lunch with me Kate?'

Millie was ready, a pink cardigan keeping her arms warm and a sweet little sunhat keeping her face cool. There was a knock at the door and she scooped Millie into her arms.

'Ready my darling? Let's go,' and she opened the door.

'Hello gorgeous!' said Josh dropping a kiss on Millie's head but looking at Kate. 'Everybody ready?'

The park was close and in no time at all they were walking along the path in the sunshine as Millie sat upright in her buggy waving her arms in the air and chattering to herself and donkey.

The unseasonably warm weather had brought out the hibernating population and the paths were full of strolling couples, children running on the grass, older folk sitting on the benches.

'This is lovely,' said Kate, aware of how close Josh was, how easy it would have been to link arms with him as she pushed the buggy. 'What a good idea!'

She didn't tell him that Alex had phoned and suggested that he take Millie and Kate out. She didn't explain how she had told Alex, quite gently, that although it was a lovely idea she had already made arrangements and couldn't join him. And because she didn't tell him that Alex had phoned in the first place she couldn't tell him that Alex had been quite desperately upset when Kate turned him down. That he had pleaded with her to change her mind, had said he was desperate to see his wife and daughter and get some sense of normality back into their lives. She couldn't tell Josh that she had been quite taken aback as suddenly the balance shifted and Alex was anxious to know where Kate was going, who she was going with, what she was doing that meant she couldn't see her husband. And of course she couldn't mention that she had snapped 'estranged husband' at Alex which had brought yet more apologies and promises. And she certainly couldn't tell him that she knew Alex was going to ask if he could come home, if they had gone for lunch he was going to ask if he could come home with them right there and then. They would eat roast chicken, smile and laugh and then go home as a family. And she certainly couldn't mention that she had suddenly become quite claustrophobic at the thought of having Alex back and the thought that everything would swing back to a life centred around keeping Alex happy.

Because that is what Kate had devoted herself to over the last few years, keeping Alex happy, a job she had failed to complete. And now she was going to have to try even harder and suddenly it seemed like a very hard task indeed.

So she told Josh nothing of the conversation with Alex that morning and instead she strolled along the path in the sunshine and imagined linking arms as they wandered to the lake and the greedy ducks.

They spent several hours enjoying the sun, Millie stared at the ducks and swans in amazement, Josh the only one brave enough to hold out bread towards the large beaks encouraged by squeals of delight from Millie and then they found some shade under a tree and ate their way through the selection of goodies Josh had brought with him, including jelly and bananas for Millie and cold meat, quiche and salad for himself and Kate. They talked of everything, except Alex. Josh told Kate about his dream to build his own home in the country. He had already bought a plot of land in a small Cotswold village although his day job as an architect meant he had no time to do anything other than sketch out his forever house. But one day, he told her with determination in his eyes, he would find the time and space to take it all to the next level. Kate told Josh of her singular lack of ambition when it came to work, how she had been happy to take any job that appealed and work until it had lost its appeal, only settling down to an office job when she and Alex were saving for their own forever house.

He told her how distraught he had been when Tanya decided that life with Josh was not giving her the satisfaction she needed. Kate said nothing about Alex wanting to come back, but needing more from Kate than polished pans. Josh spoke of how hard it had been to let go of Tanya and accept that maybe they hadn't been right for each other. Kate failed to mention that her mother had accused Kate of losing herself in her desire to be what Alex wanted rather than who she was.

And throughout the whole afternoon Kate found her eyes constantly returning to the dimpled chin and those lips that had met her own on Friday evening. She had watched him talk and gazed at his mouth, knowing exactly how it would feel if he bent forwards and kissed her. She had told herself sternly that there would be no kissing today. She was with Josh because it was a lovely day and Millie would enjoy the ducks but she was on the verge of a reconciliation and there would be no kissing of any kind. But as the afternoon had worn on she couldn't help feeling slightly aggrieved that she hadn't had to explain this to Josh. That she hadn't found the need to push him gently away and say that they couldn't kiss anymore, that they were friends only and kissing was not on the friendship charter. He behaved perfectly, he entertained Millie and chatted to Kate and although the electricity between them could have contributed to the national grid he kept to his side of the picnic blanket and there was no kiss in sight, even though Kate now found herself thinking almost obsessively about how good it would be to feel those lips on hers again.

Eventually they walked back to the car and Josh drove them home. Kate took Millie into the house and Josh brought her bag to the doorway and just as she was about to reluctantly admit that it was for the best all round that Josh had not kissed Kate and that Kate had not needed to push Josh away, he leant forward and caught in the doorway she felt his lips land on hers.

And although Kate raised a hand, the one meant to push him gently back and explain that she must prepare for Alex to come home, she actually wound the hand round his neck and found herself kissing him back and all Kate could think was how very pleasant the afternoon had been and how she hadn't really missed the restaurant, roast chicken or Alex very much at all.

Chapter 27

Kate decided they had been right to make the most of the unexpected sun when the next day brought grey skies and drizzling rain. Millie was unaccountably grouchy, the washing machine wouldn't turn on and everything seemed so much effort. Wiping porridge from her shoulder, Kate scooped Millie in her arms and took her upstairs for a bath. She took a deep breath and coaxed the bad mood away until Millie was fresh and clean and smiling once more, her eyes drooping with weariness. As she laid her daughter down for her morning nap, Kate heard her phone ringing downstairs. But she decided to take a long hot bath herself and see if her own mood improved and as she lay in the scented bubbles she heard her phone ring again.

Dressed and a little more relaxed, Kate headed downstairs just as her phone started to ring once more. She looked at the screen. It was Alex and for some unaccountable reason Kate decided she was just too tired to take the call. Not physically tired. The fresh air of the previous day, the pleasant company, a day free of stress and tears had led to a good night's sleep. Kate just felt weary. She looked at Alex's name flashing on the screen and decided that she really didn't need another round of explanations, excuses and hints of a return home. She was tired of being so forgiving and patient and she was very tired of having to bite her tongue as Alex accused her of pushing him to the side line while she looked after their daughter.

Instead she ignored the strident ringing, made herself a cup of tea and sat at the kitchen table until he finally stopped calling. She glanced at her phone, five missed calls. She remembered those first few days after Alex had left and she had been so lost, so totally alone as she tried to make sense of what had happened to her perfect husband and her perfect marriage. She had longed for the sound of her phone to ring, she had prayed that Alex would call and tell her what was happening and she went to bed desperate to hear the sound of her voice.

She pushed the phone away, well it wouldn't hurt Alex to feel a little of that abandonment himself.

By lunchtime he had called twelve times. In the afternoon the messages started.

Kate, been trying to ring you. Would like to meet and talk

Kate, can't get hold of you, would love to get together, think we need to make some plans.

Darling, you're not answering your phone, everything okay? I really want to meet.

Kate, please answer your phone. Are you out? Please let me know you're alright.

Kate I want to come and see you tonight, there's something very important I need to ask you

When Fiona called round on her way to collect the children from school, Kate wordlessly handed over her phone and watched as Fiona read the messages with widening eyes.

'Well! He sounds desperate.'

Kate shrugged. Fiona was right. Kate knew desperate, she had spent several weeks there and she could see it written in every word of Alex's messages.

'Why haven't you been answering his calls?'

With a sigh Kate sat down, fiddling with the phone. 'Oh I don't know. I just didn't have the energy. You know, I've thought of little else over the last few weeks but getting Alex back. It's been quite exhausting. And today I just …' she shrugged her shoulders again. 'I don't know, I just couldn't really be bothered.'

Fiona sat down opposite her friend. 'You know Kate,' she said carefully. 'I can't help feeling that some of your determination to get Alex back seems to have disappeared. It started to disappear the minute he hinted he wanted to come back.'

Kate didn't answer and Fiona continued. 'I know you still make all the right noises, you want Alex back, you love him, you want Millie to have her father in her life,' Fiona paused, 'It's just that you don't seem to – believe it all in quite the same way. I can't help getting the feeling that now you think the moment has arrived, the one where he says he wants to come home, you're avoiding it.'

Kate thought for a moment. Was that the problem, that she didn't believe any more? They had been happy and she'd thought that if Alex came home they could be happy once more. The problem was that Alex hadn't come home and Kate had been left with a great deal of time to think about their lives together. And the more she had thought, the less perfect the memories had become.

Another problem, one she wasn't sure she was ready to share with Fiona, was the thought of her life suddenly switching back to how it had been. Kate loved her Friday evenings of salsa. It may only be a few hours but for that short space of time she was the Kate she remembered doing something she enjoyed with people she now thought of as friends. And then there was Josh. Because whilst Kate was trying desperately hard to pop Josh in the compartment labelled friends, he had an annoying habit of escaping and finding his way into her thoughts in a way that no-one but Alex ever had.

She lifted trouble eyes to Fiona. 'I still love Alex,' she stated.

Fiona nodded her head.

'I believe he still loves me.'

Fiona nodded again.

'He says he made a mistake and - well mistakes happen, don't they?'

'Yes.'

'I want Millie to grow up with her father in her life.'

'Because you didn't have yours?'

Kate's head shot up. She had never really thought about it before but Fiona was right. Kate had felt the loss of her father's absence in the house from the moment he had left. And although she had known, quite instinctively even as a young child that it was for the best, it had never stopped hurting.

'I suppose so. But all children are better off with both parents aren't they?'

It was Fiona's turn to shrug. 'Well in a perfect world yes, but we all know the world isn't perfect. The big question Kate, is do you still want Alex back in your life?'

'Oh yes.' Kate tried to sound confident and assured but she wasn't convinced she had managed. 'Of course I do.'

Fiona's forehead was crinkled with concern. 'Really Kate? Really and truly? Because it looks as though you're about to get your wish and if you've changed your mind in any way, if you've decided that maybe you and Alex are not meant for each other, I think now is the time you need to say something.'

Eventually Kate gave in and answered the phone to Alex's relieved gasp as he heard her voice. He obviously hadn't researched Google quite as much as she had. It was absolutely not the done thing to let your other half know just how desperate you were. And the amount of times he had called, well the forums would be humming with disapproval!

'Kate, thank goodness. I was so worried, I haven't been able to speak to you all day.'

Kate decided not to point out his lack of concern during the previous few weeks when there had been no communication between them at all as he lost himself in the delights of Sandra Maddison.

'I couldn't find my phone,' she lied. 'Just come across it now, behind the cushions.'

She could hear Alex's thoughts turning round inside his head. He knew that Kate plumped the cushions up every morning without fail and the chances of a phone lying unnoticed in their immaculate depths was highly unlikely.

'Oh I see,' he lied back, 'that explains it!'

'I was wondering if I could come round tonight?'

Kate clutched the phone harder. She knew what would happen.

'Oh Alex, I really can't do tonight.'

She closed her eyes, was she completely mad. Google had said don't draw it out, when they stop wriggling it's time to pull in the line.

'I'm really sorry but I just can't.'

'Right,' Alex gave a little half laugh. 'You do seem busy these days!'

Well, thought Kate, Google had assured her that if she went out and enjoyed herself and met new people it would make Alex want to come home so of course she was busy. Shame he hadn't wanted to be part of her life before she started going to salsa and taking long walks in the park with handsome young men. At the thought of Josh her stomach contracted. Stop this contrariness, she told herself firmly. You know what to do, let him come round, let him ask, let him come home.

'Yes, well you know how it is,' she trilled instead. 'Just seem to have a lot on at the moment.'

'Yes, I understand but Kate this is quite important. I want to ask you something, something that's very – well important.'

'Yes, I'm sorry I just can't, not tonight.'

Kate wondered what response she would get if she posted a message on the 'why husbands leave and how to get them back' website. A message that said 'yes I followed all the advice and had my husband fairly begging to come home but I said I was busy because you know what, I was suddenly rather tired of the whole messy business.' The lines would fizzle with criticism.

'Okay, how about tomorrow night?'

Tomorrow seemed so soon thought Kate. So very soon.

'How about Wednesday? she suggested.

'Wednesday! Well if that's the earliest you can see me I suppose it will have to do.'

He was miffed, Kate could hear it in his voice. He was very put out.

She ignored his unhappiness. 'Right Wednesday it is then!' she said in a deliberately upbeat tone clinging onto the phone as though it were a lifebelt.

'And you can't possibly see me sooner? I could come round and …'

'Sorry! Impossible, really impossible!'

'Okay then, Wednesday. I can't wait to see you Kate.'

'Right, me too. Really can't wait. Bye!'

Dropping the phone onto the table, Kate clutched at her hair. Alex wanted to come home. Why, oh why didn't Kate feel happier?

Chapter 28

Kate was waiting in the kitchen when Alex arrived. She had already opened a bottle of wine and was sipping slowly when she heard the doorbell peal. Rubbing her hands on her jeans she went to open the door.

'Hello Kate.'

Alex was smiling. He looked pale and Kate thought he looked as though he had lost a little weight since the last time she had seen him. But he was smiling, he looked happier than she had seen him look since the morning he had walked out.

'Hello Alex.'

They walked into the kitchen and Kate sat back at the table, picking up her glass and taking a large drink of wine. She noticed he was holding a large bouquet of flowers. Beautiful flowers, not a petrol station last minute bunch.

'For you,' he said noticing the direction of her eyes. 'I know you like fresh flowers in the house.'

Actually, thought Kate, she wasn't at all bothered by fresh flowers. It was something that her mother always had, a sweet smelling spray on her sideboard and it was something that Alex had always admired, sniffing the blooms and saying how lovely to see a new display week after week. When Kate had transformed herself into the perfect wife she had of course included fresh flowers on her inventory. Personally, she found the fallen petals a nuisance, she hated cleaning out the vase and she had a habit of forgetting to top up the water and getting far less time from her flowers than Marcia ever had.

'They're lovely,' she said obediently. 'Thankyou.'

But she stayed at the table and after a moment Alex walked to the sink and sat them in a little cold water.

'You look – amazing,' he said, his surprise evident.

Kate frowned. Google had not been consulted for this visit. Kate had been both weary and wary as she waited for Alex's arrival and although part of her was cheering at the knowledge that she had succeeded, or maybe Google had succeeded, there was another rather more truculent part of her that was tired of all the rules and manipulation. She wanted Alex back but suddenly it seemed quite important that he came back for the right reasons, and those reasons were not that Kate was wearing a short skirt and had spent an hour on her make-up. Tonight Kate was just - Kate. She was wearing a pair of jeans tucked into her brown suede boots. Her top was casual and loose floating past her waist and her hair was caught up in her favourite tortoiseshell clasp with tendrils escaping to touch her cheek and neck.

She raised her eyebrows at Alex.

'It takes me back to when we first met,' he explained obligingly. 'You were so pretty, so happy. You never gave a jot for what anyone else thought of you, it was as though you lived in a slightly different world to the rest of us.'

Kate stared at him in amazement.

'Kate, you were my idea of heaven. I loved you from the minute I first saw you. And tonight – you look just like the Kate I fell in love with.'

How ironic, thought Kate. How very ironic that every article she had read, every advice column she had searched and every forum she had devoured had said that the key to a returning husband was to remind him of who he had fallen in love with. And Kate seemed to have done that not by dressing like a femme fatale or making new friends or letting Alex see that she could make a new life for herself, but by simply not making any effort at all but just be herself.

Alex had started talking again and she tried to pay attention.

'I love you Kate, I always have and I always will. I lost my way for a while, I felt – as though you didn't need me anymore. I think part of the reason for my – for Sandra was to get your attention. To make you look in my direction again.'

Kate shook her head sadly. 'There are far better ways you could have chosen Alex.'

'I know, I know and I can never tell you just how sorry I am. But I realise what a complete idiot I was Kate and I can never apologise enough. The fact that you're prepared to forgive me and let me come home, well it just makes me realise even more how very lucky I am to have you. And how stupid I was to come close to losing you.'

Kate was listening. She could hear the words and she was listening but her mind was racing. She remembered the Kate he had fallen in love with. She remembered being that carefree person who was determined to enjoy life to the full and never become obsessed with fresh flowers every week and tea poured from a pot. She had rebelled against the calm and contained life of her mother and she flitted through her own life like a leaf on the wind. Until she had met Alex.

Kate had loved him with all her heart and soul and she had been so very afraid that he would leave her one day, just like her father left her mother, so she resolved to be perfection itself. She would be everything that Alex wanted. Because then he would love her forever and never, ever leave.

Her mother had been right, Kate had changed. She hadn't just become a tidier person or learnt how to cook. She had become the person she thought Alex wanted. The carefree spirit had been carefully subdued into her vision of the perfect wife.

She stared at Alex sitting opposite her. He was still talking but she was having trouble concentrating.

'Kate?'

His hand was over her own and snapping back to the present Kate looked into his eyes. 'Kate, I want to come back. I want to come back and for us to start again, together as we should be.'

He was smiling. His cheeks were flushed and he was smiling a big smile, a confident smile, waiting for her answer. His face was the same one she had looked at almost every day for the last eight years – until he had left her because she was no longer the Kate he wanted. He looked happy, his eyes were shining, he was holding her hand, waiting.

'Kate?'

Kate looked down at their fingers entwined on the table. She had loved holding Alex's hand when they first met. She had loved walking down the road holding his hand and knowing that everybody who saw them knew they were together, a couple. Kate and her handsome golden haired young man. How she had loved him.

'Kate?'

She thought of Millie asleep upstairs. She thought of all the nights she and Alex had curled up together on the settee, watching TV, talking, reading, their bodies touching.

'What do you want from me Alex?'

It hadn't been the answer he was expecting. He frowned. 'I'm not sure I understand …'

'What do you want me to be? Because I'm so confused. You say I remind you of the person you fell in love with. But I stopped being that person for you. I became the person I thought you wanted me to be and you left. So what is it you want from me Alex, who is it that you want me to be?'

He stared at her, his face almost as confused as Kate's thoughts.

'I don't really know what you mean Kate. I want you.'

'But which me Alex? Because I think mum was right,' he looked even more confused and Kate remembered he knew nothing of the conversation she'd had with Marcia. 'You were right Alex, maybe I did change, maybe our relationship is different. But this is who I am now, I'm a wife and a mother and this is me. If you can't be happy with me, if you want the old Kate back, is this going to work?'

He let go of her hand, slowly withdrawing his own as he sat upright in his seat.

'I love you Kate, when I said you weren't the person I married I just meant that you didn't seem to have time for me anymore.'

'Because we have a baby now, because I have to be a mother first.'

'Yes, no! Not because of Millie. But in general, you just didn't seem to need me anymore, you were organised and in control and you had Millie and – I was left behind.'

'But if you come back Alex, I will still put Millie first, always.'

'Of course you will Kate, of course you will I understand that. But now we've spoken about it honestly and openly, surely we can make it better? Get back to the old Alex and Kate, the ones who love each other and were always there for each other, the ones who want to spend the rest of their lives together.'

'Do you still love me?'

'Oh Kate, more than ever, more than ever.'

'And you want to spend the rest of your life with me?'

'Yes.'

'And Sandra …?'

'Sandra was a dreadful mistake which I will never make again,' Alex said firmly. 'Never!'

'Right.'

'And you Kate, do you still love me?'

Kate nodded. She may be angry, she may be hurt and confused but she had no doubt that she still loved Alex.

'Yes.'

'And you want to spend the rest of your life with me?'

Kate nodded again. 'Yes.'

'Then there isn't anything really to discuss is there my darling? I made a mistake, it won't happen again. We'll be back the way we were, a happy family.'

'Yes.'

'So basically it just comes down to this Kate – can I come home?'

And Kate nodded once more. Because wasn't this exactly what she wanted? Isn't this what she had planned and waited for?

So Kate nodded, she nodded and she smiled at the man opposite her and held out her hand so he could wrap his fingers round hers.

'Yes Alex,' she whispered, 'yes of course you can.'

Chapter 29

It was Friday and Kate was heading out to salsa. She had put on the same black dress she'd worn the very first week and she'd taken time with her makeup. She'd already decided that she would carry on going to salsa but she had also decided that she couldn't carry on being Josh's partner. If he wanted to carry on going on a Friday night, perhaps Kate would have to find somewhere else to dance.

Alex was coming home the following day. He had wanted to stay on Wednesday night. He had wanted them to start their new life straight away but Kate had said no, it made more sense for him to move back on Saturday when there was no work to take up his time and they could have a few days together.

So Alex would be back the following morning and this would be the last time Kate would go to salsa as an abandoned wife. She hadn't mentioned salsa to Alex, it hadn't really come up in their conversation. But she would, when he was back home. She would point out that he wanted her to be the person he had fallen in love with and not the amazing housewife she had become. And the Kate he had fallen in love with used to love going dancing. She had loved salsa and she had loved spending time with friends. She had only stopped those things for Alex.

So she was dressed for a night of salsa and sitting in Stuart's car outside the wine bar. They'd been there for almost five minutes.

'You don't have to go in if you don't want to Kate,' he said after waiting patiently in a re-run of Kate's very first Friday.

'Oh I do want to Stuart, I'm sorry. I was just thinking, you know?'

Stuart nodded sitting back patiently. 'Okay no problem.'

'You'll soon have your wife back Stuart, she has been an amazing friend but with Alex back tomorrow I'll stop monopolising her time.'

'Oh don't worry Kate, it's been quite peaceful if you must know, having all her energy directed at you for a while!' But there was a twinkle in his eye and Kate was in no doubt that Stuart loved his tiny red haired wife.

'Well I'm going now, so you go home and make the most of her!'

And Kate was off, dashing across the pavement and into the wine bar.

Salsa was fun as always but Kate couldn't help a slight sense of sadness as the music finished and the usual round of appreciative applause followed. She would carry on dancing but it wouldn't be quite the same without Josh, without his strong arm round her waist, his dimpled chin and twinkly eyes. They joined the rest of their group and there was the usual clamour to the bar for drinks.

Kate turned to Josh as the others all moved forwards.

'Actually Josh, would you like to go for a drink somewhere else, maybe the little bar we went to last week? I'd like to talk to you.'

He was looking down at her and for a moment Kate thought she saw a look of resignation in his eyes but then he smiled, his wonderful, warm, gentle smile and nodded.

'Of course, I'll just tell the others not to get a drink in for us.'

They said their goodbyes and Kate smiled at the obvious excitement of the women as they presumed Kate and Josh were going in search of a more intimate evening.

Josh grabbed her coat and caught her arm in his as they crossed the street. And it felt so good, thought Kate. It felt exactly as she had imagined, strong and capable and protective.

The bar was full again but they managed to find a table and were soon facing each other, Josh's eyes on Kate as he waited.

'Josh, I wanted to tell you that Alex and I are back together. He's coming home. Tomorrow.'

There was a little silence and Kate tried to read Josh's reaction. But his face remained still as she spoke.

'I felt it only fair to tell you straight away, I mean after last week, after you – well,' Kate's face flamed as she remembered Josh's kiss. 'I didn't want you to think that there could be anything more between you and me,' she continued, ignoring the protesting leap of her heart.

She wanted him to say something, anything. She wanted him to say he was devastated, or that he couldn't live without her. No! That would be very wrong. She wanted him to say it would be okay and he had enjoyed spending some time with her but had known all along she would return to her husband. She wanted him to smile, maybe a slightly sad smile and say he'd expected it to end this way and it was okay, he hadn't fallen in love with her or anything dramatic and he would find someone else soon.

But Josh was silent. He was watching Kate and the emotions play across her face and he was silent as she struggled to tell him how she felt.

'It's just that I think it would be best if we didn't - if we don't see each other anymore. Not that I'm suggesting we were seeing each other in the first place! We weren't 'going out' were we? I'm not saying that we were and now we shouldn't. I'm just saying ...'

Oh God, what was she trying to say? What did she want to say?

'I don't want to hurt you Josh,' she carried on gently, lifting her eyes to meet his. 'I really don't want to hurt you.'

They sat in silence for a few seconds, Kate's explanation fading away.

'Are you happy Kate?'

Her eyes widened. 'Happy?'

'Yes, are you happy? Alex is coming home, are you happy?'

Well obviously she was happy, thought Kate. She had what she wanted, Alex had left Sandra Maddison and would even now be ensconced back in the family home if Kate hadn't made him wait until the weekend. Of course she was happy.

'Yes,' she said, unable to find any real fire to put behind the words. She tried again. 'Yes! Of course I'm am.'

Josh smiled. He reached out his hand and briefly covered Kate's own as it lay on the table. 'Then that's all that really matters Kate.'

'Right.'

Kate wondered if they had finished the conversation.

'I just didn't want you to think that I'd been – well you know that I had led you to believe ...'

'Kate you told me the very first time we danced with each other that you wanted Alex back, that you were waiting for him to come home.'

'Yes but I danced with you and went to lunch and we – you know.'

Josh grinned. 'I remember!'

Kate blushed. 'Well I didn't want you to think I was being ...'

Being what she wondered?

'I know exactly what you were being Kate. You were being you. You were honest from the first moment and so was I. I hoped you wouldn't let him back, I really hoped you would decide you couldn't forgive him. Because I want you for myself Kate.'

The blue eyes were looking at her with such passion that Kate felt quite dizzy.

'I told you I would happily take Alex's place if it didn't work out with the two of you and I meant it.' He smiled ruefully. 'Maybe I shouldn't have kissed you but I wanted you to at least think that there was another option.'

Kate stared back at the table, she was glad he had kissed her. Even though she was still determined that she and Alex would be back together soon, she was glad she would have the memory of that kiss.

'And there still is you know Kate,' Josh said softly.

Kates eyes snapped upwards.

What?'

'There still is another option. I know, I know,' he held up his hand to ward off Kate's interruption, 'Alex is coming home and you're happy.'

Kate fell silent.

'But you don't look terribly happy to me Kate. I think I've gotten to know you a little over the last few weeks and I certainly think I know when you're happy. Your eyes light up, you get a little flush of colour in your cheeks and your mouth turns up. They're all 'Kate is happy signs' and I didn't see any of them tonight. I heard you say that Alex was coming home and how happy you were but I didn't see any of these things on your face Kate.'

'Well I am happy, I just was worried about telling you …'

Josh continued as though she hadn't spoken. 'So what I'm saying Kate is that if it turns out that this isn't what you want, if Alex comes home and you suddenly realise that things aren't working, then there is still another option. Me.'

Kate shook her head. 'No Josh, I am with Alex, I was always with Alex, even when Alex wasn't with me. Everything will work out this time, I know it.'

Josh shrugged. 'If you say so Kate.'

'I do!' Kate wondered why so many people thought they knew her better than she knew herself. Why everyone was convinced that she didn't really want Alex back when she knew that she did. Why everyone was questioning her motives when Kate knew without doubt that the only thing that would make her truly happy, for the rest of her life was having Alex by her side.

'I do say so Josh. I am happy, Alex is coming home and all will be well. Really,' and she nodded her head fervently, wondering why it was so hard to convince everyone that she was telling the truth.

'Don't you worry that he might leave again?'

'No!' Kate bit her lip and lowered her voice. 'No, Alex won't leave again,'

'You seem very sure. Has he promised he'll stay?'

Kate sat for a moment. Alex hadn't promised anything. He had begged to come home which was of course exactly what Kate had wanted. He'd admitted he'd made a mistake, he had insisted he still loved her, something Kate had never really doubted. But they had skirted around the subject of Alex's affair. Kate found it far too painful to sit and discuss the details, asking just how and when that first kiss happened, when Alex had first decided to slip into Sandra's bed, what she had offered him that made him decide to leave his wife. So the actual affair was still a misty unpleasant fact in the recess of Kate's mind.

'Alex won't leave again,' she said confidently, 'because I'll make sure that this time he has everything he needs.'

Josh frowned, a line connecting his eyebrows. 'Everything he needs? What exactly does he need?'

'Well he needs more attention, more love; he needs to know that he's important to me and ...' Kate trailed off. In truth she was still a little unclear as to what exactly Alex needed. She had thought that she was supplying all that he could possibly want before he left. She had loved him unreservedly and together they had produced an adorable daughter. Deep down she had started to feel that should have been enough for him.

'More attention?' asked Josh, raising his eyebrows. 'Did you used to ignore him?'

'No of course not. But I didn't go to the Christmas party and I didn't make him feel special and I didn't always remember to stop what I was doing and smile at him and make sure he knew I loved him.'

There was a small pause and sliding a sideways glance at Josh's face, Kate could see he was struggling.

'And you're okay with all this – rubbish?'

Her eyes widened. 'Well I ...'

'I mean are you really okay with the idea that your husband feels you didn't pay him enough attention because you didn't go to a party?'

Kate flushed. 'He didn't leave me because I didn't go to the Christmas party!' she said indignantly.

'Well it sounds like that's exactly what he did. Kate, why don't you tell him to stop being so selfish? He should be showering attention on you right now. He should be racing home to see his beautiful wife and adorable baby. He should come home with a huge smile on his face every night because he is a very lucky man to have you Kate, very lucky and he should stop acting like a spoiled child and realise that.'

For a moment Kate couldn't speak. Her eyes were sparkling with tears, her throat tight with a held back sob. 'But I didn't …'

'No Kate, this isn't about what you didn't do, this is all about what Alex did do. You deserve more Kate, so much more.'

'But Google said I'd neglected him and when I thought about it I had. I didn't make him feel special, I didn't …'

'Google?' Josh looked confused. 'Did you say Google?'

Kate sighed. 'I went onto Google to see what I could do to get Alex back and it said, well Google didn't say anything but there were articles and people had written things and – basically I realised that it was my fault he'd gone. I didn't give him what he needed and as long as he came back I would be able to get it right this time.'

Josh was looking astonished. 'You think it's your fault he left?'

'Well Fiona said it wasn't. She said I should hit him over the head with a vase and have ….' Kate stopped as she remembered that Fiona had told her to have sex with Josh on the dance floor. 'Well she said I should tell him he was a loser and move on without him.'

'Fiona sounds like a very sensible person. I think I like Fiona!'

Kate smiled weakly. 'But neither of you seem to understand that Alex and I are meant to be together. We have a baby and a house and …'

What else did they have? Kate was finding it harder and harder to justify why she and Alex were the perfect couple.

'We should be together,' she protested. 'I need to accept it was partly my fault and forgive him and we should be together again.'

She sat for a moment, staring at Josh's hand which at some point had moved across the table and was now holding Kate's own. 'I still love Alex,' she said quietly. 'I think part of me always will.'

'But is it enough Kate darling? Love alone isn't always the answer and if you're not sure that having Alex back is right for you, then don't go through with this.

Please don't let him back into your life unless you are absolutely certain it's what you want Kate,' and he squeezed her hand as they sat silently across the table from each other lost in their thoughts.

Chapter 30

Kate felt slightly nauseous as she flicked on the kettle to make a cup of tea. Millie was busy with her porridge and Kate had about an hour to get herself and the house ready for Alex. She looked round at the kitchen which was relatively tidy but far from perfect. But instead of falling into a frenzy of cleaning Kate shrugged, her passion for living in a house that sparkled at all times had departed shortly after Alex.

But she did want to have Millie clean and ready for Alex's arrival. She wanted him to look at his daughter and wonder how he could ever have left her. She smiled at Millie. It was a month since Alex had left and she had grown so much. She was even making a noise which Kate was convinced was Mummy. She also needed to make a little effort herself and look presentable when Alex arrived.

The advice on Google had dried up. Once the hard work had been completed and the husband was back home, there had been very little written about what happened next. Maybe, thought Kate, everybody was far too busy struggling with their new lives to sit down and write anything. They were all far too busy smiling alluringly at their husband and trying desperately hard to make sure he felt thoroughly appreciated to find the time to offer any words of wisdom. So there was no advice about what outfit Kate should wear, how she should behave, whether the calm control needed to continue or whether she was now allowed to actually glare at Alex and tell him what she really thought of him, how badly he had behaved or perhaps throw something at him as he walked back through the door.

Kate paused. She had told Alex she could move on from the pain and the hurt, that they could pick up the pieces of their lives and carry on with their slightly less than perfect marriage. She had told Fiona that she wanted Alex back and she would forget all about Sandra Maddison and her charms. She had told Josh that she loved Alex and it didn't matter what he had done or what he had said, she would overcome the hurtful words and the feeling of loss and smile and laugh and try hard to be the Kate he wanted. So why, she wondered, when all the hard work had been done and she had rescued her husband and her marriage, was she suddenly feeling the need for a little old fashioned anger. Why this morning of all mornings had she woken up with a heart that was neither relieved nor happy but disgruntled as she thought of all the tears she had shed over the last few weeks.

She shook her head, taking a deep breath. Fiona had told her it was unnatural that Kate should be so forgiving. She said that at some point Kate needed to tell Alex just what she thought of him, for the sake of the next twenty years she needed to release some of the emotions from her overloaded heart. Kate had disagreed insisting that once Alex was home she would just feel relieved and although the pain may never really go she would not allow anger and resentment to cloud their future. Maybe, wondered Kate as she took Millie upstairs, maybe she had been a little naïve in her beliefs. Maybe Fiona was right and at some point Kate would look at Alex's smiling face and feel an irresistible urge to hit him over the head with a frying pan.

Kate sighed, she really must get a grip on her emotions, she decided. This was not the day to start doubting her ability to forget her husband's affair. She had Googled him back and now she had what she wanted. Hadn't she?

Exactly an hour later the bell rung and Kate froze. She had just popped Millie into her bouncing chair on the living room floor and as the bell rang out into the silent hallway she stopped and stared down at her daughter.

'Daddy's home Millie,' she said softly. 'Didn't I tell you he would be back?'

Kate walked into the hall but found herself moving ever more slowly as she got nearer and nearer to the door. For one wild moment she was tempted not to answer. To dash back into the living room and hold Millie close so she wouldn't make a sound and to pretend they weren't there. She had spent so many weeks waiting for Alex to come back through the door and now he was standing there Kate wasn't sure she was ready.

She put her hand on the handle just as the bell rang out again, making her jump.

'Sorry Alex, I was just settling Millie.'

Alex walked in. He stood in hallway, two suitcases by his feet and Kate's mind flew back to the Monday morning when he'd told her he was leaving, two suitcases by his side as he told his wife that their marriage was over.

'I though perhaps you'd changed your mind,' said Alex, grinning in a way that left Kate in no doubt that Alex thought nothing of the sort. Had he ever really doubted that she would take him back Kate wondered fleetingly?

She tried to smile, tried to relax, tried to look as though her dreams had come true. She had a feeling she had failed on all counts.

What did you do when your errant husband returned she wondered in panic? Did you invite him into his own home? Did you offer him a cup of tea, show him to his room, the room he'd left only weeks before?

She nibbled her lip, standing awkwardly in the hall. But Alex didn't seem to have the same doubts and dropping the suitcases to the floor, he stepped forwards and put his arms around Kate pulling her into his arms and holding her close.

'Oh God Kate, I've missed you so much,' he whispered, burying his face in her hair. 'I was so afraid you wouldn't be able to forgive me, wouldn't let me back.'

He lifted his head up and looked into her eyes and Kate was quite certain that he was lying. He may have missed her but he had never really worried that she would turn away from him regardless of how he had behaved. It was in his eyes, in the confident way he pushed his hand through her hair.

'I love you Kate, I love you and I'll never let you go again,' and he kissed her, deeply and passionately as his arms wrapped themselves around her body.

Kate couldn't help but respond. This was Alex, her Alex. She felt the familiar lips on hers, felt his body against her own and for a moment she felt she was capable of anything. She could forgive and forget, she loved Alex and she would forgive him anything.

Then the kiss was over and Alex was looking at her grinning. 'And where is Millie?' he asked not waiting for a reply as he let go of Kate and walked into the living room.

'Millie, darling. Daddy's here.'

Kate didn't move. She stood in the hallway and she waited. She waited for that delicious contented feeling that always filled her heart when he kissed her. She waited for that slight sense of loss she always felt when Alex moved away from her. She stayed where she was and waited.

'Hello Millie, daddy's home sweetheart. Come here and give me a kiss.'

She could hear Alex's voice, she could hear Millie's chunters but Kate remained in the hall waiting. She remembered when Josh had kissed her and the feeling of emptiness as he stopped. She remembered looking at his lips, longing for them to return to hers even though she knew she shouldn't kiss him at all.

'Kate where are you? Hasn't she grown? I can't believe how big she is.'

Kate waited. She waited and she waited until with a sigh, a small disappointed sigh she finally moved and joined Alex in the living room. He was holding Millie in his arms looking delighted. Millie wasn't crying but she wasn't smiling. She was staring at the man who was kissing her and telling her she looked beautiful and although she accepted the attention she was not grinning her big Millie grin. Alex would have to work at reasserting his place in Millie's life. Time moved on so quickly for babies. And maybe not just babies.

'Alex.'

Alex looked over at his wife and smiled.

'Isn't this fantastic Kate. Oh God I'm so glad to be back.'

'Alex, I'm so sorry.'

He carried on watching her, his smile losing just a little of its brightness.

'This is a mistake Alex. It's not going to work.'

The smile had gone. Fading into nothing as he stared at Kate in the doorway. Carefully he put Millie back into her seat.

'It will work Kate,' he said in a firm voice. 'It will work because we still love each other.'

But Kate was shaking her head, her face twisted with remorse and sadness. 'No. No Alex. I really thought I could do it, I really thought I could start again with you and I'd be able to forget everything that had happened. Well, actually I always knew I'd never be able to forget but maybe ignore? I really thought I could do it Alex.'

'And you can Kate! We can. I made a mistake and I'm sorry but we can carry on, get back to being who we were ...'

'No Alex.' The words were soft, almost gentle but so full of absolute certainty that she saw him wilt as they reached him.

'Please Kate let's …'

'No Alex. You left me for someone else, you left because I didn't pay you enough attention, you left to teach me a lesson.' She held up her hand stopping his interruption. 'And maybe I was partly to blame, maybe I wasn't the perfect wife I thought I was. But I don't think I can forgive you, not in the way I would need to for this to work!'

Alex took a step forward.

'How could you resent me putting Millie first, how could you even suggest that I wasn't giving enough attention to you! And maybe I did spend too much time worrying about cushions and pans and cleaning but that was all for you Alex. I did all this for you Alex and you left me!'

'Kate I'm sorry, I'm so sorry. You have to listen to me, you have to let me …'

'I became what you wanted Alex and you left because suddenly you had to take second place. To our child. To Millie.'

'Kate please …'

And that's what I can't forgive Alex. I can't forget and I can't forgive. I thought I could put it behind us and maybe if you'd come straight back it could have been different. But all I've had to do these last few weeks is think Alex. I've sat here and I've thought about us, about our relationship, about why you left, about all the things I've changed about myself to make you happy and how it didn't actually make you happy. And now it's too late. Because once you've sat down and opened your eyes to all of those things, you can't then forget them, no matter how much you'd like to. So I'm sorry Alex, more sorry than I can ever say but this isn't going to work. I can't take you back. It's over.'

'No! No!' Alex was pushing his hand through his hair, a desperate expression on his face. 'Kate you have to forgive me, you have to! I want to come back and we will get over this. Please stop and think about Millie, about us.'

'I never stopped thinking about Millie, it was part of the reason I was so desperate for you to come back. I didn't want Millie to grow up without a father. But this isn't right, it won't work and it won't help Millie in the long run.'

'Please Kate, please.'

His voice was low, desperate and for a moment Kate felt a wave of sympathy for him She knew how it felt to be desperate, sad and in pain. But she held firm and shook her head.

'I'm sorry Alex. It's over.'

Millie was chewing donkey's ear singing happily in her baby chatter but other than her soft rumble the room was eerily silent.

Alex looked defeated. His shoulders had drooped and he looked smaller, slighter than only a few moments before.

Kate's heart ached. She decided it was going to be aching for some considerable time. True love was not something that simply disappeared overnight. But it also wasn't something that could flourish amid resentment and distrust and Kate had to accept, however much it hurt, that she couldn't push Alex's behaviour aside like unwanted post. It would haunt her forever,

'I will always love you Alex, as someone I care a great deal about, as Millie's father. I will always love you.'

'But it's not enough?'

She smiled sadly. 'No, it's not enough anymore.'

More silence and she watched Alex as the reality of the situation settled on his face. He looked lost, alone and incredibly sad and Kate's heart ached for him but she made no move towards him as he nodded his head and walked slowly into the hall.

He picked up the suitcases lying in the corner and made his way to the front door before turning to look at Kate.

'Are you sure?' His voice was choked, defeated and Kate couldn't speak, she just nodded.

And then he was gone, the space suddenly empty just as it had been weeks before when Kate had been so surprised to hear her husband say he was leaving.

She stared at the door but there was nothing but silence and the ticking of the clock and Kate wrapped her arms around her body and let the tears roll down her face.

Epilogue

Kate was sitting in the garden. Winter was over and during the last week the sun had shone non-stop. Millie was crawling which made Kate's life more difficult than ever, she couldn't turn her back on her daughter for a moment. But they had spent many happy hours in the garden as Millie crawled around, investigating grass and plants. Kate sipped at her cup of tea and watched Millie sitting in the middle of the lawn contemplating the butterfly that was hovering above the flowers.

The house was up for sale, there was no way Kate could afford to continue living there no matter how generous Alex was with any settlement. There was only so much money to go round. She had no idea where she would end up and much to her surprise she had accepted her mother's offer to stay with her for a few months until she made up her mind exactly what to do next. Kate had looked around for a job and the phone had rung only the day before to offer her three afternoons a week in a small office not far from her mother's house. Marcia was delighted at the thought of looking after Millie for the few hours Kate was at work and Kate was looking forward to a few hours of adult time.

Fiona had wailed with distress at the idea of Kate no longer being around the corner but she had been reassured that the increased distance wouldn't affect their friendship.

Kate was under no illusion that life would be hard. She had agreed that Alex could see Millie whenever he wanted, she didn't want to restrict her daughter's access to her father. But she was essentially a single parent now and that would not be an easy task.

She lifted her face up to the sun and closed her eyes. Josh had phoned her only a few days after Alex had left. He had heard that Kate had not gone through with the reconciliation, probably Olivia or Sophie thought Kate with amusement. They would have been on the phone as soon as the news broke. He'd asked if he could come round but Kate had regretfully said no.

'I've just broken up with my husband Josh. I need time to grieve. I'm going to be starting a new life but I think I should take it slowly.'

She'd been able to hear the disappointment in his voice as he accepted what she told him.

'Okay Kate, I understand.'

She smiled sadly. Had she been hoping he wouldn't take no for an answer she wondered?

'So I'll give you some time. I'll phone you up in exactly two months.'

'Two months?'

'Yes two months. And if you say you still need more time then I'll phone you in another two months and another two after that.'

Kate had felt the smile start to tilt her lips. 'Every two months?'

'Every two months. On the dot. Unless of course you ever feel that your grieving is over and you're ready to start that new life.'

'Oh?'

'Yes. In that case ring me and about half an hour later go answer the door because I'll be straight round.'

She was grinning now. Grinning at the thought of opening her door and seeing Josh with his dimpled chin and amazing blue eyes standing on the other side.

'I can't promise anything Josh. It will take as long as it takes,' she warned.

'I know and that's okay. But I can promise you something Kate. It doesn't matter how long it takes, I'll be waiting.'

Kate had felt a tear roll down her cheek. Because she knew he meant it.

And two months later, 25 minutes ago in fact, the phone had rung and Josh's deep voice had reached out across the line to ask her how she was and more to the point did she feel ready for a visit from a close friend.

Kate had looked out into the garden full of sunshine and felt her heart lift as she confessed that she had actually missed her salsa partner very much and would be delighted if he called round.

So there Kate sat, in the warmth of the sunshine watching her daughter happily crawl after butterflies and waiting for a knock at the door so she could start the new life she had promised herself.

The End

Printed by Amazon Italia Logistica S.r.l.
Torrazza Piemonte (TO), Italy